THE
BLUE WOMAN

AND OTHER STORIES

MARY FLANAGAN

BLOOMSBURY

First published 1994
Copyright © 1994 by Mary Flanagan
The moral right of the author has been asserted
Bloomsbury Publishing Ltd, 2 Soho Square, London W1V 5DE

A CIP catalogue record for this book is available from the British Library
ISBN 0 7475 17096

Typeset in Great Britain by Hewer Text Composition Services, Edinburgh
Printed in Great Britain by Mackays of Chatham plc

The following stories first appeared elsewhere: "Truth, Beauty and Goodness",
Soho Square I, Ed Isabel Fonseca (Bloomsbury, 1988); "The Wedding Dress",
Revenge, Ed Kate Saunders (Virago, 1990); "End of Terrace", *Storia 2*, Ed Kate
Figes (Pandora, 1989); "The Octopus Vase", *Storia 4*, Ed Kate Figes (Pandora,
1990); "The Blue Woman", *Seduction, A Book of Stories*, Ed Tony Peake (Serpent's
Tail, 1994); "The White Cliffs", *Telling Stories*, Ed Duncan Minshell (Coronet,
1992); "Not Quite Arcardia", *Soho Square III*, Ed Alberto Manguel
(Bloomsbury, 1990).

CONTENTS

For Nigel

WHEN I'M BAD

When I'm bad I eat hotdogs and Cheeze Whizz and Snickers bars and food with lots of preservatives and chemicals that make me sick. I am so sick that I hit my little sister Ashley on the head with a shovel so that she bleeds and runs screaming to Mom who takes her to the hospital. I am so sick that I tear up the twenty-dollar bill Aunt Marjorie has put in my birthday card 'cause I'm sweet and she likes me. I tear it up right in front of her, throw it in her face. And Mom yells at me and grabs my arm and shakes me even though she knows it won't do any good, and Aunt Marjorie says oh it's all right, it doesn't matter at all. And I think what a schnook Aunt Marjorie is, how can it not matter, how can it be all right, the liar, the old poop. I love Aunt Marjorie very much. And I think that little shit Ashley, she had it coming, she hates me and gets everything she wants. I really love my little sister. I love her with my whole heart.

When I'm bad I wait till Mom has redecorated my bedroom. I'm getting one all to myself because we have a bigger house because Dad has this hot-shit job now. I'm having my own TV and my own phone, and Mom does the walls with this paper that's white and has roses all over it, and gets me a white bed and white furniture and even a white phone, so white you wouldn't believe it. And she puts up white curtains with ruffles around the edges, all that girlie stuff that I can't stand and she knows it. And the bedspread matches and has an even bigger ruffle to hide all those slimy things that are living under my bed, so slimy you want to throw up. All I hope is that they

3

will just stay there and hibernate like that old witch Mrs McCarthy says bears do. Please God, let them hibernate for ever.

Mom's really happy with the room — she keeps saying look, Sandy, how nice, how pretty, 'cause she never had a big fluffy white room when she was a kid. But when I'm bad I hate her making the room that stinking white, and I hate the roses, they are so gross. What I really want is a room all purple and silver and black, but with a red phone, red like Ashley's blood. So I wait till Mom's finished and one night she and Dad go out to play bridge, and I get my collection of big fat magic-markers, I've got really lots of them. And I write all over the new wallpaper and the new white furniture. I write, "Jump In The Toilet And Drown," and, "Go Fuck A Duck," and, "Ashley Is a Turd." I write, "I Love Tito and Doug and Lorraine for ever," and, "Parents Eat Shit." I can't find any red paint in the cellar so I have to paint the phone black and it doesn't look so good. I draw pictures too. A big penis, of course. I know that's corny, don't think I don't, any jerk can draw a penis, right? But I have to do it anyway. And also I draw a giant rat with Ashley's face, but it doesn't really look like her, I'll just have to tell her it's her, and underneath I write, "Rat Fuck," which I think sounds real neat. *Rat Fuck*. And then I remember I haven't put "Cunt" anywhere, so I write it on the outside of my door so they'll know right away something's been happening.

Well, they know and boy, do I get hell like I've never gotten it before, even when I hit that slut Ashley. I'm scared Dad won't stop. But he does, and at the end I get locked in the bedroom with a bucket of water and a brush and the slime under the bed. I knew all the time it'd turn out like this but I did it anyway, so what. Bad move, San.

Mom says she won't ever get over this and that scuzz Ashley says I should be put in an orphanage so she can take my share of chocolate fudge and Doritos and the Game Boy and get more trainers and U2 tapes and swimming lessons. She is so materialistic. But Mom gets over it, sort of, and I'm thinking: Mom's so great, she really cares about us all and wants us to be happy, even me she wants to be happy, except when I'm bad and don't deserve to be. When I'm bad I'm so bad that I don't even deserve food. I show them all I know this by not eating. Not anything. They go bananas then and yell and call the doctor and Mom and Dad go in the bedroom and fight except when they do it right in front of us and it's so scary.

Mom's going to the mall to shop and Ashley and I grab at her coat and hug her and jump up and down. "You're so cute, Mom," we say. "You're cuter than all the other moms. The way you walk, we love it, it's so cute, and your fingernails, they're always painted pink, they look so pretty. You're the cutest mom, cutest mom, cutest mom." And we follow her out to the Buick, jumping around and singing. And she waves goodbye with that cute little smile, oh God, it's so great. Then I go and see if she's left any of her money in the desk.

When I'm bad I fail my English exam. My big brother Charlie says I'm Denise the Menice and he puts his arm around me, and it feels nice, it feels good being all squashed up against him. I tell him he's a fuck-face and he laughs. I'd hug Charlie all the time, only they'd never let me.

When I'm bad I get real clumsy and like bump into everything and spill milk and Pepsi on the rug and fall off the garage roof and break my arm and my foot gets caught in the bicycle spokes so that my ankle looks like a rare cheeseburger that somebody stepped on and bang my head on the side of our swimming pool and nearly drown. But the worst fuck-up I make is shutting Sylvester's tail in the refrigerator door. Sylvester has the most ginormous tail and he

5

yelled his head off. When I looked at the tail it was all bent and Mom said he was traumatized and that's why he wouldn't let me hold him, and I said won't Sylvester love me any more? And it's so awful, you know what happened? They had to cut half his tail off. His beautiful tail, and now I don't think he'll ever forgive me and I cry and cry but he just acts so funny all the time. Mom says he'll be OK but I don't know. So my idea is I don't eat so maybe he'll know by that how much I'm sorry I hurt him. Maybe he knows but it's real hard to tell. And it's so sad because I love Sylvester and sometimes when I look at him I think he's just so like perfect that my hands start to shake and I cry and I love him so much I want to be *inside* him, you know? Like I'll even pass out. I can't explain it, even to Charlie. So I grab Sylvester and hold him real hard and say I'm sorry, I'm sorry, beautiful kitty, I didn't mean to, until Mom comes and takes him away from me. But he wants to stay with me, I yell. Me, me! But Mom is so mean she wants to keep me and Sylvester apart. So I hit her with the pancake flipper.

When I'm bad I play my music real loud and there's more yelling till I turn it down which takes me about half an an hour 'cause I pretend I can't hear them 'cause I got rights. Mom says it's more than she can take and I say all the songs you listened to when you were young were only about dances and dating. At least U2 sing about what's wrong in the world. Dad is the worst about our music. He likes all that stuff with saxophones, yuk. And sometimes I think he's crazy too because he doesn't want *any* music. I mean he wants *silence*. How can he live?

Especially when he gets home from the city and sometimes that's not till nine-thirty and Mom's real busy. She's got meetings and stuff and about two million messages on her machine, and we have call-waiting 'cause she says us kids are driving her nuts with the telephone and he yells about the bills. She says she won't cook for that creep any more and they hardly speak to each other except when they fight. She leaves his supper in the microwave and he eats it all alone at the big table in our dining room. This dining room is hot shit, Mom's real proud of it. The table is so gleamy you can see Dad's reflection in it like there's two of him, so maybe he's not all that alone.

Sometimes when I get bored of that butt-head Ashley I sit down with Dad when he's eating and tell him about school and everything. About me and Lorraine and Natasha and Christine and what we get up to in that disgusting pig Mr Sach's history class and sometimes he even smiles. I can see him trying not to and he thinks I don't notice but I do. And he'll say, "You did *what*?" and surprise, surprise, we're all flunking. And I tell him who's got the hots for who and how Christine's got a real live date, sort of, with this guy Rob. And he says but she's only ten and I say how dumb can you get. 'Course I don't tell him about the cigarettes and how we spend our lunch money on make-up or sometimes if they're selling stuff through the fence.

Then he says he's too tired to talk and goes to bed. At least he doesn't do anything. Guess he's too tired even to get mad. He leaves his dirty dishes on the table. That's disgusting, I yell, that's really gross, but he just closes the bedroom door. So I go to the family room and watch TV with Ashley and we eat potato chips with sour cream and onion dip and Chocorama ice-cream and laugh at all the ratbags on TV and then have a fight and usually break something and try to hide the pieces. The dirty dishes stay on the table till morning.

One night Dad's eating his revolting miked food and something happens. I tell you, I can't explain it, but it's really bad like my brain's on FF and I can't find the off-button. I don't know. It was the silence maybe, and him sitting there and we're not allowed any music even though we have rights same as him. But what I felt was I wasn't even mad at him. It could have happened anywhere, any time, anywhere, without sounds and the thing that happened, well, it would have happened. Maybe 'cause I'd been drinking a lot of Diet Coke and that's real bad for my allergies, Mom says, but it's always in the refrigerator. Anyway I started talking, not normal talking but crazy talking like I can't stop. And I'm going hey, Dad, this this this and hey, Dad, that that that and Natasha and Sylvester and REM and the field trip to the Natural History Museum last week. I said how boring it was, but not just once it was boring, that's it. I was finding a million different ways to say it was boring, they kept coming and coming and I was getting scared 'cause I knew it wasn't me controlling them and I couldn't stop them. Then I was jabbering about some stupid thing Lance Maloomian said in maths class, and then I was just saying numbers, whatever came into my head, on and on because numbers never end, that's what Mrs Harmon said, and I couldn't stop thinking about that and I was laughing and counting like I was a machine and at the same time just a kid. And then Dad was looking at me funny and I could see he was scared too and there was Ashley standing in the doorway with this dumb expression, for once not saying drippy things every minute. And he was yelling shut up, shut up! And I wanted to, I really did, but I couldn't and he threw a plate and Ashley was crying and he was dragging me up the stairs, bump bump, it really hurt, but I still couldn't stop, but I could tell he'd decided he was gonna make me stop.

So he did. For a little while. And it was the worst time, I tell you, he never hurt me that much before. He locked me in my room and I lay on the floor sort of holding my knees to my chest and rocking and making all these noises but soft now. And I fell asleep.

In the middle of the night the talking starts again and Ashley's banging on the wall, she's so selfish she doesn't care about anybody but herself. And I'm praying please make me stop, please make me stop. And I did other things, I guess, I can't remember. And then he's there again and Mom right behind him. And she says you leave my daughter alone and calls the ambulance. And all the time I just want to hug them and them to hug me.

So now they're sending me to this special school for flakes and retards where everyone will be as bad as me so I'll fit right in. But I miss Natasha and Lorraine and Christine and even Tito. Please can I see them on weekends. Yes, if you're good. I promise I will be, but how can I promise when I never know what I'll do? They tell me that from now on I'll have this medicine that Mom says will make me feel much better. I don't, but maybe that's because sometimes I flush the medicine down the toilet. I gave some to Sylvester to make him feel better, but he just walked away with this expression like get real, kid. Then I paid Ashley to take it and that little bitch took all my allowance and then *she* flushed the medicine down the toilet and bought all these comics, so I smashed all her mirrors so she couldn't see her ugly face.

We go to see this guy, I guess he's a shrink because he asks me a lot of dumb questions that Mom's always trying to answer, and he says please, Mrs Callister, let your daughter talk and I say hey, dude, my name is Sandy. Anyway he keeps bugging me with questions till finally I say maybe he should go stick his head up a pig's ass, and that sort of ends the meeting. I hear him telling Mom and Dad that one in four children suffer from some kind of mental disorder and mainly nobody notices. Then I think how awful it must be to be crazy and I get real scared. He says it's the stresses of the modern world. He says it's because we're Americans, but I don't believe that, do you? The modern world's great. America's great. TV and CDs and computers are great. Everybody knows that. And this guy's supposed to be smart?

The school's costing Dad a whole bunch of money and I'm glad 'cause he doesn't care about the environment. Me and Christine do. We're gonna go live in the rainforest and talk just to Indians and no one'll tell us what to do. But the school's not so bad. At least I'm away from home more. I'm away from *him*. I'm glad because Mom and *him* fight all the time now and sometimes she's screaming and crying in the bedroom and I think: He's doing it. He's in there doing it right now.

Then it's Hallowe'en when everyone's out pretending to be bad and guess what, that's when the big disaster happens. Not me, I didn't do it. It was Aunt Marge, can you believe. She comes over one afternoon and Mom isn't back yet so we talk, only it's more I talk and she listens. She's brought pumpkin bread special for me and it's real yummy, and I'm feeling good, all sort of cosy with her. I'm her pet, everyone says so, even if I tear up her money. And I'm eating all the pumpkin bread. It's not made with white sugar 'cause Aunt Marge doesn't believe in white sugar which around here is like not believing in God. And she's laughing at all the things I'm telling her about school and she says I'm a very entertaining little girl, and I say I'm not a little girl, I'm a killer clown from outer space. Then all of a sudden she grabs my arm and says what's that, how did you get that? And I say Ashley and me were fighting, we didn't mean it.

Then comes the big scene. She and Mom are sitting at the kitchen table drinking beer and handing out candy corn and peanut butter cups to the Trick or Treaters, all with their parents to take them around now it's so dangerous for children, oh gee whizz, how pathetic can you get? Then Aunt Marjorie suddenly notices Mom's face. She sure has good eyes for an old person, 'cause Mom's covered the thing with tons of make-up. And Aunt Marge says what's this like she's real upset and Mom says don't be dumb, it's nothing.

Then it happens. Dad gets home and there's no dinner. She's forgotten, maybe on purpose, and all of a sudden he's yelling and she's yelling and then they're in the living room with Aunt Marge right behind them, and then he does it, not the hardest he can, but right in front of Aunt Marge. Big mistake.

Then it's all quiet like they're trying to hear a sound from way far away. And Aunt Marge says what about these kids, what about Sandy? Me and Ashley are sitting on the stairs eating Little Debbies and watching like it's a movie. Dad says for her to mind her own business and to get out of his house, so Aunt Marge leaves only she's just pretending 'cause pretty soon she's right back and this time she's got the police. By now we're all in the family room watching NYPD Blues. And Mom says why, everything's fine, it was a misunderstanding. I don't know what my sister's talking about, she was never quite right, you know. Ashley and me just stare at the cops and Dad's standing with his hand around Mom's shoulder, can you believe. Aunt Marge looks like she's gonna have kittens. And I'm thinking where's Charlie, he's always out, surprise surprise, 'cause who'd wanna live here? So the police go and they look at my aunt like maybe her brain's turned to mashed potatoes. She kisses me and Ashley and then she leaves too.

The four of us all sit together on the big plaid couch and eat Häagen-Dazs and watch some more TV and it's nice to feel everyone so close, like touching, one body next to another one. Our family sticks together, I say.

We all have our picture taken for Mom to put on the Christmas card. There's a new picture every year. Mom's kinda corny like that. And the card says, "Merry Christmas and Happy New Year from all the Callisters." We're all smiling, see, and everyone's had their hair done and they're wearing their best clothes, the ones Mom buys us, the ones we never wear, no jeans or trainers, and it's like the card's saying look how happy we are, look how neat and clean the kids are and how they've grown since last year, how pretty Mom is without her black eye, how much money Dad's making, we're a nice normal American family with a swimming pool and shrubs on both sides of the front door. Aunt Marge doesn't get a card this year. We don't see her for a while.

So now it's the shrink three times a week, which is costing Dad an even bigger bomb. I keep trying to call Natasha and Lorraine and Christine but they're always doing their homework, only they never do any homework. Their moms just want to split us up. They don't want their daughters to be friends with a loony, so I just yell down the phone at them and say they've got herpes and Aids and crabs and I'm telling everyone. They rat on me to Mom and complain and Mom goes bananas and she's real mad, like *real* mad, and says how dare I say such disgusting things to people she *knows*, oh gee whizz, I say, and will you calm down for one mother-fucking minute, and well, that does it. She flips and we're fighting in the kitchen and then there's Ashley too, natch, has to get her nose in everything. And suddenly it's all out of control, like nuts, we're all screaming and I guess I grab a kitchen knife or something. I didn't mean to, but I sort of did. But it's not true that I tried to slice my sister, don't believe her if she says that. Mom takes it away, even though I wasn't going to do anything. And she says so it's all starting again. I thought it was getting better, but it will never be better. And now I'm crying, so Ashley has to cry too. Mom yells I've had it with you, young lady. This is the end of the line. Get to your room and stay there till your father comes home.

So I'm sitting here now. A young lady in the dark. I've turned all the lights off. I don't know why, maybe so's he can't see me, won't find me. I've pushed my white bureau against the white door, 'cause he can open the lock with his American Express card, he's done it before, just like a crook. I sit in the dark and I hold my knees right up to my chest and make myself as small as possible. I pretend I'm shrinking, shrinking, and pretty soon I'll be nothing, invisible in the dark, and I'm almost believing it when I hear the Cadillac in the driveway and the kitchen door opens and it's him. Be tiny, Sandy, be a piece of dust. Downstairs Ashley's playing my Nirvana tapes. All innocent. It's quiet for a while. Then I hear his steps. He's coming up. Maybe he's only going to the bathroom. I'm small now, I'm real small. Maybe he's not going to do anything. Maybe just talk, just yell. Or maybe he won't be able to move the bureau. I tell myself all this stuff, but I don't believe it. Maybe it will be OK. He loves me really and I love him and anyway, he doesn't do it all the time. He only does it when I'm bad.

MAY DAY

The house I grew up in was big and yellow. It had green shutters and stood on the corner of Garden and Pearl Streets. A busy corner, a blind corner. My father Frank lost three collies there. The last one, Bobby, had been his favourite, and when he and the distraught driver of the 1947 Ford had knelt together over the broken body, its fur still lustrous but with the brightness fading fast from the intelligent eyes, he'd decided such pain could not again be endured. And so, despite the fact that our yard was large enough for apple and pear trees and four tall maples and a picnic table and a cement-floored clothesline with metal arches strung with six long ropes, and that I was in love with animals, I was never allowed a dog.

There had been accidents too, though not fatal: children knocked from bicycles, head-on collisions. Which was why, my parents explained, we had to start locking Grandma in.

"Don't forget," they said. "Never forget to lock the storm door and the screen door behind you." And I didn't forget, though sometimes I wanted to.

On the first day of May when I came home from school to find the screen door not only unlocked but wide open, I was surprised, then puzzled, then alarmed. It was a beautiful day, edging towards summer, practically there, with tight red leaves opening to green, so fast you could almost hear the squeak of their unfurling.

Our windows, I could see from Garden Street, were wide open, as if to receive and make room for the glory of the day that entered into the house the way the nuns told us Christ enters into the purified soul. As though the house had been to confession and was now in a state of grace. Saved. Its yellow paint was bright as the May sun, and the bedroom curtains fluttered like angels' wings. But when I mounted the three wooden steps to the porch and stood on the threshold my heart was pounding and I was afraid. You see, my mother was always there when I got home from school, busy in the large kitchen that shone from her attentions, ironing, cooking, polishing the copper bottoms of her wedding-present set of Revere Ware. The radio would be on, and she would be singing along in a voice that was sweet and uninhibited and that she used to give free rein to a part of herself that otherwise went unexpressed.

I could not move, my feet were screwed to the linoleum floor. I clutched my ringbinder to me and my schoolbooks, covered in thick green paper. I held them like I would hold a doll at night, tight, for protection. I looked down at my black Mary Janes and white ankle socks. My cotton print dress came to my knees, and from under it peeked the frills of a fresh pink petticoat. The collar of my dress had been perfectly starched by my mother so that it stayed crisp without scratching the back of my neck. Tucked under it was my green cardigan with its matching pearlite buttons. I was normal but also not. The clothes, the books, the Mary Janes and the gleaming lino beneath them were inadequate defence against recent events, unknown but palpable.

I had not experienced such a sensation of dread since the day Grandma came to stay with us. "Just for a while," they said. In fact, she had moved in. Yet permanence was never mentioned, even when my mother redecorated the spare bedroom. So her presence was an affliction I assumed must end, like measles or chicken pox.

*

She came through our kitchen door in the mouse-coloured coat she had worn for so many winters. The knot in which she tied back her long grey hair was slipping from its pins, and her face, creased with wrinkles, looked confused and distraught. My father's arm was around her shoulders.

"Welcome, Grandma," he kept saying. "Welcome home." My father was famously kind.

My mother rushed around as usual, arranging everything. You could see she was assuming a burden, glad to do it, glad to martyr herself. My Uncle Harry brought up the rear with my grandmother's two suitcases, all she possessed since her house had been sold. I watched for a while then returned to the den and the rocker and Nancy Drew. I could not understand what was happening to my family and I didn't want to. Understanding would involve pain. I preferred my book which offered insights I did not need into a world that did not exist. What I needed to know I could not bear to look at. That was how I was.

I'd always found my grandmother harsh and distracted. Even at the big Christmas dinners she gave for her ten children, their spouses and their children, when she looked and should have been happiest, she did not seem to me the way grandmothers ought to be. Watching her from one of the tables where all the children ate together, I would be thinking: Even now she is not a real grandmother. She didn't exhibit any of the comfort or indulgence or silly obsessive love that a parent's parent is supposed to dispense so liberally. Too busy for indulgence, she was more like a wicked stepmother than a grandmother.

My mother Nora was devoted to her. They had always been close, best friends more than parent and child, with an intimacy no one else could penetrate. They even had the same name. Mummy did not appear to be troubled by the Belfast accent that alienated all the children, nor by the bare gums, nor by the shock, whenever she smiled, of seeing no teeth, not a single one. She would mash away at the food my mother diced into soft pellets for her, slurp, gurgle and lick, mostly with her mouth open, hideous to see. Gravy and mashed potatoes and soup were her favourites. (Sometimes I was unable to swallow my food, and I pushed my plate away and went off to watch television.) Mummy didn't mind her skin cross-hatched with a thousand wrinkles, destinationless trails across the desert of her face, nor her thick, camel-coloured stockings that bagged at the ankles but were not coarse enough to conceal the knotted lumpy veins beneath; nor the black old-lady shoes with heavy heels that thudded wherever she went and were never laced properly. The only thing she didn't do was smell. My mother ensured that she bathed daily and washed her hair once a week. She did it herself, bending over the tub while my grandmother knelt on the mat. My mother would empty jugs of water over her head, waiting while the water cascaded through her long grey hair, rinsing and rinsing, until it squeaked when she rubbed it. Then she would sit her by the grate in the kitchen floor, a towel around her shoulders, and the hair with its wide-apart waves spread out over her back to dry in the hot air that rose from the coal furnace in the basement. She would sit for forty minutes like that, just waiting.

"Why don't you read something, Grandma?" I'd ask. Sitting with nothing to read or look at was incomprehensible to me.

She would shake her head. "I won't read right now."

She wasn't interested in printed matter save for the *Boston Herald Traveler* which my father brought home for her every evening and which she called her "wee book". I didn't discover until years later that she could not read very well and had been illiterate when she arrived in America. No one ever talked about this until after she was dead and my Uncle Harry showed me the X on her marriage certificate.

When her hair was dry my mother would braid it with the same care she had mine in the days before I wore a pony-tail. Then she would wind the plait into a flat spiral at the base of Grandma's head and hold it in place with big black hairpins which looked to me like insects or electrical-machine parts or even science-fiction weapons, easy to conceal and lethal. Then she would seem for a while almost a real grandmother, with those cotton house-dresses that you didn't see any more except in old movies and that not even my father's sisters wore. She was old. She was ancient. She was only sixty-four.

I didn't know then how old she was because no one talked about it. In our vast family of more than forty people, not one person spoke of her age. They spoke of other things — of the way she was "before".

"Everyone came to your grandmother with their troubles. All the neighbours. They loved her. She understood 'cause she had so many of her own."

"We never had any money and the salesmen, they was always after Ma, wanting payment, you know. One of them, he gave her a real hard time about a bill and finally she said get out I don't have it, and do you know what he did? Picked her up, picked her right up and set her on the coal stove. Right on the burner. She had burns all over her bottom. Great big welts. Can you beat that?"

"Your grandfather used to say she had the prettiest face and the prettiest legs in all Ireland." My grandfather who had left her with ten children.

"She'd slap us and then she'd cry," my mother told me many times, as though this were added proof of my grandmother's adorableness.

I searched in vain for this wonderful person I was assured had existed. For this kind, heroic, beautiful woman. This creature of almost mythic fecundity which everyone who knew the original held in such esteem, such almost holy regard. But I could not find her.

"She's an old witch," my cousin would say as we'd whisper

together, watching her from across the dining room. Comparisons with the Wicked Witch of the West and with pictures in my fairy books were unavoidable. I saw in her the vengeful old woman turned into a sunflower and waving her cane in fury at Ragged Robin, borne heavenward by the Orange Tree Fairy. She was the cave-dwelling hag in the Line of Golden Light, a princess under a spell for a hundred years. Who had cast the spell on my grandmother? By what magic had she been changed from madonna to hag?

I kept trying to find a way back into my grandmother's "before", to find the princess beneath the hag. I did so right until the end, led on by clues and hints purposefully or inadvertently dropped by my parents. The phrase "hardening of the arteries" kept coming up. What was an artery? I imagined these purple tubes clogged with clay, mud, hair, excrement, slowly fossilizing, turning into geography-book specimens of stone-captured pre-human creatures. Sometimes I thought it meant she simply couldn't shit. My parents alluded to these afflicted arteries for several months before finally issuing a proper grown-up bulletin: Your grandmother is sick because she has hardening of the arteries. Was hardening of the arteries the spell she was under?

Her arteries, it seemed, had begun to harden, to make her sick and crazy, while she was still in her old house on Harrison Avenue, her big house, suddenly empty of children, their friends, their spouses and their children. Everyone in the family had lived with Nora Winkle at some time or other. She was the kind of mother you brought people home to. They stayed for months, years. Even with five bedrooms there was never enough space. She'd looked after others her whole life, my mother told me (it was part of her litany of virtues, as if my grandmother was the Holy Virgin when she wasn't even a Catholic), her own irrepressible brood as well as the strangers whose houses she cleaned, her hands reddened by soap, bleach, detergents, her nails and the lines of her palms permanently blackened by coal dust.

When they all left she might at last have stopped and taken her permanent deserved rest. But just at the point when it was possible, rest was cruelly denied and restlessness put in its place. She did not know how to stop either working or worrying. She could not simply *be* without reason to be. And her reasons, all ten of them, had gone, no longer present and selfish and adoring and demanding. And their absence left a void where there was only furniture and plumbing and tasks which no longer maintained or benefited anyone but herself.

The time "before", the mythic time, had actually been one of drudgery and over-population, and her pleasure had been derived from precisely that. Whatever enjoyment she found must have come in the interstices between the drudgeries — little moments of madness or gaiety. Or it arose from the subliminal hum of the constant presence of others, the uninterrupted assurance of some-one you loved being always around. She was never the princess, I realized. She had always been the old woman who lived in the shoe.

"Her life just stopped," my mother said. "There was only silence and nothing to do. Nothing."

Put that way, I was able to sympathize a little. The feeling of loneliness, the need to expend energy: that I could understand.

And so my grandmother became absent and forgetful and lived in a permanent muddle illuminated now and then by lightning flashes of recognition. She who had looked after everyone could not look after herself. Her authority usurped by her own offspring, she was taken, lured by tricks, from the house where she had lived for forty years. Taken to us. Why us?

She had only been in the house a few weeks when she began asking to leave.

"I want to go home," she'd say. "I want to go to my own house."

"This is your home now, Mama."

"Harry'll take me. Where's Harry?"

"Harry's at work. He's in East Rochester."

"Call him up."

"I can't, Mama."

"Call him."

"Mama, the house has been sold."

"Who sold it?"

"You did, Mama. We all did."

"Why did we do that?"

"Because you couldn't take care of it any more."

For a long time my mother believed that if she just explained matters over and over, patiently and calmly, my grandmother would understand and accept. But it never happened.

"You live here now, Mama. With me and Frank and Moira. We're taking care of you."

"I don't live here. I don't want you to take care of me. I want to go home."

She grew devious. Determined to find her way back to Harrison Avenue, which was eighteen miles away, she would wait until my mother went down to the cellar to oversee the next phase in our endless cycle of laundry or was talking on the phone to one of her sisters and bolt for the door. She was so nimble she'd be at the top of the rise and outside the Lanouettes' front porch before anyone noticed. Sometimes she got as far as Orange Street where the traffic, even in 1952, was heavy. Mrs Lanouette and Millie Furbush opposite were enlisted to keep watch lest she escape, but they couldn't always be looking out the window for Mrs Winkle; they had families of their own, after all.

One afternoon she got as far as Green Street. She was wearing a slip and no stockings. Her hair was loose and her shoes untied. The temperature was 25 degrees Farenheit. Rose Delahandy invited her in for a cup of tea and promised to drive her to Rochester. Then, treacherously, she rang my mother. After that we locked the doors.

No one knew what to do about my grandmother. How to occupy her all day. How to prevent her escaping. It was the first time I had witnessed the fearsome energy of old people, the terrible force that was wearing my mother out. She was forever chasing after my grandmother, leaving the housework then returning to it, constantly worried that the old woman was "up to something", like slyly removing the contents of all the upstairs drawers and hiding them in the attic, stripping the beds for the fourth time in a week, dressing and undressing herself like a little girl, inventing preposterous costumes, emptying the rubbish bin on to her bedroom rug, approaching the cat with malicious intent. Day after day my mother set straight the mess, got my grandmother back into a clean housedress and stockings, tied her shoes, rescued the cat. Her eyelids looked as if they were growing grey scales. But Nora Winkle went relentlessly on, killing her favourite child.

Only my father Frank could pacify his mother-in-law's demonic restlessness. She would wait for him when he returned from the office at five-thirty with an account of my mother's abuses, the mean measures she'd invented to thwart and mistreat her.

"What's the matter, sweetheart?" he'd say, leading her into the den, his arm around her shoulder. "What's happened? Let's hear all about it." And she would sit with him and recount every slight, real and imagined, still at last. And he would absorb all her complaints and neutralize them. Sometimes, though, not even he could contain her wild resentment, and then he would take her hand, unlock the door and walk her round the block so that she might expend a little of her rage. He would placate her with promises of a ride after supper. He understood her need for movement but was not above empty promises of returns to Harrison Avenue. Even when these did not materialize and we ended up back in our own driveway at eight o'clock, she would not hold his betrayal against him. She would behave herself for the rest of the evening and happily watch the television. He was her cavalier, her father, lover, son. All the good things men are to you if they are not your husband. He was the only man she trusted. She'd pressed my mother to marry him, pleaded, insisted, cajoled. It was a way of marrying him herself. And he seemed always to have known that the two Noras would share him and that he would spend his middle years being gallant to them both. And gallant to me. There was always me, who watched the painful proceedings across my Rice Krispies and from behind my Nancy Drew. The three of them were characters in a drama that mesmerized and frightened me. But I remained the audience, separate and removed, no matter how much the play might grip my emotions.

Yes, my father was smoothly attentive to us all. What was the source of his facility? He did not appear torn by our diverse requirements, but had affection and interest to spare and distributed them with scrupulous and easy fairness. I was not like him but lived divided between my need for my mother and my growing hatred of my grandmother. A hatred that soon turned to fear.

The fear crept up gradually. I could not name it at first. Perhaps because it seemed to me so wrong, a sin, and therefore something to be confessed. I did not need any new sins. And so I locked my sense of transgression away in the container I kept inside myself for such purposes and which functioned as a kind of Pandora's box in reverse.

What upset me most were the mad combinations she made of her ugly clothes, sometimes stealing one of my mother's hats and clapping it backwards on her head, completing an ensemble of the mouse-coloured coat worn over baggy pink underpants and a scarf that had recently been the bathroom curtain. That, even more than the havoc she wrought with the drawers or the bad language spewed out in her Belfast accent, marked her as the usurper of order, the instigator of chaos, the Mistress of Misrule. The costumes had an element of obscene humour, making her not only witch but clown. She carried something alien into the house, something that originated in the dirty back corners of carnival tents. Something you went to visit but did not allow into your own clean and tidy space. She was clutter and menace and destruction, and her antics, like those of a hyperactive child, demanded more and more of the attention that was draining the blood from my perfect mother. I could see her spirit waning. She was running down, not able to keep pace with my grandmother whose exorbitant drives were fed by a source that was unfathomable and malignant and that was making our lives a poisoned heavy dream.

She was sick now, really sick. They tried to keep the extent of the damage from me, but I could hardly ignore the weekly visits of the district nurse. Mrs Noonan was kind and efficient, a deceptively frail woman who was in fact possessed of great strength of character which was apparent once you'd taken time to study her posture and her defiant little chin. Nothing upset her. In that way she was good for my mother who always assisted when she came on Tuesdays to attend to my grandmother, whom Mrs Noonan respectfully addressed as Mrs Winkle.

I wasn't supposed to know, or they were reluctant to tell me what happened upstairs during these Tuesday afternoons. Eventually I found out. I listened, as I often did, to my mother's telephone conversations with her sisters, those transactions in an adult dimension that I could not reach and that for years would remain a mysterious territory requiring passwords and riddles and initiatory rites before I might gain admittance. She was speaking very quietly, but my hearing was sharp, like all my senses, and I was able to catch the word "enema". So my instincts had been correct. The old woman could not shit.

One Tuesday I confirmed this repulsive discovery. I'd convinced my mother to allow me to stay home from school with an upset tummy, a frequent and indulged complaint. (I think my mother simply liked to have me with her and was glad of company.) They were especially noisy that afternoon. Above Grandma's protests and curses I could hear my mother's pleas and the nurse's firm instructions. "Lie *still*, Mrs Winkle." "Up we *go* now, Mrs Winkle." Absorbed as they were, they'd be unlikely to hear me, so I laid aside my book and crept upstairs in my red woollen bathrobe and rabbit slippers, pausing four steps from the top when I sensed imminent action.

Sure enough there was a sudden rush from Grandma's pale-green bedroom. The exodus was so rapid I could only see the three women from the back, in a kind of awful flurry. My grandmother, struggling and swearing, was gripped at the elbows by my mother and Mrs Noonan who were hurrying her into our tiny bathroom. My grandmother was naked, though she wore her black shoes, unlaced as usual. Her hair had come loose in a swampy tangle. I saw the doughy marbled flesh on her back and bottom. Then they were inside, the bathroom door locked behind them. I backed down the stairs to the accompaniment of more cries and curses and despairing entreaties. I returned to my book.

I have since learned, as everyone does, that things are not always what they seem. I have learned to interpret appearances and behaviour and events as though their real significance lies hidden behind them, a face beneath a mask, a nut inside a shell, to be removed by clever analysis. But I also know that once in a while something happens that does not yield to this sort of analysis. The event is only what it is, immune to rationalization. The sight of my grandmother naked, mad, and being dragged to the bathroom by two well-intentioned women was such an occurrence; a fact, irreducible, a wall at which you could only stare for a minute, defeated by its stubborn, pure reality.

My mother was always exhausted after these Tuesdays. She was being worn out, ground down to nothing, but she would not let go. She was determined to hold on to my grandmother and never be separated.

My grandmother now spent nearly all her waking hours on the other side, in a world that was entirely her own, peopled by phantoms and full of anguish, where she was pitched to and fro by mysterious compulsions and which overlapped our world at no point save that of her agitated physical presence. She was pitiful, tragic, but I did not feel sorry for her. I envied other children who had real grandmothers or whose grandmothers did not live with them, children who had no grandmothers at all. And I had a reason.

She'd forgotten who I was. I don't know when this lapse occurred; perhaps long before I finally noticed, before she began to say things.

"Who's that girl?" she'd ask my mother as though she'd only just noticed me over the top of the *Herald Traveler*. "Why is that girl here?"

And I would sit, pinned to the chair, unable to read, unable to move, fixed by her eyes so bright and hostile, in shape like my mother's but with the expression all wrong.

"That girl's been here a long time," she'd say at supper. "Doesn't she have a house of her own? Who is she?"

Then a silence would fall, full of invisible sparks from the electrical current that connected the four of us, switched on at highest voltage, a silence my father would break with some piece of local gossip or a comment on the editorial in the *Boston Globe*.

My mother said nothing, did nothing. How could she, being the object of this cruel competition? I pitied her, divided between her mother and her child. But I blamed my grandmother. I wanted her to go and put an end to my mother's constant pain. Meanwhile my father floated among us, undismayed. Perhaps he didn't mind how his women behaved provided he remained surrounded by them. Perhaps he was simply adept at hiding his concern. He believed in being positive, I knew that.

Only Dr La Plante would say the unsayable, give a name to what could not be uttered by us who were struck dumb under my grandmother's spell. His were not words to be spoken aloud, in daylight. They were like weapons, these words, like sex, something dangerous which must be concealed in darkness. Yet I knew he had spoken them and that they concerned me and the harm that my grandmother might do me. I knew that since he'd taken my parents aside and whispered his words, something had changed. That whenever my grandmother asked, "Who's that girl?" the ensuing silence was deeper and more debilitating, rendering us even less capable of action. Something was coming that my child ignorance could not articulate, and I was sunk in primitive dread.

When she was not staring at me, plotting my destruction, my grandmother prowled the house searching for an open ground-floor window, a secret tunnel out of the cellar. I started sleeping with a knife under my pillow. I imagined ways of strewing my bedroom floor with broken glass, laying it out at night and removing it and storing it away in the morning if I had slept safely and my grandmother had not crept towards my bed to murder me. That was when I thought of leaving the kitchen door open, hoping she would run into the road and be killed like the collies.

Perhaps, after all, I should go away. But where? I did not want to live with one of my aunts. And if I went, who would keep my mother company, alone as she was with a mad old lady? I decided I must stay for her sake. And I did, though I think now I was no use to her, ensconced behind my books, waiting to pose the question I could not ask.

The question was answered that afternoon on the 1st of May when the doors and windows were opened at last, and the spring wind blew through the house and I clung to my books in the kitchen. It was a Tuesday, but there was no Mrs Noonan, there were no shouts nor pleadings, no heavy footsteps overhead. There was no radio, no singing, no smell of hot clean cotton, no stacks of my father's shirts, precisely folded, on the table. Had everyone gone away, moved to another location to perform their play without me? Had I become superfluous to the drama and was my punishment to be confinement in this once-loved house that was now hateful in its emptiness?

Then I realized that the house was neither empty nor silent. I'd been deafened by my panic, that was all. But now the awful noise reached me and opened my unwilling ears. I tiptoed to the foot of the stairs. I knew I was not mistaken. I really was hearing the sound of my mother's crying. Her sobs grew louder and louder. The house shook with them. They came from the root of her being, as though she were parting with pieces of herself, having a baby, dying. Her sobs cut me off from her. They rose and spilled out like vomit from the grief deep inside her that was a private sickness, hers alone. And then she spoke the terrible word.

"Mama," she cried out. "Mama."

She shouted it over and over, gasping it between sobs which went on and on, gathering force like waves piled high in a sea that would wreck and drown her. I felt how small she was on that sea and how alone. How could she love that horrible old woman? Then I understood. My grandmother had gone. She was never coming back. My relief and joy were huge, brilliant as the day. But they were brief, the life of a Mayfly. I saw soon enough the price that had been paid for them and which would never allow me to live in the light they promised.

"Mama," I whispered, knowing I should go to her and knowing she did not want me to. I was convinced she had a right to her exclusive sorrow. I sat at the kitchen table for I don't know how long. Over an hour, I think, until her crying began to subside and I heard the bed on which I had been conceived creak as she rose from it. She was going to the bathroom to wash her face, to put a cold cloth over her red eyes, so that I wouldn't see, wouldn't know.

"Mama, Mama," I said, mouse-quiet, so that she couldn't hear me. I should have gone to her, spoken to her, but what could I have said?

When I heard the bathroom door open I went out into the yard and sat at the picnic table with my book open as if I had been there reading all the while.

A week later I found out that my father and my Uncle Harry had taken my grandmother to the state mental asylum at Concord. By what ruse, I wondered, what stratagem? But it wasn't hard to guess. They'd told her, naturally, that she was going home.

Years later, when my mother was dead, my father alluded to that May day when Grandma left. He told me my mother had not been the same afterwards. "Something went out of her eyes after that," he said and looked away. I wondered what that something was and where it had gone. I think he wondered too, all the time, and that he never found out. We didn't talk about it any more.

THE IMMORTAL
GIRLFRIEND

I knew a goddess once. She lived across the street from me. Her name was Estelle Vachon, and she was a small-town Venus.

What made her a goddess? Her magnetism, but also her surroundings. Picture the fifties — a small American city going to seed since the textile mills closed. Everyone just getting by and not a lot of local colour. Bars, pool rooms, an Elks Lodge and one movie theatre in need of repairs. Oh, and the leaves turn red in the Fall. Urban renewal and sexual liberation still coming attractions. What the Pope says goes. Then rock and roll arrives, and with it danger: riots after concerts (we watch them on TV), black people, flaming pianos, men with kiss curls, men who wiggle their hips; our leaders in a moral panic and the priests lecturing kids on how it's a mortal sin even to listen to Fats Domino and Little Anthony, and all the while the 45s go round and round in our brains — "Whoooo do you love? . . . Whoooo do you love?" In such a place and at that radical moment Estelle stood out. She was like rock and roll.

I can't think of Estelle without thinking of the boys. Raymond La Chance, Demo Eleftherion, Frankie McCrillis, Bobby Wentworth, Mo St Onge, Chester Langevin. Kanuck, Irish, Greek, Yankee. Names I never hear any more. Faces I never see. And there were other names and other flames, plenty of them, some of whom I knew only slightly, like Eddy Foss. Poor Eddy. Eddy the Last.

Every boy I knew, including my little brother Marty, was in love with Estelle. He never dared make a move, rejection being a foregone conclusion, even if she did always tell him what a cutie he was. But Marty had the unique advantage of living across the street from her and knew things the rest of them would have given a lot to know. I was constantly catching him with Daddy's binoculars, and for a while he supplemented his allowance by peddling eye-witness accounts of our foxy neighbour's activities. Grown-ups, especially women, didn't go for Estelle. Even at eight she was a scandal, and my mother, normally a generous Christian lady, mistrusted her and complained that she was too sexy for every-one's good, as if Estelle were a dish the cook had mistakenly over-seasoned and would have to throw out. Mom seemed to see the future and didn't approve of my playing with her, though there wasn't a lot she could do because of our physical proximity.

In fact Estelle was a good-natured and affectionate child, but already with that hint of mischief and subversion that enhanced her charms. She'd run up to you and kiss you for no reason at all, then run away laughing. She was always giggling, and her laughter, like her voice, had this crackle in it that was a mystery. No one we knew had a voice like that, like the taste of chocolate and lemons mixed up, I don't know how else to describe it. She and I belonged to the same girl gang until, at thirteen, she moved out of our league and into that of the fearsome Laurel Carberry – by means of some very public foreplay. Estelle liked an audience.

She was never much on clothes. Her father worked in the Bleachery and had five kids and earned even less money than mine, so, until her teens, she wore only hand-me-downs. I remember a lavender dress with puffed sleeves, much stained and washed, that served for school, mass and birthday parties, usually paired with a letter sweater that had belonged to her sister Carol and that she wore most days in place of a jacket. Later on, she dressed basic: pencil skirt and tight sweaters in blacks and browns, and the white socks we all wore, held up with rubber bands that cut off our circulation and left red rings around our calves. No frills, even on her prom dress; nothing to enhance her appearance. Fashion just didn't interest her, nor did jewellery or make-up, items you'd expect any normal Venus to regard as indispensible. Yet something distinguished her from your bouncy breathless brunette of transient high-school fame. People found her disturbing, not so much because of what she did — at least at first — but because of what she had. What she had, I guess, was what my parents' generation would have called It.

Estelle was nice, often sweet, but never innocent. There was something Estelle knew way before the rest of us, if we ever did know. Even when we were kids she made me feel that she was at the centre of life and I was on the periphery. She made me afraid I would never reach that centre where the sacred fire burned. Her charm was potent, her ardour real, her flattery irresistible. She was hot, that's what she was. Everyone must have sensed that the reason she was burning bright was that she was burning fast.

That's why she did everything first. She was the first to get chased home from school by the Riley brothers, waving the gory segments of a dead grass snake as she screamed with pleasure. She was the first to be asked to dance, even at those adolescent balls where the boys shuffled and muttered on one side of the empty floor while the girls squirmed and giggled on the other. Someone — usually pretty thrilling, but even if he wasn't she'd be nice to him — would approach and take her hand and together they'd break the socio-sexual stasis. She was a good, but not outstanding, dancer with easy, unselfconscious movements. Not a dedicated bopper who could win dance contests like me. She didn't need contests, and as far as I know never competed for anything except cheerleading, for which she was immediately selected but didn't show much enthusiasm. She didn't need to win because she didn't need to prove anything. She was already living proof.

She was the first of us to get her period, the first, aged twelve, to go on a date. What, fumed my Mom, could her parents be thinking of? But Mr and Mrs Vachon were never big on restraint. They understood, just as her friends did, that romance was their daughter's destiny, her divine nature and right. They knew better than to interfere. They seemed proud of her power.

Estelle had what was called a Reputation. Boys were "wild" or "cowboys" or "punks", but only girls had Reputations. They were like breasts. On the one hand getting a Reputation was the worst thing that could happen to you. On the other, you were secretly, universally admired and envied. At the age of twelve, Estelle established and maintained a five-star, gold-medal Olympic Reputation, founded in part on her taste for flagrant necking, especially at parties.

Most of us would sneak off to another room or at least a dark corner, but not Estelle. She smooched openly — standing, sitting or horizontal if there was room — with Frankie McCrillis or Bobby Wentworth or Clovis Nedeau or whoever was favourite of the night. And these were not just five-minute interludes. They were marathons. I mean flesh was glimpsed, kisses timed, records set. And what infuriated the rest of us, male and female, was that she was having such a shamelessly good time. On Monday mornings reports, true and false, would sweep through high school like a brush fire. The idea was that a party just hadn't been any good unless it was followed by whispers in the corridors and phone calls among snoopy outraged moms. Of course if the priests got involved that was the best, and from then on everyone would kill to get invited to your parties even if you held them in a cowshed. A mention at mass meant star billing. Something really dirty was sure to have gone on. Usually I hadn't been there and would eat my heart out along with the rest of the good (read locked-up) girls. The number one problem of early adolescence is lack of transport.

We were jealous of Estelle; we wanted to be with her; we wanted to *be* her. And then we lost her. As I said, she left our gang around this time, though she was always nice to us and I still talked to her a lot because she lived across the street. I'd see her skating at Black Pond or Long Swamp or Filion's Field. Always hand-in-hand with a boy: Chester Langevin, Vincent Kennedy, Elmer Verville. Then she stole Frankie McCrillis from me. Not that much was going on between us, and I know he saw other girls too, but it was exciting having him hanging around. Frankie was cute and lazy and we all thought of him as a rebel, our own private Jimmy Dean. He and Estelle had an on-off thing for maybe four months. I was pretty upset, but that didn't stop me from being Estelle's friend. I regarded it as inevitable that she would take whomever and whatever I wanted.

It was with cars, though, that real romance began. Robin's-egg-blue Chevy convertibles with fox tails on the aerials, huge black 1949 Buicks that took up two-thirds of the road and could hold eleven people; '51 Fords with engines tuned to sound like gun battles, all with WBZ turned to maximum volume, all driven by sixteen and seventeen year olds, cruising the main streets and the back roads and the surrounding towns until the small hours of the morning or whenever the gas ran out, and all parked, at one time or another, outside Estelle's house. Their owners would stop by after school or at weekends, and in good weather Estelle would stand and talk to them for hours, her head inside the window, one leg crossed over the other, her classy ass highly visible. My Dad found it irritating.

"Why?" I asked. "They're only talking."

"It looks cheap," was his verdict.

Late at night you could always hear a motor running as she and Ray or Frank or Chester said their long goodnights or pursued their regular quarrels. Everyone said why didn't her parents put a stop to it, insist she come home at a respectable hour like other girls her age. Why were they so indulgent with her? But her parents knew that Venus needs new men. Though Estelle, limited as she was by a population of only 9,956, operated more on a rota.

She was the first of us to lose her virginity — in the back seat of Raymond La Chance's car. We knew because she told us all immediately. No one could call Estelle discreet.

"You feel so close after you do it," she enthused and advised us wide-eyed virgins to follow her example on the double, though not with Ray. It was love, you see. It was exclusive. She wore his class ring on a chain around her neck and sat practically in his lap as they cruised around town. He was obsessed with her, wasn't interested in anything but being with her, a weak passionate guy who was heading for trouble. Everyone said so. Ray's father, a nice man but very religious, tried to intervene. After five months in Venus's service, his son's normally good grades had dropped to Cs and Ds, and he was concerned for Raymond's future. He even came to see Mr and Mrs Vachon to suggest they rein in their horny daughter. The meeting was supposed to be a secret, but Marty and I watched him come and go from Mom's bedroom window and timed the length of the visit, information which gained us a lot of kudos once we began passing it around. More than anything, Mr La Chance was afraid Estelle would get pregnant.

There was nothing he could do, except maybe hate her. Her parents remained infuriatingly tolerant, acted like they didn't know what he was talking about. He just couldn't face the fact that his son was a casualty of *l'amour*. He had plans for him, you see, wanted him to be a lawyer. Poor man, it was plain to everyone but him that Ray wouldn't end up being much more than a fool for love, though maybe a holy fool. He was clamped on Estelle emotionally and physically, almost like he was trying to commit suicide by taking an overdose of her. Every night there'd be sightings of his car parked in various remote locations: dirt roads, fields, deserted beaches, even the church parking lot. We all knew what went on in that car. We were all jealous.

Venus needs new men. The wheel went round and soon McCrillis was back on the scene. He didn't own a car, but like I said, he was so cute with that lopsided smile and slouchy feline walk that nobody cared. Besides, Estelle never went for heroes. She wasn't interested in football or basketball stars. They had to go to bed early and waste all that energy on exercise. Mars bored her.

She and Frankie borrowed cars or else he'd come round to her house for an hour in the afternoons when her sister was working in the doughnut shop and her brother was rehearsing for the school play. When the news reached Ray, he flipped. There were raised voices in his car at 1.30 a.m., tears in the corridors, and, finally, a fist fight outside the gym during the biology club dance. The police came, but Estelle was driven safely home by Mr Beamis, the biology teacher. Rumours flew. The two of them certainly had flirted in class, and he seemed to enjoy the way she played saucy and stupid at the same time. He'd give her a B minus whatever mess she made of her exams. On one famous occasion when he caught her passing a note to a girl behind her, he reprimanded her, but what he intended to be, "Miss Vachon, please turn around," came out as, "Miss Vachon, please turn over." The class went wild. It took him twenty minutes to calm the uproar and regain his composure and for his face to go from boiled lobster back to normal white.

She was a universal flirt. She'd flirt with the cat, the furniture, the tree, the priest, anything. She was always voted Class Romeo in the Yearbook Supplement. Yet she loved going steady. It was what she wanted most. She was like Liz Taylor, the way she went on getting married and divorced. She just needed to do it, and maybe, like Liz, every time she believed it would last. Her attachments and break-ups were top of the gossip charts and the subject of long and urgent speculations from the locker room to the old *mémères'* tea parties. We all knocked her and we all wanted to be her best friend, even the meanest and toughest girls like Laurel Carberry. Estelle was the focus of all our attentions, and what she did mattered.

Some say she blew her life on giggles and romance, but I don't think so. She just needed, more than the rest of us, to express love. I remember the way she would touch everyone, male or female, young or old, animal or human. Simple physical contact gave her so much pleasure. You could see it in her eyes as she danced with her boyfriends to "In the Still of the Night" or "Since I don't have You" or "Smoke Gets In Your Eyes". (She especially loved the Platters.) They'd dance close, too close, and were constantly reprimanded by Mr Hegarty and Miss Chick. I'd watch her from where I sat on the benches or from over the shoulder of a less glamorous boy. The look in her eyes was ecstatic. It revealed complete surrender — to the music, to the boy, to her own emotions. Until then I thought such expressions existed only in the movies or in the raised faces of saints. Where did such rapture come from?

For a while it came from Demo. Demosthenes Eleftherion was cool, wore pegged black trousers and pink shirts, quiffed and greased his hair and cultivated a cynical attitude. Demo smirked at life. It was pretty impressive. It certainly impressed Estelle. He was a challenge, this new Adonis. For him she was a trophy, she was sex. He was proud of himself because, unlike her, he needed to prove something. It was the most evenly matched of all her loves, and maybe that's why they lasted nearly a year. Meanwhile Ray was failing English, algebra II and American history. Mr La Chance still blamed Estelle, though we all thought this was unfair since she was screwing, slapping and smiling at Demo alone. Demo was strong, with a negative strength. He was a Resister and could therefore handle Estelle. For a while. Almost.

1959. Elvis was in the Army, Alan Fried resigned as America's Number One disc jockey over the Payola scandal and Estelle's behaviour took a turn for the worse. It was at the end of our junior year that her own big scandal broke. Her gang, led by the ferocious Laurel, had been torn for weeks by internal strife. Tension was mounting, and we had a feeling that something had got to give — and violently — pretty soon. Then one day Estelle didn't show up for school. And she wasn't sick. Something had happened the night before that everyone was talking about but that no one could explain. The gang had driven over to Chandler's Hill around ten at night. Several strange boys had turned up and there followed what I imagined to have been some sort of ritual in the dark, involving all of them but mainly Estelle. What act could be so shaming as to send even defiant Estelle into hiding and turn the entire gang against her? They called her a whore and more besides but refused to give any details, as if bad behaviour were their exclusive preserve. Or maybe, this time, they really were scared of repercussions.

We didn't see her for five days. Marty kept watch on the house, but she didn't come out. The place looked like someone had thrown a shroud over it, and all the shades were down. Then on Tuesday a Mercury driven by Laurel's boyfriend, Dave Seavy, squealed round the corner and five of the gang got out, sending Dave on his way. I was outdoors watering the lawn so I could see and hear quite a lot, but not the specific, crucial words. I did hear yelling and crying. Then silence. At five o'clock Dave was back in the Mercury. He gave me a wave, unlike Laurel and Solange and Mary Lou and the others. They'd decided I was the enemy because I'd just got straight A's. I knew they were planning some humiliation for me. They piled into the car and took off, sending me dirty looks and burning rubber all over the street. The next day Estelle was back in class and back in the gang, though it was understood she was on probation. No one ever talked about what had happened that night on Chandler's Hill, and it remained their glamorous and terrible secret.

A couple of weeks later Estelle went back to Ray. She claimed he was still the best lover.

I think she got so upset over her expulsion from the gang because she really loved women. Her girlfriends were very important to her, even if only as confidantes. She was affectionate with them and they were devoted to her, despite the jealousy they had constantly to suppress. If the outcome of her life had been different, or if she'd lived in a later time, another place, she'd probably have had affairs with women as well as men. Same as the boys, no matter how angry girls got with her, they just couldn't leave and forget her. She had this effect on you that you had to be with her no matter what. She was where the action was. Action followed her around.

Venus was gaining weight. The imp-like child had developed, in adolescence, a firmness that could verge on solidity. She was five foot seven with good posture and she moved well. She could handle the extra pounds and people continued to see them as luscious, until the spring of the year we graduated, when her thighs were bulging from the black Bermuda shorts that she wore with a plain white blouse and black sneakers. Still no frills. Some said, with relish, that she was becoming like her last name, Vachon — *vache*.

Or else, they snickered, she was pregnant. But Ray didn't care. She still had her thick olive skin that had never betrayed her with a blemish, that gleaming dark hair, those clear teasing eyes, so brown they were almost black. He was as much her slave as ever, and his father was broken-hearted when he failed to make the National Honour Society.

In fact Estelle wasn't pregnant, though everyone expected the announcement daily. While other girls were rushed to the altar practically in their graduation gowns, she continued to enjoy herself with divine impunity. For Demo was once more slinking around the margins, and soon they were again having fun on the sly. In addition there were rumours of a last fling with Bobby Wentworth before he went off to Fort Dix.

Then she did it. She dumped them all and for a whole month proclaimed celibacy. No cars were parked outside the Vachon house. She went with her girlfriends to dances and to the beach and shopped at the Factory Outlet. She got a job as a typist in the fish-packing plant. What was going on?

Ray went into sharp decline, and Mr La Chance at last accepted that the most he could hope for was that his son would emerge a sane and functioning American citizen. But even this modest dream was wrecked when Ray appeared one night at Estelle's house, drunk, to beg her to take him back. She told him their love was over and that she didn't want to see him again, and he set fire to the Vachon's front porch. All the neighbours stood outside in their bathrobes and watched the fire engines arrive. Ray was hospitalized with second-degree burns then sent away to an aunt in Illinois to recover and calm down. Mr Vachon said Ray was a bum. Mr La Chance had his second heart attack. Ray's excuse — the only one he thought he needed — was that he'd seen Estelle with some old guy.

We all agreed with Ray. Thirty-two was old, and Eddy Foss was thirty-two. He was tall and strong with red-blond curls and green eyes and his face wasn't cute but serious and full of what my mom called experience. Old. He'd been in the Navy. He'd been around. (Estelle had never been further than Boston.) Now he had a job in the brickyard, a pretty good one, they said. And he owned a yellow Oldsmobile convertible. People said he was from Delaware, but it turned out he was from Pittsfield. After dating her for two weeks, he asked Estelle to marry him and she said yes. Ray's father tried to keep the news from him. No one wanted any more flaming porches. His boss at the garage where he'd got a job as a mechanic did eventually tell him, but instead of cracking up, Ray just quietly crumbled. It was a couple of months before he'd speak to anyone, even his mother and father.

Now the yellow Oldsmobile was stationed like a faithful Palomino across the road. Eddy and Estelle were together every night, holding hands and watching TV with her parents and brother, Marty reported. He was sixteen but still not above binoculars. One night I looked too. They sat like married people, not saying anything. I never heard her giggle, not even on hot nights when all the windows were open. During that summer there were no rumours or scandals about Estelle. She'd created a gossip vacuum, which the town abhorred, and everyone resented her for it.

In September, a few days before I left for college, I had a conversation with her, she on her side of the street, I on mine. I'd been raking the first of the fall leaves, and I put down the rake to go and speak to her. She was waiting for her sister to pick her up and take her to the new Portsmouth Mall where they'd start their search for the wedding dress, which I assumed would be without frills. She'd had her hair cut short and permed, and the effect wasn't so good. Her face had gone from round to full, and there was — I'm sure I saw it — the shadow of a second chin. She laughed a lot and was sweet to me, and I felt the old seduction, the pull of her aura on mine. She seemed happy, but then she always seemed happy.

When I came home at Thanksgiving, she was dead.

She'd started having headaches in October. New glasses, the doctor said, but that didn't work. Migraines, maybe. Only a migraine eventually stops. And during the first week in November came a pain that did not stop but whose intensity grew until the highest potency painkillers short of morphine were prescribed. Then morphine was prescribed. For five days she could eat, sleep and move. She touched Eddy again and wanted him to touch her. He was so happy and relieved to see her better that he cried. He cried, some people said, because maybe he thought, like they thought, that Estelle was having headaches because she didn't want to get married. Of course she never said such a thing. But now that she was defenceless, people seemed to want more than ever to put words in her mouth.

A week later the pain began all over again, becoming so terrible that she screamed in agony. That's what her white-faced mother said: in agony. Estelle had stopped going to work or trying to do anything except lie on the couch or in her darkened bedroom. One afternoon her oldest sister dropped by to see how she was and found the door locked. She banged and called but no one came. She panicked and put a stone through the kitchen window and discovered Estelle in a bathrobe, lying beside her bed that had been neatly made and covered as usual with stuffed toys and heart-shaped cushions and dolls with large circular skirts that surrounded them like ruffled haloes. She was dead of the tumour that had been feeding on her brain, perhaps for a long time, the doctor said to her weeping parents and brothers and sisters.

I couldn't help imagining it there beneath her shiny hair, behind her knowing eyes, slowly growing, even while she'd been flirting and giggling, while she'd been dancing to "Smoke Gets In Your Eyes" and wearing that expression of bliss, while she'd been making love in the back of Ray La Chance's car. Even then it had been eating her alive.

You had to force your way into the undertaker's parlour. I'd been going to wakes and kissing corpses all my life, but I'd never seen Mr Guilmette's establishment so crowded. Estelle's mother was too stricken to come to the wake, but Mr Vachon was standing beside the coffin, his rough hand on its edge, as though he were rocking a cradle. I approached him reluctantly. I was more afraid of him than I was of Estelle's dead body. He seemed shorter and stubbier and balder than before, and tears were streaming down his flushed face. I couldn't bear to see his grief. I told him how sorry I was and that I would always love Estelle and remember her. He held my hand, not realizing how hard he was squeezing it, and gazed at his daughter laid out before him, a doll in a blue velvet box.

"She looks so beautiful," he kept repeating. "Doesn't she look beautiful?"

She did not. They'd rouged her lips and her olive cheeks as if determined to turn her into a rosy blonde. She wore a pale-green taffeta dress, all flounces and fuss, like you'd put on a ten year old. Her hair, its gloss and bounce gone for ever, looked as if it had been done at the poodle parlour. Someone had entwined a crystal rosary around her plump folded hands. I kissed her forehead. That is what you did.

All my classmates were there, trying to look subdued but feeling totally crazy. For many this was their first death. We took turns going to the parking lot for a hit from a bottle of Four Roses which I'd never tasted before. It was awful, but it made me feel better. The next night I went back. That is what you did. Again I kissed Estelle's forehead and this time hugged her mother who could barely stand and who said what a good friend I'd been to her daughter. Over her shoulder I saw Eddy sitting alone at the end of a long row of folding chairs that were backed against the wall, as was the custom. He leaned forward, his arms resting on his thighs, his head bowed, holding a can of beer between his large hands. You weren't supposed to drink in the funeral parlour, but no one complained. Eddy was a Protestant.

That night it snowed. Then the temperature fell to 22 degrees. But on Friday morning, St Joseph's was so crowded that people stood outside on the steps, stomping their feet and rubbing their gloved hands together, saying how lucky it was the grave had been dug before this weather set in. The sky was so blue you could hardly look at it. I can't remember what Father Gilraine said when he stopped halfway through the mass for the Dead to deliver the funeral oration; it seemed to have so little bearing on events. There was too much to feel and think about and look at. We'd been late, and had to take seats at the back, but that was fine because it meant I could see everyone present. I could see the coffin draped in white silk stitched with a yellow cross, topped with yellow and white flowers and carried up the church aisle by Raymond La Chance, Demosthenes Eleftherion, Frankie McCrillis, Bobby Wentworth, Mo St Onge and Chester Langevin. The main altar wouldn't hold any more flowers, and they were spilling down the steps practically to the Communion rail, in front of which the boys set Estelle down.

We were all crying. I could recognize the distinctive sobs of each of my old girlfriends, sobs I'd heard since they were children. Even Laurel cried. Even my mother. I was astonished to see her flooded face and her silently heaving shoulders. Only Marty stood like a zombie among the mourners. I think he was in shock. People held each other by the arms, rested their heads against each other's and wept. Even her enemies, even those snoopy moms and disapproving dads. All of us, whoever we were or whatever we'd thought of Estelle, believed that eighteen was just a bad age to die, and we were crushed by the monstrous injustice of it. Maybe some also cried because they recognized, now that it had gone out, how special her fire was.

But nothing that day was as interesting to everyone present, nothing was so much talked about for years after, as the six pall bearers; boys who had hated and feared and fought each other over the girl whose coffin they carried in a single unified effort. Yet their presence, like their task, seemed entirely appropriate. Who else should walk her home? They regarded Eddy with what looked to me like a mixture of contempt and pity. Maybe they were just sorry for themselves since he was a reminder that they too had failed to own her.

He maintained a brave front and supported poor hysterical Mrs Vachon. It was Ray who was looking fragile, but he composed himself until we reached the graveside. Once his job was finished and he had relinquished Estelle, he collapsed and sobbed like an exhausted child and was led away by his parents.

When I was home again at Christmas, I saw Eddy's car parked outside the Vachons' house. For a minute I wondered if Estelle was really alive and it had all been a mistake. My mother told me that he came to see Estelle's family all the time, that he hardly did anything else, besides drink. It was like they'd adopted him. He'd sit and watch television with them, as though he were trying to keep close to Estelle's genes, to the stuff from which she'd been created. Everyone said he was a sad case and that the Vachons were worried about his drinking. Then one night he had a bad accident on the way home, and his right leg was never very good after that. Eventually he left the brickyard, because of the leg, he said, but the story got round that he'd been fired. One day he went away and never came back.

Two years ago, when moving house, I came across my high-school Yearbooks. I sat and flipped through the glossy pages, scanning photographs of faces I'd nearly forgotten: fourteen year olds who looked as if their lives were already finished, and maybe they were. Others, myself included, with features blurred by adolescent gloom, features unformed or unbalanced that didn't fit together properly, as if they'd got mixed up with someone else's component parts. Only a few stood out, fresh and shining with what used to be called the bloom of youth. Estelle's was not among them. I was amazed I could have missed her and went through the four volumes again, searching for her. I was surprised to find she didn't look all that special. Cute, but that was it. The photographer had failed to capture any of the foxiness or the warmth. Or else she just didn't care, wasn't trying, wouldn't give it to him.

I read through her senior list of accomplishments, which were meagre. Aside from cheerleading and a perfunctory membership of the French Club she hadn't been interested in much. Academically she'd been mediocre. She disdained ambition. Only being Venus interested her, being the Immortal Girlfriend. What would she have done as a wife?

Dissatisfied but aroused by the Yearbook pictures, I went on to look through an earlier batch of photos. I pulled out several, feeling as if I were following Estelle back through time. One of them, my favourite, was a little snapshot taken by my mother, of all people, at my ninth birthday party.

Estelle is laughing and her mouth is open, showing her bright teeth. She wears her sister's letter sweater. Her eyes dance with happiness. Sometimes I take out this picture of Estelle and study it, holding it far away then close, looking for clues, I suppose, looking for anything I might have missed. Once in a while I dream about her. I wake up and wonder what happened that night on Chandler's Hill.

ALICE'S EAR

She was young, poor, struggling in the city. She never had enough money and her boyfriend had left her. The manager of the sandwich bar where she worked for £2.50 an hour had recently fired her when she'd repelled his advances. The flat that she shared with three other people was the property of a fierce landlord who was demanding his overdue rent. She was beginning to feel very hungry, and her name was Alice.

Because she was hungry she thought of the future. Because she was hungry she accepted Cyril's offer.

Alice had never thought much about the future. She might have children, that was all. She began to think about the future while standing in the bus queue outside Brixton Station. The queue was long, the bus was late, and the evening was hot. She shifted from foot to foot, watching the gospel singers with their white robes and taped accompaniment, the traffic warden shaking her hips to the music in spite of herself, the incense and T-shirt vendors, the sociable drunks. The scene reminded her of the temple of some loony religion, like she imagined India — primitive, vital, not very clean. Usually, she would lose herself in the spectacle, addict of a dreamy observation that had no end but itself. Now the street claimed only part of her attention, and she thought also of the Doc Martens she needed but could not afford, the overdue rent, the dole office, the Job Centre, and someone called Richard who slept in a doorway on the Strand and who had invited her to share that doorway.

A black man with black teeth and short, bead-studded dreadlocks gathered into a top-knot asked her for money and she complied, holding out a hand full of change and inviting him to help himself to eight pence worth of copper.

"The rest is for my bus fare," she said and did not lie.

He smiled and bowed and cheerfully worked his way along the queue. Alice hoped someone would give him a ten-pound note but knew it wasn't likely. She was eighteen, halfway between innocence and experience and unable, as yet, to tell which was which. There was a part of her that drifted towards that doorway.

I'd give him more if I had it, she thought, and with the rest I'd visit the McDonald's on the corner. Perhaps she should become a vegetarian. She really was very hungry.

All this time Cyril had been standing behind her. She felt his eyes on the back of her head and the freckled skin across her shoulders grow hot under his gaze. When she turned round he was looking straight at her.

"Will it ever come?" he asked, smiling.

"Will what?"

"Will the 196 ever come? That's the one I'm waiting for. What about you?"

He didn't look much like a guy who waited for buses. More like someone used to slick cars, Golfs with Vodaphones and the latest CD players. More like someone who never waited at all. More waited on than waiting. Like someone on whom she might wait. And this he recognized because he was assessing her in that way already familiar from the sandwich bar and the pizza parlour and the bistro. He was swish, was Cyril: designer shirt, trousers with the right sort of bag, creased linen jacket, black briefcase like you'd see on Charlotte Street or Long Acre. And she was Grunge all the way home, provocative but full of baby fears. She had drifted (there was that word again) down from the North. And he could tell, he could tell.

Except there was something he could not tell — she was changing her life. She had just decided, so the decision didn't show yet. She listened to him being plausible — like his car had broken down and was in the garage, like he didn't know how to spell "molestation" — unaware that the girl he addressed was rehabilitating herself as of one minute ago. And all rehabilitation begins with a good dinner. So when he asked if she'd care to join him for a meal, she thought of the future and said yes.

The city offers infinite possibilities. A cab, for instance. A cab can appear out of a hot mad dirty crush of traffic when there hasn't been one for half an hour and guys not used to waiting are forced to join the rest of humanity in the bus queue. Such guys are always rescued. And now Alice was being rescued with them.

"Shall we grab this?" he asked, pushing her into the back seat.

He looked at her, taking in the tightness of her top, which ended five inches above her midriff, her crocheted waistcoat and floppy trousers, her frayed espadrilles, her ankles, her fringe, her ears.

"Nice to be spontaneous."

She considered it. "Yeah." But she hadn't smiled yet. He'd have to wait for the smile.

Alice wasn't coy, but she had her moods.

They were driving through parts she didn't recognize (her knowlege of London being confined to main arteries), past a stretch of land by a railway track where houses of nasty yellow brick were under construction, so fragile they looked as if a child had built them.

"This land used to be completely wild, protected by the council. There were foxes . . ." Maybe he meant to be nice after all. This was only her second trip in a black taxi.

In minutes the city grew green, the houses large and looked-after, attended by shops catering to little whims.

"It's not far now." He must have heard the rumblings of her tummy. "I know this place. I've been once before, and I'm sure they'll have us if we ask politely. And here we are." He rapped on the glass divider and handed the driver a ten-pound note. They stepped out of the cab and on to the wide unlittered pavement.

"There are breezes here," remarked Alice.

Cyril stepped aside and let her precede him through the door. The colour came first and then the owner. The pictures, which were really the most important things, were initially only a blur across the walls because the colour stopped her in her tracks. It was pink and brown and mauve all at once; roses and cream and clay. How did you make such a colour? She'd seen similar shades before — their coral and green equivalents that adorned restaurants and shops — but only from the outside, through a window. They were new, these shades, though not, she supposed, to trendy Londoners who took them for granted: She had never been allowed inside such colours. She'd stood and gazed at them, a beggar at the feast. They seemed to offer comfort but not to her. Still, she'd grabbed as much as she could of them under the circumstances. She was a thief of colour.

The paint on the walls didn't just hit your eyes and bounce off. It had taste and smell. It got behind your eyes; you could roll it around inside your mouth like a hard and delicious sweet. Yet it contained something of the earth, a brown bit hidden underneath which was what made it tasteful, though why Alice couldn't work out. Roses and cream and clay. Near to what her Mum called dusty rose, only the restaurant walls had this other quality that sheltered and veiled and flattered the people rich enough or good enough to be admitted to their opaque glamour. They were nothing like the walls of her flat. Nothing like her mum's walls.

Their glow was deepened and enhanced by the sunset light. (For La Cigale faced west.) The light came filtered through the trees opposite which waved their leaves like little hands. It lay round about you, over the tables and the cutlery, silky and powdery on your skin. Alice felt she ought to have had a bath, that her London grime would prevent the light penetrating, doing her the good it ought to do. The others in the restaurant looked bathed and smooth and at ease. They wore clothes collected that afternoon from the dry cleaner's. Not one of them was young.

She was all wrong, she suddenly thought, and turned as if to leave, but Cyril placed a restraining hand on her shoulder. Oh-oh, she said to herself, here we go. His touch had claimed her and she became his pliant hostage. Then they were at their table and he was explaining everything to her. Barry, that was the owner, the guy who'd met them at the door, well, he ran the place with his mate Peter. They were gay, Cyril informed her. (The fact didn't faze him, so she assumed he must be tolerant even if he did have a briefcase.) They'd kept the place small on purpose. Most of their customers were regulars and on a first-name basis. And sure enough, there was Barry, his foot resting on an unoccupied chair, chatting sympathetically to a married couple, both of whom were dressed in white, about the problems and setbacks they were experiencing with the sale of their house. He and Peter had built La Cigale from nothing, it was very pleasant, wasn't it, did she like it?

"I don't really have the right clothes."

"But you dress so imaginatively."

She looked down at herself, back at him. "I don't think I have much of an imagination."

"Of course you do. Everyone does. Even I have an imagination. Now let's get you something to drink."

Barry produced the wine list. Cyril spent a long time over it. Meanwhile she picked at her face, stopping when he looked up.

Barry was beside him in a flash and Cyril uttered a name in French that seemed to give them both a lot of satisfaction.

Cyril put his napkin in his lap so she did likewise, fingering it under the table. It was a deep green, its surface smooth with a low sheen. The crockery, she noticed, was painted with little flowers and animals out of a fairy-tale. It looked old-fashioned and rustic. Apparently, all these dry-cleaned people were pretending to be peasants in Barry's comfy cottage, regardless of the BMWs and dispatch riders whizzing past the windows.

Cyril went on talking and she sat mute until the wine appeared. She was surprised at how yellow it was and how cold. She tasted it, then drank some more. Now that Cyril's generosity was actually inside her, she supposed she'd better smile at him. Now that their bargain was serious and sealed.

"So what do you do?"

"I work for Preston Television." He was so casual.

"Do you make programmes?" She knew she sounded impressed but couldn't help it.

"Not exactly. It's more administration, more executive, you might say. Do you like your wine?"

She'd never been quite sure what executives did besides make lots of money.

"I'm getting used to it."

"Well, you should get more used." He smiled and filled her glass. He smiled but he never laughed. "You'd better decide now," he said, as if there must be no more nonsense, and tapped her menu with his finger. She noticed he didn't wear any rings, unlike her who wore many, all silver, but none with stones in them. Her only stones were in her ear.

She studied the menu which was full of words like *terrine* and *tiède*. There was no chilli.

"The Summer Salad is good." His eyes had an encouraging expression. They were nice eyes, and his hair was nice too, black and shiny and falling on to his forehead. Once when she was fifteen she'd had a crush on a boy like that. A boy with black hair and blue eyes. It was such a long time ago. But she remembered him now.

"But I think I'm going to start with the grilled peppers and goat's cheese and then go on to the veal," he went on. "The duck is very good here."

"Oh yes." It was his jaw she didn't care for, so prominent and packed out with flesh.

"You could have that. And then the gigot's great or the salmon in pastry. Depends if you like fish."

"Not a lot."

"Then have the gigot."

She hesitated. She felt she ought to be making her own decisions, and besides, she didn't know what in hell a gigot was. It might be like brains or liver, and, even hungry as she was, she just couldn't — maybe they were going to put a whole brain on her plate and then she'd just be sick.

She took a dizzy risk. "I'll have the duck breast," she said.

Cyril commended her choice. He was in complete control. "And to start?"

"Umm, the Summer Salad." Now that grim decisions were over, she hoped they'd bring the food fast. Meanwhile what would she say to Cyril? She helped herself to more wine, neglecting to offer him any, but he was not offended. He went on talking about his work, making it seem inconsequential while clearly captivated by the subject. Alice's attention span was limited, and her eyes kept wandering off towards the pictures, dozens of them, that covered the walls of La Cigale. The more she drank, the more absorbing the pictures became until at last she realized that they had something in common.

"They're all of the same place," she announced straight into the middle of his sentence. Again he wasn't offended. He was the flatterer, she the flattered.

"You mean the pictures? It's the island where Barry and Peter go every year for their holiday. How did you know?"

She shrugged. "It's obvious, isn't it?"

"It's obvious you have a good eye."

"They must like this island a lot if they go there every summer and want to look at it all winter too."

"I suppose they do."

Each picture was slightly different in terms of size, angle of view, time of day, human and animal figures, type and colour of frame. But they shared a quality of light and atmosphere, and then there was the sea, the little house, the hill beyond and the two dark trees close by. The pictures covered nearly all the wall space, floating on the rosy haze behind them.

One in particular attracted Alice. She couldn't say why, but her gaze returned to it over and over again. Maybe it was the wine, but the painting seemed to call to her, to invite her in, to sing a song for her alone. There was something so familiar in the way the trees hugged the little house, the angle of the path, the corner of the bay you couldn't see in the other pictures, the glimmer of sunlight on the water, the cloud that moved stealthily to cover the sun. The more she looked the stronger the call became. She could hear the wind, the human voices that were carried on it, the distant lapping of the waves, as if she, not Barry and Peter, were the person who'd spent so many summers there. It was the antithesis of Richard's doorway.

"Well, Alice, this seems to be nearly gone." Cyril inspected the bottle as if its condition came as a great surprise to him. "We'd better have another. Are you game?"

"I don't mind," she said, then added, "I've never been outside Great Britain."

The starters arrived. Her Summer Salad, which was composed of thin shreds of undercooked meat scattered among an assortment of beansprouts and frilly lettuce, gleamed in its sesame-oil dressing. The meat was both sweet and salty in a totally unfamiliar way. Cyril's peppers were a jungle-flower red, partially cooked, so that when he offered her a thick strip to taste, raising his fork to her mouth like a mother with a child, she felt as though she were eating lips. The rolls, brown and white and nestled in their delicate basket, were more cake than bread.

Alice had never imagined her body could be gratified in this highly specialized way. She looked at the other diners who probably ate like this all the time. Barry produced a second bottle. Wine, she thought, more wine, and glimpsed what gluttony was. She would never refuse another dinner invitation as long as she lived. Even if she did have to be the sweet.

Her starter was gone. She stared at the shiny surface where it had been then returned to the picture. Her flat and the Job Centre and the dirty street where she lived seemed galaxies away from this rosy interior and these well-dressed people. And she, Alice, was with them, here inside the restaurant. And inside the restaurant was the picture, and inside the picture was a safe world of beauty, calm but never dull, a womb within a womb. A place where she might go, she and Cyril. Why did it fill her with such giddy happiness? She realized she had not experienced such happiness for a long time now, not since she had left home.

"There was this picture in my mum's sitting room." She interrupted him again and still he didn't mind. She just went on, not bothering to explain her train of thought, not apologizing. He seemed to understand. "When I was a kid I used to stare and stare at it. Whenever Mum got angry and yelled at me I'd take it upstairs to my room and look at it for hours. I'd imagine I was living in it. It was a place where no one would ever get angry with me."

"What was in the picture?" Their main courses arrived, and he began to eat, quickly and efficiently, his eyes darting from his plate to her face and back again, back and forth.

"I don't know. A canal, I think, or a river. Holland or something. And snow. The sun was setting through a kind of mist so you could barely see it. And there was this titchy house with a light in the window and smoke coming out of the chimney."

"You should eat before it goes cold."

"And I lived there, you see, in the house next to the canal, in this other life. Some other me. Oh yeah, there was a person too, a boy or maybe it was a man, walking along the dyke. And sometimes I'd tell myself this boy was my brother. My brother in my other life that was going on inside the picture. Where everything was nice."

She could not explain to him, never could to anyone, the strangeness of the possibility of meeting herself in her other life. The meeting never happened, of course. It was only always about to happen. Nor did she meet the imaginary brother or find out what was going eternally on behind the lighted window. Yet she was tied to the picture as by an umbilical cord. It promised shelter and transformation. She yearned to be part of its magic world that was so consoling and mysterious. Like an hallucination, without substance yet entirely real. It was a world in which you were safe but aroused, with all your senses at work, as in a good dream. A world as static as heaven.

"Do you have a brother?" Cyril brought her back.

"No." She gave him a weak smile.

He leant across the table and touched her right ear, briefly caressing its contours and fingering for a second the garnet earring embedded in its tiny lobe like a drop of blood.

"You only have one ear-ring." He returned to his meal.

"I lost the other one. I always lose them, so I decided to give up and just wear one." Alice laughed, though the remark wasn't really funny.

He squinted at her. "But there are lots of holes."

She touched them. "Yeah. I got a bit bored with all that junk I used to stick in them. The holes are closing now, so I guess I'll just let them."

"Well, perhaps I'll buy you some ear-rings."

She stared at him in disbelief then began to eat. Her duck was pink, almost the colour of the walls, with a crispy crust and a sauce that tasted like a higher octave of Ribena and was probably a near relation as there were several plump blackcurrants arranged across the fan of its display. She bit one with her front teeth and its jellied contents popped into her mouth. Its taste was so huge it seemed to engulf her. For a while she forgot the picture.

"Where did you get the garnet?" Cyril suddenly asked.

"It was my mum's," she said defensively, as if he had accused her. "I told you. I lost the other one."

"They were a present?"

"Not exactly."

"Were they expensive?"

"Who knows?"

"Then you have a sentimental attachment to them?"

"I guess."

"Does your mother know where you are?"

"No." She touched her ear which was small and round, its curls and crevices soft as a flower and folded neatly against the side of her head.

Her eyes met Cyril's.

"I have to make a phone call," he said. "Will you excuse me?"

"Sure." She realized their conversation wasn't exactly fluid.

She ate, drank more wine, stared at the picture. He was gone a long time. Perhaps he was buying condoms. Not that she minded his absence. She was happy eating and watching the customers and going in and out of the picture. Happier than when Cyril was distracting her with talk about his job and questions about ear-rings. She supposed there were far worse people for whom she might be the sweet. Then Barry approached, probably worried she was bored or self-conscious, unaware of her sense of security, her perfect ease. How odd and out-of-place she must appear to him.

"I'm completely exhausted," he confided, leaning on Cyril's empty chair. "I've had a terrible day, I don't mind telling you — a terrible week, really." He behaved as if she were no different from the woman with the white suit and the house problems.

"Why is that?" Alice tried to be polite.

"Jury duty." He bent towards her and almost whispered the words, as though he were divulging a secret or confessing to an embarrassing affliction.

Why is he telling me this? Alice wondered. What am I supposed to say?

"Did the case go on all week?"

"*All* week," he sighed. "At least we've removed one lunatic from the streets."

"What did he do?"

"Brained some poor woman in a car-park. She was outside Sainsbury's and had just finished loading up the boot." Barry maintained a balance of horror, resignation and intimacy. "This psycho appeared out of nowhere and asked her to hand over the keys. Unwisely, she refused. So he hit her with a cricket bat. Very hard."

"Christ."

"She's in hospital. In a coma. Three kids, a husband, a career. Now this." He folded his arms. "Turns out he'd done it before. Twice, though not lethally. He'd been a mental patient until two years ago when he was 'released into the community'."

"But if he was a nutter then it wasn't his fault."

"No. But whose fault was it? The *woman's*?" For a moment Alice thought he was blaming her. Then he smiled regretfully. "Excuse me," he said, "Mrs Hepplethwaite seems to be signalling."

Alice slid her knife and fork into a four o'clock position as she had seen Cyril do. The walls of her sanctuary had cracked and let in the world. The world was staining its rose-coloured walls, dimming its bright pictures with pollution. It was all true, what Barry had said. She'd seen dozens of disturbed Londoners on the Underground, cursing, punching the air, slamming their palms against the windows, carrying on impassioned dialogues with themselves, frightening the other passengers. Barry was right. People do fall off the deep end. They go mad and hit you with a cricket bat, stab you on the common, strangle you and set fire to your flat. There is no redemption, no remission, no reprieve, and your life can end well before you die. Why had Barry chosen her to tell his story to? Perhaps he told to it to everyone.

She looked around at the smug diners who were pretending not to notice her clothes, her tangled hair, her dirty nails, her enormous glaring difference. What was she doing among such people besides single-handedly lowering the tone? They were unacceptable to her and she to them. They were what her mum aspired to, what she admired. How surprised she would be to find Alice among them. Surprised and, yes, envious. "Comb your hair," she would say. "Don't look so mardy." Horrible that some people were worth dressing up for and others not. What determined it — how much money they had? You should be able to look like a slag or like Madonna, Alice fumed, depending on how you felt and not on other people. But why was she thinking of her mother? She was Alice, and she was not interested in anything that was like the life she used to have. The life before London that was really death, locked up in a coffin with your parents, all dying together. It had certainly been OK not talking to them for eighteen months. She was only thinking of her mother now because of this place, these people, and Cyril's questions about the ear-rings. Why stay here, surrounded by everything for which she'd practised contempt?

"Sorry I was so long." Cyril slid into his chair, looking sleek and scrubbed. Alice was even more aware of her dirty nails and her greasy hair and her urban pallor. She wanted with all her heart to get back into the picture. But Cyril was looking at her hard, and she read requirements in his blue eyes. Once they were out of here, at his place, she supposed it would be easy enough to entertain him. But now . . .

In desperation she said, "I stole the ear-rings."

"What!" At least she'd produced a reaction.

"My mother's ear-rings. I stole them when I left home. She never said anything about it. I kept waiting for her to ask me if I'd seen them, something, but whenever I spoke to her she never mentioned them. I think that's really peculiar, don't you? Then, like I said, I lost one and now we don't speak at all."

To her amazement Cyril burst out laughing. He threw back his head and opened his big jaw and emitted a huge noise that silenced two adjacent tables.

"You sneak," he exclaimed. "I knew you were bent, little Alice, I swear." He certainly had a weird sense of humour.

"I don't know why I did it. I've never stolen anything except packets of fruit gums when I was a kid." She smiled, pleased to have pleased him. "I didn't even really like them. I didn't like the earrings either."

"But you wear them."

"They're all that's left."

"Alice the jewel thief," he teased. "Alice Malice."

"I'm not," she pouted.

Again he laughed, and this time she laughed with him.

"I'm going to order us something really special, I've decided." He was wearing his "spontaneous" look, the one he'd worn in the taxi. "We're going to end on a high." He summoned Barry with a glance and ordered something that sounded like Venice muskrat which arrived in two tall glasses, very cold.

"This is magic, Alice," he said, raising his eyebrows and taking a sip. Then he stopped her hand. "Hang on, we haven't toasted yet."

"Oh *that*." And she clinked his glass with her own.

It was very sweet, the Venice stuff, almost too, but Alice liked it. Liquid pudding, he called it, and after the third sip she felt she could never get enough. It and Cyril's laughter had restored her completely. Not only was she able to forget Barry's story, but all remnants of fear and loathing had dispersed, and she felt nearly at home among the people she could not bear to look at five minutes before. The future, which had menaced her from outside the restaurant windows, had vanished, leaving the view of plump trees unimpaired.

"You're really quite pretty, Alice," he said as if he had only just realized. Was he serious? She looked down at her bright-orange trousers patterned with swooping green ferns. They belonged to her flatmate who had found them in a charity shop. She compared them with the colour of the walls, and somehow the contrast didn't seem as great. Her eyes headed once more for the picture — her picture. For it did not belong to Barry and Peter any more. She had taken it over, acquired it, and she could go there any time she liked. She was going there now. Cyril was taking her.

It was dark when they stepped on to the street, a beautiful summer night. She could hear the wind gently rustling the two trees, the distant beating of the waves, human voices that teased each other in tender ways.

The stars were very bright. They were even brighter in the park. Alice had expected the taxi to carry them straight to Cyril's flat and was surprised when he suggested they go for a walk. It would be nice, he said, to be alone in the dark and experience the full effects of the Venice muskrat. Fine. What did she care? Delays only enhance a journey when you're on your way to somewhere wonderful.

During the middle of July the sun in London rises around four o'clock. So a park attendant is at work early, long before the first dog-walkers appear or meths drinkers stir or the homeless begin to gather their few belongings and move on.

He approached his task in a leisurely style, savouring the sweetness of the air while it was still fresh, before it grew tainted and stale with the day's advance and the influx of humans. Despite the heat he wore the orange plastic waistcoat of his trade and pushed his dustcart before him like a pram, stopping every now and then to gather the abundant litter — crisp packets, used condoms, the remains of Indian takeaways, the odd syringe. He was slow, steady, and not much escaped him. He pierced, prodded, swept, deposited and moved on, straying occasionally from his route whenever he spied an object bright enough or large enough to catch his attention. Stabbing at a shopping list then at a brown sock, he made his way across the patchy grass towards a clump of trees where he invariably uncovered diverse tokens of the night's events.

A bright-red spark tugged at his eye, inviting inspection. He drew his cart up to some dusty shrubs and knelt down for a closer look. There, among the McDonald's cartons, cigarette packets, bus tickets, crushed Tennant's tins and expired travel cards, was Alice's ear.

TRUTH, BEAUTY AND GOODNESS: A REPORT

Early in the autumn of 1962 Frances Marion Hodgkins's name was changed to Cal. This pleased her because she never had liked Frances and because Cal was a shortened form of Calypso, implying an allure she had not thought she possessed.

A group of her fellow students often gathered in the lounge of Marigold Quadrangle to play Botticelli or Exquisite Corpse, and when the weather was good they went outside for Capture the Flag. They also invented a diversion of their own which they called Casting the Classics. Zelda Turpin became Dido, Mark Lasky Aeneas. Ralphie Sajovic, clever, dissolute and cynical, found no contenders for Ulysses, and Nancy Phoner, the best-natured girl in the Sophomore Class, was Penelope. No one had suggested a role for Frances until Harlan Getz proposed her for Calypso. Assent was unanimous, and so as Cal she went on, much improved.

Harlan previously had discussed her suitability for the character with his room-mate Jay. They agreed about her. They sensed the secret glamour behind her small-town exterior. The corduroy shirtwaists and round-collared blouses hid something dark and flexuous, an unconscious greed that wanted to hold on to everyone, binding and clinging without being aware of what it did. They had glimpsed the seductress. She just needed someone to tell her who she was.

Cal admired Harlan, and she loved Jay. But she hardly dared speak to them because they lived in an apartment off campus. Here they entertained friends who wrote poetry and involved themselves in radical politics. They contributed to the university paper and the *Bruckner Review*, went on peace marches to Washington, and were members of SANE and SNCC. Professors of English, Psychology and Economics were regular dinner guests. Cal felt intimidated.

"She just wants to watch people and play," Ralphie Sajovic told Jay.

"Uh-huh, Ralphie. She's a woman of mystery." Jay nodded towards Cal across his living-room which was crowded with students, all very drunk. It was the first time Cal had come to one of his parties. Later that night the police answered a neighbour's complaint and dispersed the company. Jay hid Cal in his room where they talked until morning and fell asleep on the only bed in the apartment with sheets.

Cal spent more time in the house on Flood Street. She came to know all Jay's friends, but was herself known for nothing in particular apart from her consistent appearance on the Dean's List and a prettiness which she now exposed with black jeans and sweaters. She liked the anarchy of the cold dirty apartment and returned with reluctance to the pink cinder-block walls of her dormitory and to her melancholic room-mate Stephanie, regularly asleep under the soft plastic helmet of her hairdryer. When Stephanie was thus occupied, it was impossible to talk to her about Jay. So Cal lay on her bed in Fenwick Hall in Marigold Quad, in the middle of Bruckner University — small, academically exclusive, and politically febrile, crowning the highest hill in the Boston area and overlooking the dismal town of Waterville — and thought about her lover.

Jay and Harlan shared their chaotic apartment with Joel Cheevers. The three of them were ardent friends, and Cal loved to sit on their collapsing sofa, holding herself in her own arms, while the others listened to Shostakovich and Charlie Mingus and argued about Behaviourism and Zen and Marcuse. She understood little of all this. She listened and hardly spoke. They were better-read, worldly-wise, city-raised, and she wanted to learn. An intense curiosity about everything in life kept her quiet until invited or compelled to talk about herself. She was amazed they wanted her there, aside from the fact that she was Jay's lover.

Early in the autumn of 1962 the four of them were eighteen and had known each other throughout their Freshman year. Harlan and Joel were without girlfriends, and so attached themselves to the couple.

Joel adopted a light, lofty view and enjoyed relating literature to life. It was he who first compared himself and his two friends to the Platonic virtues. Harlan was Truth, Joel himself Beauty, and Jay was Goodness. The personification was lightly made, as if Casting the Classics. But to Cal it was serious and real, and she saw her friends as the tangible manifestations of those ideal qualities. Truth, Beauty and Goodness: from then on she called them by those names.

Beauty and Cal had won scholarships. Truth's father, a police inspector, managed, just, to pay outright for his son's education. But Goodness's family was well off. Only he had a car, and so he drove the others, and numerous friends besides, to Cambridge and the movies and "Jack and Marion's". He lent money to Truth and Beauty and paid the rent when they fell behind, ignoring his parents' complaints of extravagance. Cal had given her virginity to Goodness. He wrote her poems, dutifully used prophylactics and read sex manuals to increase her pleasure. He felt bound to her. He changed the sheets once a week and kept the heater in his room on High. Cal loved him, but not because of his kindness to her. Not at all. He was an image she had picked out right away, watching him from a distance, imagining him her own, drawing him nearer by her

77

passivity, feeling him yield and watch her, then finally touching him, sure of his attraction to something in her she could not name.

He was big and fair and ruddy and well-made. She liked his little nose and blue eyes, his dry-cleaned Levi's and open tweed sports coat and bare feet in penny loafers; the kind of obvious things, she later realized, that appealed to inexperienced girls from small towns. He was not exciting, but she wanted him because he seemed the kind of boy she ought to want — she could not say why, except that no one who had known her before she became Cal would have expected her to get a boy as good as him.

Truth, Beauty and Goodness were all in love with Cal, and their love made her glamorous. More and more they let themselves be held by her secret greed which they had discovered and defined. They continued to discuss at length their favourite topics: literature, politics, the Bomb. They gave parties which were terminated by the arrival of the police. They talked about their futures, and about what they might do with their lives, as an alternative to remaining exactly where they were — in a cold bare apartment on Flood Street, lying on naked mattresses, smoking grass, bathed in the presence of Cal. She never questioned why they loved her. Her expectations had been low. She was surprised, pleased. She let them continue.

When they asked her if she loved them too she sometimes said yes, sometimes no; sometimes she just got in a bad mood. She stayed with Goodness and let herself be seen as his, but in the autumn of her Sophomore year she was restless, wanting to tell others about herself. She had poured as much of herself as she could into Goodness, but he proved an inadequate vessel. He could not contain all she told him, and it spilled over and flooded around their feet. She needed new listeners.

Goodness was not anxious about the feelings of the other two. It seemed natural to him that everyone should love Cal (except

Ralphie Sajovic who maintained that she was nothing special). She possessed an unconscious grace, she was innocently provocative, she had the right to be selfish. But he did like being alone with her in his own room, with clean sheets and his grandmother's dresser and the heater on High, either in bed or trying to study.

Goodness studied hard. He had entered university with commendable grades and was devoted to learning, holding it high against the backdrop of his father's supermarket chain. He and Beauty and Cal were enrolled in English 221a. They read Wyatt and Sidney and Spenser aloud to each other and gossiped about the professor. The men complained that he showed favouritism to Cal, who always managed better grades than they. Cal conceded that their work was more original.

Truth and Beauty seldom studied or attended classes. They ignored their reading lists and immersed themselves in current fiction, politics, critical theory and drugs. All their term papers were late. Goodness rose at seven to make an eight o'clock Physics class, devoured his reading lists, received Bs and Cs for his pains. Cal lived in procrastination, preferring Flood Street to the library where a stack of books was on hold for her. She began her term papers the day before they were due and handed them in untyped. During finals and mid-terms she would go forty-eight hours without sleep, living on black coffee and No-Doze, cramming her brain with the facts, quotes and ideas she should have been absorbing over the previous weeks. She would retain everything just long enough to pour it, during the course of three hours, into the pale-blue ruled notebooks provided for the purpose. Then she would collapse, fall ill, get straight As. The professor of English 221a stopped her outside the classroom and kissed her hand, congratulating her as she blinked at him. Beauty teased her without malice. Truth accused her of telling the authorities what they wanted to hear. But Goodness was wounded. There were tears in his eyes as he protested over what he had begun to regard as the pervasive and adamant injustice of this world. Beauty laughed at his indignation.

Cal needed new listeners. Goodness was neither suspicious nor jealous. When his grandmother suffered a stroke he drove alone to Albany, sacrificing Ralphie Sajovic's party and leaving Beauty to accompany Cal. In the crush, they stayed close to each other all evening, finding at last some space on a sofa where they selfishly kept a bottle of wine to themselves. Beside them Ophelia and Agamemnon were necking casually. Cal felt relaxed and accepted and very close to Beauty. She looked into his face. When he ascribed Beauty to himself, he had not been referring to his looks. (Goodness was much more vain. It was one of his few little failings.) He had meant rather that beauty was his first love; that he valued art more highly than being virtuous or objective; that he worshipped Apollo and the Muses. Still, he was the most charming of the three, with his fresh smooth skin, his cherub curls, his round grey eyes and lips so ready to smile and his light short body which he carried with ease. She held up his hand, hardly bigger than hers, and pressed her own against it, fingers splayed.

"We're so alike," said Cal.

He quoted her something from a Donne sonnet as she passed him the bottle. He returned it and recited some e. e. cummings. They slid downwards until they nestled against Agamemnon's back, then did as their illustrious companions. Truth watched them through the open doorway, But they didn't notice him. They were perfectly happy and saw nothing but each other as the room went round and round.

At 3 a.m. they woke up in the municipal playground. They thought they had gone home. There was no more wine. They supported each other unsteadily past the swings and seesaws, found the gate, and turned into Flood Street, talking about their child-hoods as the moon cast shadows through the maple leaves. It shone purple-white into the window of Beauty's room, lighting the walls which bore reproductions of Goya's *Maja* and Vermeer's *Head of a Girl*. The books lined up along the wainscoting were mainly poetry. Cal saw the titles on the spines appear and vanish as she and Beauty changed positions on the mattress. She wasn't thinking of Goodness at all when Beauty smiled at her and said, "Guess what, I'm a virgin."

She thought I hope this isn't the beginning of a trend.

She sensed that he intended to make sex with her into an exercise in romanticism; now she would be the Experienced Woman. She put her barely experienced arms around him and stroked his curls and let him imagine whatever he pleased.

In the morning he threw open the window and leaned out and called, "Hello Waterville, you ugly city!"

Cal giggled, then she moaned and turned towards the wall. Truth did not come back for two days, and they regretted his absence because all of Saturday they were very sick.

Goodness returned on Sunday night with two dozen of his grandmother's frozen blueberry blintzes. The three of them sat at the kitchen table under a bare light bulb and devoured them in contentment. There was no hot water for baths.

Cal met Beauty whenever she could — at the furthest end of the cafeteria, with cups of black coffee and packets of Oreos, until they were joined by Truth or Goodness at whom they would smile in perfect innocence; between classes, leaning against a high stone wall, dangling their green book bags; in the woods behind the chapels on a golden floor of leaves, or, when it was cold, in a borrowed room in one of the boys' dorms.

They knew they were special, as though a god or goddess had declared them sacred offspring. They repeated to each other how alike they were because their hands were the same size and they loved the same poets and believed that art was all and nothing was higher than art. They could afford to be careless.

Beauty was very prolific. He kept journals, wrote one-act plays and essays on aesthetics — in short he did everything but hand in his term papers and pass his exams. His parents lamented; Dean Bags admonished him. He also wrote letters, mainly to Cal. He took great pains and derived great pleasure in describing her to herself: her shiny brown hair and hazel eyes that sometimes went yellow like a wicked little she-goat's; her long white legs and the place where they joined. He was reading Byron and Henry Miller and both crept occasionally into his one-sided correspondence. He left the letters at her dormitory or recklessly slipped them into her biology textbook. She read them once through and put them away in her brown accordion file. On nights when she stayed in her own room, she would take them out and look at them while Stephanie snored heavily under the hair-dryer.

At Flood Street Beauty and Cal behaved as if nothing had happened — until Truth forced Beauty to tell Goodness the truth. Candour appealed to Beauty almost more than deception had: When Goodness begged her to discuss the matter with him, Cal lay on the bed and refused to speak. She lay there for two days until Goodness returned to normal. She wasn't being cruel, and he understood this; she simply didn't know what to say. Her responsibility was diminished; she was blameless. And he could not hate Beauty for following his nature.

Cal loved being with Truth. She would sit beside him as he argued about politics, besting the other students with his conviction and his integrity, making them appear pale dilettantes. One of them reasoned that nuclear arms prevent war through fear of war and implied that fear was a necessary and natural balancing factor in all of life.

"Fear!" he replied, "fear is shit."

He introduced her to Jung and Lorca and Hannah Arendt and was never contemptuous of her *naïveté*. He did try to force her to examine her preconceptions. He was the only one of the three occasionally to criticize her. She clung to him because she knew he had the best mind, and she reserved for him that part of her which wanted to think better of herself and to go forward. He seemed to represent some future attainment which involved great difficulties but was still comfortably far off and vague. He helped her to hold on to that vision of attainment. Therefore she wanted to protect him, even though she was unable to protect anyone. She did not want to sleep with him. He was the one she never slept with.

Truth was dark, lean, angular. He had a kind of rolling walk which was pleasant to observe, but he took no trouble with his appearance. His eyes were too large, his cheeks sallow, his neck scrawny, and his hair like a black Brillo pad. There seemed not to be enough of his face. He didn't care about food and never minded what he ate. He was all veins and tendons. Like Beauty and Goodness, he made no secret of his love for Cal.

One night in that autumn of their Sophomore year, Cal discovered how much she had hurt him. Late in the evening she tried the door to his room, but it would not open. He had locked himself in with a packet of razor blades and a bottle of Nembutal and was threatening to commit suicide because she would not be his lover. Goodness, Beauty and others present attempted to reason with him, alternately pressing their faces to the door and drinking Thunderbird. Cal sat in Goodness's grandmother's armchair, her knees pulled up to her chest, her arms wrapped around her knees, saying nothing, but sipping the Thunderbird when it was passed to her. She stared at the wall, not knowing how she ought to feel; feeling one thing and then another.

At five in the morning Goodness shouted that he intended to break into the room, and Truth finally opened the door. Then Cal unwound herself and went to Goodness's bed where she lay down with Fast Eddie the cat and pulled the covers over them both.

Goodness came and stood beside her. From her horizontal point of view his developing paunch appeared more exaggerated. His kind eyes seemed smaller.

"I'm not enough for you, Cal. Whoever thought you'd turn out a femme fatale?" He sighed. "I guess I did."

Cal looked up at him. "I wish you wouldn't say things like that."

Goodness was gaining weight, growing a beard. He was very comfortable to sleep with. Cal stayed with him, and let it be known she was still his, though she could not resist flirting and did so more and more, listening to other boys with complete attention until she erupted in a compulsive need to expose to them her innermost self.

The morning after Truth's attempted suicide she rose at seven and began her biology paper which had been due the previous day. At four the paper was finished, and she showed it to Truth. It was a report on a book called *Sick Minds, New Medicines*.

"It's about the use of drugs in psychoanalysis," she told him.

He smiled at her. "I like the crudity of the title."

The paper got an A minus. She had done it again with her blind intelligence. They pretended to be bitter and complained about the male professors. But they knew she never went to bed with any of them. She was interested in her peers because only they could reflect her back at herself.

The four of them lived in physical lassitude (athletics were not compulsory at Bruckner) and in emotional and mental excitement. Whatever happened to one affected the other three, and everything that happened was special. The world was packed with phenomena, symbolic yet personal, riddled with secret messages to be deciphered by them alone. And these messages arrived direct from the Power, whatever it was, that took a constant and avid interest in them. They held intense communication with the gods, whom they were sure were meddling in their lives. It was an absurd attitude, but they were not yet adults. Adults do not make unqualified identifications with cats or political causes. They do not feel branded by the books they read or translate life through them or embrace them like lovers. Adults see the world neither as code nor as secret garden.

In October 1962 Truth, Beauty, Goodness and Cal were still taking life in this unadult way. Their reaction to the Blockade of Cuba was therefore not surprising. They were convinced of the malicious intent of all parties. Like the other students at Bruckner, they had been tuned for three days to their radio. No one at the school attended classes, many of which had already been cancelled by professors anxious to keep close to their televisions. Everyone listened to the president's announcement that as of the 24th Cuba was to be quarantined. They saw for themselves the photographs of the missile bases and learned that Soviet ships were crossing the Atlantic with their provocative cargoes. Inside the claustral atmosphere of the university the crisis was inflated beyond its already perilous limits. A confrontation was inevitable and the result would be Armageddon. They had talked of it for years; it was what they expected.

Even Cal was worried, though she did feel as if she were watching herself in a film — a film about the end of the world. It was running an awfully long time. When would it be over? She remained at Flood Street where Truth was attempting to rouse the others from their lethargy.

"It isn't a question of politics any more," he argued. "It's survival I'm talking about. You live like creeps in your Bruckner dream. And in this dream all that's required is that you talk and read and talk and talk and talk. You spend your time elaborating your positions and your blame and joining organizations whose purpose is to do exactly the same thing. And so you think you're on the right side and that you've risked a little danger. Well, the dream is a trap and Bruckner is a trap and you'll just sit there talking as you die. Do you want us to be like them?" He gestured towards the hill. "Well I don't. I want us to live."

Beauty frowned. "You're saying we should split?"

"Split! We should run like hell's behind us. Which it is. Jay has a car."

Goodness sighed. He knew Truth was right. The entire Eastern seaboard was doomed, and eighty million people were living the last days of their lives.

"Where can we go?" he asked. "Where's the safest place?"

Truth did not hesitate. "Mexico," he said.

They left that afternoon, stopping at the campus for Cal to pack a bag. Their friends were impressed by their valour. A few were envious of their escape. But no one else wanted to leave. No one had any plans. Ralphie Sajovic told Truth that he was crazy. Either there *was* no escape or nothing would happen. They'd come back and feel like assholes.

Truth, Beauty, Goodness and Cal were not worried about coming back. As they drove along the Mass. Pike, Cal beside Goodness in the front seat, they watched the landscape, the towns, the woods in autumn colours for what they were certain would be the final time. They were sad but not afraid. An unknown future with nothing to cling to but each other was a great romantic adventure.

The radio issued half-hourly bulletins on the progress of the

Soviet ships. They would listen in silence then resume their speculations about Mexico. They might be forced to start life anew, as in the beginning. Now Cal would *have* to sleep with them all.

Beauty began to sing.

The others joined in, Cal barely moving her lips. She was thinking how New England sunsets were best between now and Christmas. The wet light both heightened and softened the mad colours of the trees. Wooster and Springfield looked grimly poetic with the sun, like a descending firebomb, at their backs.

How lonely America was. It would be even lonelier soon. She had not called her parents. Perhaps she would never see them again. They were not taking the crisis as seriously as she, and would be worried by the idea of a trip to Mexico. They would not understand how she was perfectly safe and protected for ever by her three best friends. She might call them from a phone booth, only she didn't have any money. She tried to imagine what life in Mexico might be like and looked forward to the beaches and the swimming and to climbing ruined pyramids in the one pair of shorts she had brought. She planned her French paper which was due on Monday. The preliminary notes for it were secreted in her suitcase, as well as the book which was to be its subject — *Adolphe*. She watched the sunset like someone hypnotized, and thought about Mexico and the end of the world and her French paper. In her mind everything coexisted peacefully, without contradiction. She was ideally suited to be educated.

New York looked like a city on the edge of the universe, glowing with greasy light. From it you jumped off into nothing. Truth said it represented what Madame Blavatsky had called a Ring-Pass-Not. The half-hourly news broadcasts were having a peculiar effect on him — on all of them. There they were walking down Mulberry

Street towards Hong Fats and no one hungry. Cal watched the people and played with her noodles, paid for by Goodness, and listened to him and Beauty talk while Truth made telephone calls. None of what they said made any sense.

Truth had not been able to reach his friends. He suggested leaving immediately for Washington, he could get Goodness some amphetamine. Instead they drove uptown to the Bronx and paid a surprise visit to Nancy Phoner's parents. Benjamin Phoner was a kind man, in appearance not unlike Truth. He was much admired among Nancy's friends because he had been blacklisted during the McCarthy purges. He had lost his professorship at NYU and now worked in his brother-in-law's furniture store. They'd had no money and no one dared do anything for them. He had been heroic. Cal was especially fond of him. When Truth explained how they were on their way to Mexico to escape nuclear holocaust Mr Phoner looked at him in disbelief.

"Go home," he said impatiently. "Finish the education your parents worked hard to pay for."

They argued for two hours. Mr Phoner was convinced that the CIA had manipulated the military into its present situation, that Kennedy simply wanted to force Khrushchev to back down, that the Russians were in no position to attack.

When Mrs Phoner offered to make Cal a bed on the couch and Cal accepted and went off to brush her teeth, Truth put on his thin jacket and made for the door. Beauty followed him. Mr Phoner said at least they should wait twenty-four hours, at least they should think of Cal and protect her if they loved her as much as they claimed to. He said the very fact that they had come to see him meant they didn't want to make the journey. They were just seeking an authority figure to confirm what they already knew and to let them off the hook of their cracked commitment. Truth and Beauty said again that they were leaving. They looked wounded and worn out. Goodness said he must stay with Cal, he was sorry, why didn't they all meet here tomorrow.

"Goodnight, Mr Phoney," snarled Truth on the way to the elevator.

At ten the next morning Beauty returned to the Phoners'. Truth was not with him. Goodness and Cal were in the kitchen with Mrs Phoner eating toasted bagels and reading the newspapers. They looked relaxed and happy.

"We're driving back to Bruckner," they said. "Are you coming? Whatever you do we love you and we understand. Mr Phoner lent us twenty dollars."

The half-hourly radio reports confirmed that U Thant had flown to Cuba. As they drove past Springfield, not singing, they heard how Castro was refusing to allow international inspection of the missile dismantling. Even so, the tension had eased. By the 3rd of November Kennedy had announced that the Cuban bases were being dismantled and Cal had received an A on her French paper. Goodness grumbled and Beauty was amused, but neither was behaving like himself, Cal could tell. She too felt distant, almost disembodied; relieved and yet let down.

They were worried about Truth. His absence was palpable, a collective ache. He telephoned every night from New York. During the calls Cal would sit in the big armchair, twisting her hair into a knot and letting it fall, listening to Beauty and Goodness trying to persuade him to return. The missile crisis was over. Why stay in Manhattan, smoking dope and sleeping somewhere different every night? Truth insisted that he would go on to Mexico. The crisis had been a sign, warning them and everyone like them that they must break out of the Bruckner dream. Sometimes he cried. He said he refused to concede that it was no longer possible to live heroically.

He refused to allow the others to concede it. They said they could not understand why he thought they were conceding anything.

The next time he rang, Goodness snatched up the phone.

"We're coming to get you," he said. "We're leaving right away. Give me your address and just stay there and wait for us." It was 11.30 p.m.

Leaving the apartment unlocked, they headed once more for the Mass. Pike. They drove as fast as possible, listening to all-night music stations and laughing and singing.

"My head is spinning," said Beauty.

"Mine too," said Cal.

The outskirts of the city had a sobering effect. They took a wrong turn off the Bronx expressway, drove around for an hour and made another wrong turn into a deserted industrial estate. They sat and looked at it, suddenly exhausted. The place seemed to emanate an almost radioactive glow.

"God, this is sinister," whispered Cal. "Where are we?" She had never imagined that being awake in a car at three in the morning could produce such feelings of desolation. By four they had found the apartment that belonged to Truth's friend who lived in a building on the Lower East Side. 2nd Street was funnelling a freezing wind from the broad barren channel of Houston Street, and inside the apartment the light was as cold and dead as the radiators. Truth sat on a cushion in a corner holding a grey cat.

"This is No-Name," he said. "He's a bum and a Buddha and he's coming back to live with us."

Truth looked paler than ever. They hugged and kissed him but he did not rise, and they remained on their knees beside him, tenderly testing No-Name's ears and tail. Then Cal drew him to his feet and made him go with her to the car. He lay on the back seat, his Brillo-pad head in her lap, and clutched the cat who seemed secure in his future.

Goodness nibbled a No-Doze as the sun made its appearance in a smutty Hartford sky. Beauty sang along with the Vivaldi "Gloria". Their spirits were high because they sensed that something great had been accomplished. They were regarding this fourth and final journey as a triumph.

There was snow during the second week of November, then a warm spell. Stephanie complained of being lonely because Cal was always at Flood Street. She said Cal had drifted away and that she had become weird. Cal didn't realize how much Stephanie was hurt. She was held too tight in her quaternity. She lived with three men in a secret garden from which everyone else was excluded. They could not and would not be separated. Their friends turned and stared after them as they walked past. What had happened to them during that trip to New York?

They too began to wonder. They did no work and hardly ate and did not want to see anyone. They did not go to the movies or to SANE meetings. The other students, Bruckner, the whole world seemed a mirage. Truth said that a potent energy had been invoked and that they were all in its grip. They were exalted, they were displaced, and Cal was the most displaced of all.

"What's happening," said Truth, "is that we're having a collective hallucination."

"We're under a spell," Beauty replied.

"We ought to tell someone," said Goodness.

Cal was frightened. So much had gone on without her noticing. What was it that had captured her mind? She felt as though a spirit were watching, as though it had come too close to bear, too close for their own good. She could feel the eyes and breath of the spirit. They *were* under a spell.

On the 20th of November the Blockade was officially lifted, but they paid no attention and felt no relief. They went to the office of Dr Wolff, professor of Psychology and expert in Eastern religion and philosophy. They told him how, since the journey to New York, an occult power had broken down the normal barriers between their minds and was causing them to see reality in the same twisted way. They told him that they were passionately in love with Cal and could not give her up, and that she might be crazy and they did not know what to do about it. They described to him how at first their unification had been beautiful, but that now it was terrible, that they wanted both to be set free and to remain in their present exalted state. What did he think was the matter with them?

Dr Wolff was interested. He took them seriously. He invited them all to tea, then told several of his colleagues that he had never met with anything quite like this four-way romance.

"Possession," diagnosed Dr Wolff who knew a good deal about daemons in the brain. "Her." He put down his teacup and indicated the only one of the four who did not talk incessantly. Goodness spoke up like a man.

"I'm responsible for Cal," he said.

"No," Beauty interrupted. "We all are because we're all in love with her."

Dr Wolff made a sympathetic noise in his throat. He smiled at Cal who smiled back. He could see the daemon right there in her eyes. He was a big man with a sharp wit who commanded respect.

"Come and see me again on Wednesday. And don't smoke any grass and don't talk about this to anyone else."

"We can't talk to anyone else."

"We can only talk to you."

"Come on Wednesday."

Was the quartet becoming a quintet? Was Dr Wolff saving them from this dangerous romance or was he falling victim to its charms?

They began to feel as though it was impossible to be separated from Dr Wolff.

They went for walks. They ate lunch in the cafeteria under envious eyes, aware of their uniqueness. Then one day Dr Wolff told Cal to come alone. The others waited for her at the entrance to the library, but she did not meet them. The afternoon light withdrew to concentrate itself in the setting sun, and still she did not arrive. No one had seen her. They were worried, and went to Dr Wolff's office which was closed until the Monday after Thanksgiving. Later she called at Flood Street to say she would spend the night in the dorm preparing for an exam.

Over Thanksgiving Goodness telephoned Cal in Rhode Island. She said she missed them all and hated Thanksgiving, that her mother was very irritating and that she was bored. He told her so many times that he loved her that he put her in a bad mood. Two weeks later at Flood Street she informed them in an offhand way that she had been going to the Psychological Counselling Centre. On Dr Wolff's advice.

"They'll give you pills and fry your brain," said Truth. "They'll tell you not to smoke grass and to quit SANE."

"Please don't," Beauty entreated. "It'll destroy all your creativity."

"It's interesting," Cal replied.

Goodness asked her what had happened during her last visit to Dr Wolff.

"He asked me how I felt, so I showed him a poem by Wallace Stevens which he said he couldn't understand."

"And is this supposed to untangle you?"

"We talked after."

"But you're so beautiful as you are."

Cal shrugged. She was drifting away from him and from Truth and Beauty. They sensed the way she had come down out of their

93

collective hallucination, which they remembered now with sadness. They likened themselves to a civilization that had reached its peak and must now commence its inevitable decline. When they asked Cal about Psych Counselling she would answer only that it was interesting. She could not say how it offered her a whole new way of talking about herself and describing herself. After all, she was only a small-town girl, bound to be entranced by the new and different reflection in the glass that was now held up to her.

"Cal," Goodness approached her as she was lying on his bed studying for her mid-terms, "I don't think I'm enough for you."

His voice bore the trace of a whine, or so it seemed to her.

"Please don't say things like that," she answered.

Truth was still the only one to be critical. His interpretation was that Cal wanted to see herself while simultaneously being distracted from herself. "She wants to see herself better lit."

One night, as she sat holding Beauty's hand, Truth looked at her fiercely and said, "You've been going to bed with Ralphie Sajovic."

Cal stared straight back at him and laid her head on Beauty's shoulder. Truth walked out and Beauty continued to read to her from an open letter of protest he had written to Dean Bags.

Beauty and Truth discussed the way in which they had been revelling in their hopeless love for Cal. Perhaps it was the idea of her that they loved. Her drifting away had blurred and weakened the focus of their feelings. Ideas and actions they had held in abeyance for months came to fill the place she left. They had been frustrated for a long time by Bruckner. Suddenly they were eager to seize their real destinies, free of the restrictions of academia.

During the Biology mid-term, which was compulsory for all Sophomores, they sat together in the deserted cafeteria drinking black coffee and reading *Evergreen Review* and borrowing cigarettes from the staff. At lunch they talked briefly with those who had survived the morning, then went upstairs to the lounge and spent the afternoon listening to Sam Daley improvise an ersatz Bach fugue. They leaned back lazily. They decided to leave school and go to New York.

Cal and Goodness joined them in the lounge. They had just finished the Renaissance Lit. exam and looked as though they had spent two weeks on a liferaft. Beauty and Truth explained their decision as Cal sat gazing at Sam, perfectly quiet and holding tight to Goodness's hand. She admired Sam as she had once admired Goodness — from afar, simply waiting to be noticed and seized. She had this feeling that Sam could tell her about herself. In her mind everything coexisted peacefully, without contradiction.

She went less often to Flood Street where there were no more parties. Goodness's new room-mate, Dexter Wapshot, was not a substitute for Beauty and Truth. Those two called or wrote to her from New York where they lived any old way, without money, just reading and going to films and staying up all night and getting crazier, she could tell. She missed them, and what they had done impressed her. They were the first of her classmates to take a year off. Eight months later students left in legions for the Lower East Side and the West Village. Cal adored New York; she imagined it as she read Beauty's letters.

"I am under severest pressure from my parents and Dean Bags to get myself shrunk. Dean Bags says, "It will go well with you before the administrative board if you take corrective therapy.""

Don't, she thought. You don't really want to be readmitted.

Goodness was by nature domestic, and he tidied the apartment and made it quite comfortable with more of his grandmother's furniture. He fussed in the kitchen, cooking elaborate meals for Dexter and Cal who sometimes failed to turn up. Then he and Dexter would eat alone under the kitchen light which now had a shade. He knew Cal was unfaithful to him but he did not dare to think how often. Once in February he met her going up the hill to the library. He had not seen her for six days and asked her point-blank about the other men in her life.

"I love the way everyone is so different," she told him.

He could see her assessing him, thinking how fat he was getting. His back had thickened like the stalk of an old vegetable, and he hid his second chin under a beard. Deep in his florid face his eyes were still kind. He put his hand gently on her arm.

"You just want to get away from me, don't you?"

"No," she lied.

Truth wrote her long letters which she guessed he had composed after hours of smoking grass because they were very abstruse and mystical. Cal gave up trying to decipher them and wrote back simply, "This is what I think: the universe is order and it's chaos. Orderchaos. That's all." What did he think he was doing? But she added the postscript, "I miss you."

Beauty wrote, "With the passing months there is no longer any reality about you . . . I don't wish to be a Byron, wandering around the world never able to love because I once idealized someone. You cannot idealize something that is there, and so I am begging you to release me by sleeping with me. You have nothing to lose, never having loved me. I certainly cannot come out any worse."

Cal felt embarrassed. Then she cried.

"What a stupid letter," she said aloud through her tears.

Two years later Cal received a Bachelor of Arts with Honours. Goodness was not awarded Honours, but was admitted to a graduate school where he obtained a Ph.D. in English. He kept his beard, gained more weight, married and taught Renaissance

Literature at a college in Tennessee. Truth wandered the world. When he returned to America he drove a truck and rose high in the ranks of his labour union. Beauty developed an incurable illness and died in his twenty-fifth year.

THE WEDDING DRESS

They meet at a dance. It is the Saturday night after Thanksgiving and the York Beach Casino is filled to capacity. Nora wears a white angora sweater which Frank notices right away, because of its contrast with her dark-blue eyes and what he likes to call her apple cheeks, a feature which in 1935 is greatly admired.

They spend the rest of the evening in each other's arms. Couples step aside, making way for them as if the whole floor were theirs by right. During the last dance he dares to hold her a little closer.

Nora's brother Jimmy is driving her home. Frank expresses concern about possible snow, the condition of the roads and the number of whiskies Jimmy has consumed. "Oh it will be all right," she says, and he suspects that she is not unhappy about going home with this brother of hers. As they separate, Nora sees that Frank's blue serge suit is covered with angora fluff. He looks as if a dozen Easter Bunnies have capered on his chest. Nora feels badly but can't help laughing. Frank laughs too, for he is a good-natured man. He is also, like Nora, a sharp dresser. She tells him he can call on her. They part.

Frank presents his sisters with the fuzzy suit. They manage all his domestic difficulties. Always have.

Lizzie and Sadie exchange looks.

*

"Jimmy! Jimmy, stop it!" Nora, in her bathrobe, leans from the bedroom window, trying to shout and whisper at the same time. "Please, Jimmy."

In the street below, her brother is attempting, as he does every morning at seven-thirty, to start the motor cycle which he bought second-hand from the White Mountains Garage.

"Son of a bitch! God damn!" He kicks it. "God *damn!*" He kicks it again.

"Please, Jimmy!"

"You go to hell, Nora." His breath and the cycle's steam and billow like an enraged dragon's.

"Jimmy, the Floods . . ." Neighbours have complained. Harrison Avenue is a Methodist stronghold.

"Fuck the Floods," he shouts and tries, again without success, to jump-start his ornery machine. "And fuck you too, Nora, you dumb bitch."

Nora slams the window shut, her hands trembling. She throws herself on the bed which she shares with her sister Frannie and sobs. The continuing racket of the machine serves as a background to Jimmy's curses.

Frank does some investigating. As a reporter for the *Daily Democrat*, he knows how. He is good at it, he enjoys it. And he is acquainted with nearly everyone in the Tri-city area.

What Frank discovers: Nora Winkle is a Methodist (may present problems), born in Belfast. Emigrated to the US in 1913. Mother cleans houses. Father estranged, works in a box factory in East Rochester. Nora Winkle is the eldest of ten children. She is secretary to Huntley Bates, boss of the paper mill, a good job for a girl of her background. She is known for her contralto voice and her ladylike behaviour. Nora Winkle has also been engaged three times and she has broken each engagement. There was even a medical student from Montreal, but she changed her mind and wouldn't have him. They say he had a nervous breakdown.

Nevertheless, Frank feels encouraged. Frank is an optimist.

Poor Nora: a mother to her brothers and sisters, a husband to her mother.

She stops crying. Oh, she thinks, to be alone. Alone in a room with a few nice things; where it's all new and clean and mine. Where nine people and their friends are not continually fighting and needing you to settle the arguments, losing things and asking you to find them.

But there was that one time, that only terrible time when she *was* alone. One afternoon during her last year in high school she came home to find the house empty. She called for them all, called every name, but heard no reply, no complaining, no music or arguments. And she felt her heart tighten then abruptly stop. Alone. A black helmet was descending over her eyes. Her head was cold and her body hot. Alone. She was sweating — or rather perspiring. "Mama," she murmured. Slowly she backed out the front door, clutching her books. "Mama." She staggered across the front porch and sat on the hammock, unable to move, her eyes searching the street for one of them. Any one. "Please," she whispered, "come home." Then Frannie and Ellie turned the corner into Harrison Avenue. Just at that moment her grandmother emerged from the house across the street. She was taking her three pugs for their afternoon constitutional. Immediately Frannie and Ellie crossed the road and made for the trunk of a large elm tree where they huddled together.

"Ha!" cried Grammy Glick. "I see ye. Ye can't hide from me, ye dirty wee things."

Nora pressed her head against her books. Oh, to be just alone.

Nora goes to the mirror, takes out her curling tongs and crimps her short blonde hair. Even with red eyes, she is, as they say, a stunner. Yes, high colour is the thing. And white, very white skin. She is healthy and exercises with Indian clubs. If only she could get rid of the giveaway Irish freckles. The bleaching cream doesn't really work, despite the promises on the package. Might as well admit it and stop spending precious money on it. Be careful, Nora. You are becoming vain. It is such an easy thing to slide into. The Bible says so.

She has a passion for clothes and spends whatever is left after she hands her paycheck over to her mother on fabric and accessories. She haunts the sales. Her sister Lillian is an expert seamstress and at thirteen was already earning cash by mending silk stockings — so cleverly that her work was almost invisible. Together they "cook up frocks" from the latest fashion magazines.

Do not be vain, Nora, she tells herself again, studying the back of her head with a hand mirror, be grateful. And she is grateful, because she is an American now, the citizen of a great and good country that has agreed to accept her and her boisterous family and be responsible for them; to offer them jobs in box factories, in linen and paper mills, in bleacheries and shoe factories, to teach them to read and write so that they may buy galoshes and orange pekoe tea and second-hand motor cycles. She offers thanks every night when she says her prayers and every Sunday at church.

At eight precisely Nora leaves for the mill. On the street she passes Millie Flood who smiles, as usual, as though she had not been awakened yet again by foul language. The Irish cannot control themselves, thinks Millie Flood. God help them.

Fresh from his bath, Frank dons the shirt so carefully laundered by his sister Lizzie. Frank is not handsome, but Frank has "got something". He checks the auburn curls which he fears are beginning to thin. Never mind, he reckons he'll have them for just about as long as he'll need them.

On the cedar chest is a three-pound box of Whitman's Sampler. He has discovered that the only woman he has ever loved, and to whom he will be faithful until he dies at the age of seventy-six, is a chocolate addict. He will attend the Democratic City Committee meeting then drive the twenty miles to Rochester to deliver his gift. Deftly he loops his striped tie and adjusts the knot.

It has been a terrible week. The week before Christmas always is. The dress she and Lil have been working on has had to be completely unstitched. Timmy has brought home three friends for an indefinite stay. She trips every morning over the bodies on the landing. Her mother cannot say no to Timmy. His friends love Mrs Winkle and they love her cooking. She is an even more cheerful slave than their own mothers.

Frannie has been sleepwalking again. Clayton Flood, who once found her wandering by moonlight in his vegetable patch, thinks it has to do with changes in the weather. Whatever it is, something must be done about it. She's becoming dangerous.

At 3 a.m. on Wednesday, Nora woke to find her sister standing over her with an old tennis racket. Nora screamed and Frannie fainted. Timmy complained that he'd been looking for that racket for months.

Normally her behaviour was merely strange, even funny. Someone would hear her on the stairs and wake everyone else. Whispering, on tiptoe, they would follow her to the cellar and watch by flashlight as she lifted the wooden cover and looked down into the well.

"Gives me the goddamn willies," Jimmy would say.

"Shhh!"

Then on Saturday there was the incident with Uncle Brendan. At fifty, Brendan Beckett still lived with his mother, the monstrous Grammy Glick. Everyone said she'd had eight husbands, only two of whom had been legitimate, and that she'd only married Solomon Glick, the Jewish tailor from Boston, in order to sneak her disorderly family into the Land of Opportunity by the back door. No one knew what had happened to Mr Glick, though Frannie was convinced her grandmother murdered him with a chamber pot and fed him to the pugs. At four feet eleven inches, she was the bane of Harrison Avenue and its environs, and her memory still struck fear into the hearts of men, schoolchildren and cats throughout County Down.

Nora knew something really bad was going to happen. The sign had come just after breakfast. From their sitting room, the Winkles could look straight into the Glick kitchen opposite. Harry, Timmy and little Vinnie saw Grammy Glick descend her permanently snow-covered front steps (the Floods complained they were a health hazard). She cast a malevolent glance at Number 27, but she wasn't quick enough. Anyone who happened to be in the sitting room knew exactly when to hit the floor. Off she went with the pugs, knowing she'd been outsmarted and swearing vengeance.

"Close call." Harry breathed a sigh of relief as he got to his knees and peeked over the windowsill to make sure the coast was clear.

"Oh-oh," he cried. "Fire! Fire!"

Nora, Mama and Ellie ran to the sitting room where they could watch Uncle Brendan shoving log after log into the big black stove.

"Oh God help us!" wailed Mrs Winkle, flapping her apron. "Not again!"

Four columns of flame from the open burners shot as high as the ceiling. Uncle Brendan liked it warm.

They all ran across the street in pyjamas and bathrobes, just in time to save Number 28 from conflagration. Mrs Winkle tried to make her half-brother understand how upsetting this sort of behaviour was. She said that she would have to tell his mother if he went on this way. This made Uncle Brendan very sad. He said he was truly sorry. He would never do such a terrible thing again. But he had promised before, and his promises only brought more disaster in their wake.

Sure enough, Sunday morning, as Nora was grinding cranberries for the relish, she heard the front door open. She knew with an awful certainty who it was. She called for Jimmy who was in the garage, tinkering with the motor cycle, but Uncle Brendan already stood in the kitchen, wild-eyed and wielding an axe. Jimmy burst in. Too late. Uncle Brendan dashed to the sitting room and proceeded to chop down the Christmas tree before they could lay a hand on him.

"Why?" Mrs Winkle wept into her apron. "Why?" Hearing her, the younger Winkles began to cry, then Harry and finally Nora. All of them crying together and Uncle Brendan too, not understanding.

"What saps," Frannie observed.

I must live somewhere else, thought Nora.

Jimmy said, as he always did, that Uncle Brendan ought to be locked up. And one day he was. He has been in the Concord Hospital for more than thirty years now. Only Harry, Nora's favourite, still visits him. Of course Uncle Brendan has no idea who Harry is.

For once Frank's instincts are not aligned with his famous brain. He jumps the gun and proposes too soon. She isn't ready for this.

"No." Nora says. Then more kindly, "It's been an awful week. Just awful." And then, "I can't leave Mama."

Ah, Frank thinks, and kisses her and cheerfully departs. Now he understands why the three engagements were broken off.

Nora feels badly. She respects Frank, knows he's kind and smart. But she has told him the truth. She cannot leave her mother. A life of hard work and anxiety has left her looking fifteen years older than she is. Already Mrs Winkle wears old ladies' shoes and thick stockings that bag at the ankle. Her hands are twisted and raw with veins a quarter-inch high. (All that yellow washing soap, all that bleach and polish and disinfectant and starch.) It isn't possible to abandon her for something as selfish as one's own home, one's own children, one's own husband, one's own wedding dress. Not when she is Little Nora and her mother is Big Nora, and that is how it's been all her life.

She spies the Whitman's Sampler, lies down on the sofa and devours the entire top layer while listening to Rudy Vallee.

"I'm just a vagabond lover . . ."

Nora hums along. As she bites into a butter-cream centre she remembers the words of her best friend Vinette. "It's getting late, Norrie. You're twenty-six."

She cannot stop eating the chocolate. Chocolate stills her mind and heart.

The next morning she wakes up covered in hives. Mortified, she refuses to come downstairs for a Christmas dinner laid for twenty. Of course there is no tree. Mrs Winkle could not afford another since every year the Winkles spend their last penny on Christmas then go into debt for the next eight months.

Harry brings Nora her turkey and cranberry relish in bed. Nora loves Harry best of her six brothers. He was the easiest to rear and is also the one most like her. She'd held him in her arms all the way across the Atlantic while her parents spent the journey in the lavatory. She cannot leave Harry either.

*

Frank is a smart person. He has "got something". This something is not lost on Mrs Winkle and Frank knows it. It has been many years since Mrs Winkle met a man she could trust, and this too is not lost on Frank. He calls her sweetheart and gives her presents. He always remembers to bring her the *Boston Herald Traveler* which she calls her "wee book".

He takes the three youngest Winkles for rides in his Ford and lets them scream and bicker and jump up and down on the back seat. He buys them candy and takes them to Saturday afternoon matinées to watch Tom Mix and Hopalong Cassidy. He, too, is partial to Westerns.

Nora teases him about being in love with Mama. He answers that he only misses his own mama who died when he was fourteen.

"Poor Frank," Nora says and strokes his cheek.

"But I have the girls."

Oh yes, the sisters.

Frank drives twenty miles four nights a week to see Nora. Much of his visit is spent in the kitchen with Mrs Winkle. He has added honey and sweetie-pie and old darling to his repertoire of endearments. Nora he calls Nora.

Politics are his obsession, and he talks to Mrs Winkle about them with great animation and in a way she can understand. She likes this. No one has ever talked to her about serious things, aside from dog bites, broken arms and unpaid bills. She listens. She asks questions as she makes the tea and rolls out the pie crust. She does not mind that Frank Murnane is a Catholic and a Democrat. Once not minding would have been unthinkable, but this is America, the greatest country in the world. None of those bad old feelings here. And good riddance too.

He says there will be a presidential election soon and will she vote. Oh yes, Clayton and Millie Flood (staunch Republicans) always arrange for her to be driven to the polling booths. The Floods are good friends and neighbours. Fine people. Very kind to her and her family. They even introduced her to the Methodist minister, though of course she never has much time for church. Nora and Harry go. They seem to like it. Nora was even in the Salvation Army, did he know? And Harry will soon be a fully-fledged Mason. The minister likes Nora because she has a beautiful voice. At home Vinette plays the piano while she sings. She sings in the choir too. Gets lots of solos. She'd heard her daughter once in church and cried. Where did it come from, she wondered, this beautiful voice? Of course Mr Winkle is musical in a way. Played the bagpipes in a Black Watch band. Kilts and all. My, she'd been proud of him. But not like Nora. Bagpipes never made her want to cry.

Frank tells her stories of the great FDR, how he saved the country of America that she loves so much and of which she is so happy to be a citizen. Roosevelt is a hero, he says, omitting the fact that it was the great FDR who repealed Prohibition. The youngest Winkles come and listen too. Then Nora then Harry when he returns from a Masons' meeting. They all move to the big dining-room table in order to accommodate Jimmy, who has been sulking in his den over a letter from his estranged wife, and Timmy with his three friends. Their supper has been kept warm for them by Big Nora.

The talk moves from politics to poker. Frank tells funny stories of late-night sessions and tricks played on slower-witted cronies, forgetting the Methodist line on games of chance. But no one minds. The Winkles begin to tell their own stories, all of which involve disasters. They giggle and guffaw and let the children stay up until one. Harry is pleading, "Shhh, shhh, she'll hear us," then laughing louder then anyone else. But they are not so hysterical as to neglect to turn off the porch and sitting-room lights. They want no visits from vindictive grandmothers. One of Timmy's friends falls off his chair and cuts his lower lip which Little Nora treats with mercurichrome. Big Nora brews more tea and produces a banana-cream pie.

The Winkles adore Frank. All but Jimmy who says he's a phoney. He hates the way Frank always calls him Seamus. Who the hell does that Harp think he is? Nora tells him he's just jealous.

New Year's Eve. There is a dance at the York Beach Casino. Frank takes Nora. Alone this time. No siblings. No little Winkles. She looks like a million dollars, a real lady. He's so proud of her. He will still be proud of her when she shrinks and sags and the colour has drained for ever from her cheeks — especially then.

"Marry me, Nora," he says as, the objects of every admiring eye, they sway to the music of Glen Glenn and his orchestra.

"I can't leave Mama," Nora replies.

When they arrive home at four in the morning, Nora makes them cold baked-bean sandwiches, her favourite after-dance snack which Frank is slowly learning to love.

By spring they are close enough to exchange confidences and make confessions.

"I've raised nine children," Nora says. "Each one as it came along. When she was forty-four and told us she was pregnant with Sonny I said, 'Oh Mama, not again!' Wasn't that awful of me? I was angry because she wouldn't stop seeing Papa. We were all angry. Except Frannie. She loves her father best. I still feel guilty about saying that."

Frank likes her trace of brogue. He asks her about Belfast. He wants to know everything. She tells him her first memory. She was Queen of May, the prettiest little girl on the Shankill Road — at least that's what they all said. She wore a white dress and a wreath of flowers and sang a song, she can't remember the words, and held the maypole while everyone danced round her, entwining their coloured streamers. It was so pretty. But the festivities were brought to a sudden end by a raid of Catholic boys. They threw stones. Then there was a big fight and the police came. All the children ran away scared and crying. Someone, she never knew who, picked her up under his arm and ran with her, her bare legs and feet dangling, all the way to the Winkles' door where he handed her over to Big Nora.

More confessions. About her clothes. She knows it is a vice. The minister said so in church two Sundays ago, and she is sure he was looking straight at her.

"But I don't spend a lot of money on it," she hurriedly tells Frank, almost as if she were assuring him that she would make a thrifty wife despite appearances. "Just the little I have left over when I've given my paycheck to Mama." He says he realizes that. "Lil and I go to the sales. We look in the magazines and get ideas. We don't even buy the magazines. We read them in the news shop and memorize the photographs of the models." She does not say that clothes are the only things that are hers alone. Her clothes and her voice. Vanity.

She does not tell him that her birth forced a marriage between two unsuited people; that no one was sure of her mother's maiden name; that her father was an Orangeman and had jumped many times over the imaginary bodies of dead Catholics; that when she came to America her mother could not read or write. Nora is ashamed of these things. I must tell him, she thinks. And then, I must tell him later.

"Now you confess," she says. "Isn't that what good Catholics are supposed to do?"

He pretends to consider the matter.

"I hate my sisters' cooking." They laugh.

"Well," she urges after a moment, "go ahead. There must be more."

"They'll be leaving soon and know what? I'll be glad."

"Leaving? why then you'll be — "

"All alone."

Alone. In that big wooden house on the corner with its four bedrooms, its three apple trees, its big back yard with the Bridle-wreath hedge, its large sunny kitchen . . .

"Sadie's been transferred to the mill in Manchester and Lizzie's finally getting married."

"Really?"

"There's one more thing." He hesitates. "Don't you want to know it?"

"If you want to tell me." She presses his hand. She looks so appealing, innocent almost. Frank resists the impulse to kiss her. He's never sure how she'll react.

"I've seen you before."

She looks at him, nervous suddenly, quizzical.

He saw her at a bean supper in South Berwick. Her colour was especially high. Vinette accompanied as she sang numbers from their favourite collection, *A Treasure Chest of Songs We Love* — "I Dreamed I Dwelt in Marble Halls", "Just Before the Battle, Mother", "The Letter Edged in Black" and "Whispering Hope". It was the loveliest thing Frank had ever heard.

"Well, my goodness. But you shouldn't flatter me."

He does not tell her that on that night he resolved to capture her voice.

Summer. Excursions to Rye and Wallis Sands and Old Orchard Beach in Frank's black Ford. The youngest Winkles run wild at the amusement park. They are completely unmanageable. Frank buys them candy apples and cotton candy and popcorn. On the way home they are sick. They fight and cry and finally fall asleep, their faces sticky and dirty, their noses running, their soiled socks runched down into the backs of their shoes. Nora tries not to be embarrassed. She begs them to blow their noses. She always carries a small packet of Kleenex.

During the drive she holds Frank's hand. She feels better when she holds his hand. She thinks of a large kitchen, three empty bedrooms, a white dress . . .

Nora cooks Frank a special Sunday lunch. Mama is to rest (she doesn't) and Frannie is to help.

"Please," Nora begs her brothers, "no wells."

They laugh until they remember that Nora takes wells very seriously. They argue that potatoes taste better with wells. But they promise: just for today. Of course they forget. They heap up their mashed potatoes, make large craters in the centre with the backs of their dessert spoons then fill them to overflowing with gravy. They spend a moment enjoying the effect of their accomplishments then mush the potatoes and gravy into a beige soup. Wells.

Frannie sets the table in a leisurely way, practising a dance step as she does so. Nora inspects her work. She adjusts the salt and pepper shakers by a quarter-inch.

"There." She smiles at Frannie. "Isn't that better?"

Frannie smashes a saucer on the floor. "You wanna see a mess?" she cries. "I'll show you a mess! Clean it up yourself, Miss *Just So*!"

November, 1936. The presidential election. The Floods arrive promptly at nine in their recently polished car to drive

Mrs Winkle to the polling station, then to the house she is cleaning that day. They have done so ever since Mrs Winkle moved to Number 27 nineteen years ago. Mrs Winkle sits in the back seat thanking them repeatedly for their kindness. They nod and smile and are pleased with her and with themselves. They are killing the two birds of civic and Christian duty with one stone. It's not every day a person has a chance to do that.

Mrs Winkle votes. The Floods vote. They wait for her, the motor running, as she chats to the mother of one of Timmy's friends. Mrs Mallon hasn't seen her Michael for two weeks and she's getting a welfare report from Mrs Winkle.

"Well," says Clayton Flood when Mrs Winkle has climbed into the back seat. "Feel better now that you've helped put Landon in the White House?"

"Oh," says Mrs Winkle, always cheerful, "I didn't vote for Landon, Mr Flood."

"You didn't?"

"I voted for Roosevelt." She smiles, hands folded in her lap, pleased with her wonderful country.

A silence descends which has no effect whatever on Mrs Winkle.

"Bye-bye, sir, and all the best." She waves as she steps from the car. The Floods do not speak to the Winkles for nearly a year.

"When were you happiest, Nora?"

"In the Salvation Army," she answers promptly.

Frank laughs, but when he sees the expression in her eyes he stops. He tries to be serious.

The Floods introduced her to Captain Daggett. It was one of many efforts to civilize the Winkles. No one but Nora was interested, but her enthusiasm more than compensated for their disappointment. Captain Daggett was taken with her voice. She'd got to sing lots of solos and play the cymbals. She even loved her uniform.

The others were kind and decent people who never spoke ill of anyone and eschewed the drink. Nora admired them. With them she felt protected. It was a world safe from the likes of Jimmy.

"And when have you been happiest?"

"Right now."

She understands she might not have given the correct answer.

It's official. After dances, drives and amusement parks; after innumerable evenings in the Winkle kitchen and twenty boxes of Whitman's Sampler and Candy Cupboard; after Vinette has warned, "Don't wait too long, Nora. You're twenty-eight;" after Frannie and Lil vow that if she won't have him they'll make a play for him themselves; after the three children beg and plead and Mrs Winkle cries into her apron; after Harry proclaims Frank a wonderful man (he has got Harry an assistant managership at the Ben Franklin five and dime) and promises to drive Mama over to visit Nora twice a week; after thinking for months about the four-bedroom house (empty of sisters), of her own furniture and china cupboard and most of all the wedding dress — the white dress in which she once again will be Queen of May but with no street fighting this time and satin slippers instead of bare feet, and no stranger carrying her home but her own dear Frank — after all this she says yes at last.

Now Frank's Ford is parked outside 27 Harrison Avenue every evening. And now the moment has come that everyone has been dreading. Grammy Glick cannot be put off any longer. At seven-forty-five on Wednesday morning she storms in, the pugs yapping about her long skirts and lunging at Skippy, the Winkles' yellow mongrel, and announces that they will not succeed in "sweeping her under the carpet", that they are a bunch of damned ingrates and that she insists on meeting this bloody Papist. She announces that she will not be made to wait another day and bangs her cane on the floor at which the pugs whine and cringe and roll on their backs and Skippy flees, the screen door banging behind him.

Nora has warned Frank and Frank believes he is prepared. He has faith in his charm.

She is waiting for them. She sits in her kitchen by the big black stove, the pugs at her feet, quiet for once, her skirts spread round her like the Queen of the Gnomes. Uncle Brendan is safely locked in his room, for she wants no ructions but those she creates herself. She wants to look long and hard at this Papist. She wants to see an example of this religion that practises idolatry and makes hamburger meat out of Protestant babies.

"Grammy, this is Francis Martin Murnane."

Grammy Glick does not answer. She leans forward and peers at him as though giving him the evil eye. Frank lets her look.

"Be nice, Grammy. Say hello. Frank's my fiancé."

"I know that," she roars. Nora is silent for the rest of the interview.

"You've tricked Little Nora" (by whom she means Mrs Winkle). "She was always feeble-minded. They'd all ha' perished without me. Not a brain among 'em." She points to the house across the street. "'Twas I got 'em all in, you know."

"You're a very smart old woman, Mrs Glick."

"And don't you just wish I wa'n't Mr Murnane. I've got your measure and you know it. You cast a spell on that poor imbecile Little Nora."

"You've got me there," he smiles, and winks.

"Shameless," she sniffs. Then she sniffs again. Oh no, thinks Nora, here it comes. She closes her eyes.

117

Grammy Glick lifts the hem of her black skirt and folds it carefully back over her lap. Underneath is a grey petticoat which once had been white. This too she raises and folds back over her lap. Then she lifts a yellowed petticoat which might once have been pink and repeats the process. Finally she arrives at the red flannel petticoat, the ragged ruffle of which she lifts to her face. With a noise like Captain Daggett's French horn, she blows her nose into the ruffle, examines her achievement and blows again. Then she unfolds the red petticoat and smoothes it over her knees. The might-have-been-pink one follows then the grey and lastly the black skirt. Nora can open her eyes now. Grammy Glick turns to her.

"Ye daft thing," she says. "You'd give up your religion, surrender your children to the priests, eh? For this *spiv*!"

"Oh Frank." Nora speaks at last. "Let's go."

"Catholics!" she shouts after them. "Never trust 'em. They're not Christian."

"It's true, Frank, isn't it? I'll have to promise to — "

"Plenty of time." He pats the hand that rests on his arm. "Plenty of time."

"It's true, isn't it?" Nora asks Vinette. "I can't be a Methodist any more. I can't go to my own church or sing in the choir."

"Nora." Vinette looks at her hard. "It's worth it."

Lizzie and Sadie are calm. They are concerned but they are calm. They would never express disapproval of their brother Frank. But as he leaves to pick up Nora and take her to her first interview with Father Happny, Sadie remarks quietly, "You know they say the Scots-Irish have the worst tempers in the world."

Frank waves and blows a kiss and genially orders them not to wait up. When he's left they discuss the rumour of insanity in the Winkle family.

Sadie and Lizzie have never been in a Protestant church. They treat Protestants with respect, though it is hard for them not to giggle when Toddy McVeigh makes fun of their Bible reading, the fact that their congregations all sing together, and in English, and that they are too cheap to smarten up their churches with a couple of statues.

Father Happny is a kind man. Still, Nora is nervous of him. She has never spoken to a priest before. She says she understands about the children's baptism and education. They will go to the school next door where for eight years they will be taught by those saintly women, the Sisters of Mercy. She understands that they will make their First Holy Communion and their Confirmation here in St Patrick's. Won't it be a wonderful thing says Father Happny, when she can receive the Sacraments with them?

"Wonderful," says Nora.

He stresses that she need not take instruction immediately, though of course it would be preferable to be married as a Roman Catholic. She agrees, trying not to show her panic.

Frank, she wants to say when they leave, I'm not ready. But he speaks first. "See? What did I tell you? Plenty of time, plenty of time."

Frannie is awakened by Nora's sobbing.

"For Christ's sake," Frannie moans. She puts her arm around her sister's heaving shoulders. "Come on, Norrie. It doesn't matter that much. I'd get married in a Men's Room if I could marry Frank Murnane."

"Oh you're disgusting!" Nora cries even harder.

"Well, why not?" Frannie squeals.

"Shut up," hisses Lil at the door. "Will you just please shut up. Oh-oh. What's the matter, Norrie? Oh no, is it because — "

"It's *because*," Frannie sighs.

"Look," Lil embraces Nora. The other two make room for her on the bed. They can see the silhouettes of moving leaves and branches on the green window-shade. "It's not really so important."

"Naw," reasons pragmatic Frannie. "So you can't do it in the big church. What's so bad? The chapel's still part of the church. I mean God's there too, I suppose, if that's important to you."

"I don't want to be married in an old chapel!"

"Shut up," yells Timmy and bangs on the wall.

"Oh go stick your head in a bucket," says Frannie.

They can hear Mama in her heavy black shoes going down the stairs. It is 5.30 a.m.

"It's not just the chapel." Nora collects herself. "It's — the dress!"

"Yeah, that stinks," Frannie agrees.

"His sisters said an off-white suit would be 'appropriate'."

"Well, beige is almost white."

"Beige! With my high colour?"

"Your high horse, more like it."

"Shut up, Frannie."

"It's as if I'm not good enough," Nora goes on, "to wear a proper wedding dress and be married properly in church. It has to be all hidden and quiet somewhere way out back where no one will see. They're ashamed of me. Even Frank — ashamed."

With her sisters on either side of her, Nora sleeps at last. The alarm goes off at seven. Bravely she rises, crimps her hair, skips breakfast, leaves for work with Mrs Winkle chasing her down the front steps with a cup of tea.

"At least drink this, Nora my darlin'. Drink it for Mama."

"She wants beatin' not babyin'," shouts Grammy Glick from her porch as she gathers up the pugs' leashes.

All day Nora thinks about the white dress that will exist for ever only as an idea. She thinks how terrible a beige suit will be, even with one of those showy orchids pinned to the lapel. She looks awful in beige. Everyone looks awful in beige.

Huntly Bates admires Nora Winkle. She is hard-working, conscientious, honest. Best secretary he's ever had. He decides to give her a wedding present of $200. It is more money than Nora has ever had at one time.

"Well, honey, you've earned it," Frank says. He tells her they'll be lucky together. Look, their luck has already begun. Yes, she says, she is holding their luck in her hand, right this minute.

"Wish my sister Lizzie would get lucky."

"Why?"

"Marriage postponed again." Lizzie has been engaged for four years to Eddie MacMahon, the local policeman. A nice man with a sick mother.

"Does that mean?"

"'Fraid so, Norrie. It won't be for long, I promise."

So the house with the four bedrooms will not be empty and hers after all. She will have to share meals, conversation, a kitchen, with a reticent and unsympathetic woman who will be sure to have fixed ideas about how everything should be done.

"Then I think I'll keep on working for a while," she says, not showing her disappointment but chastening him all the same.

"Sure, honey. Plenty of time."

Plenty of time to turn Papist. Plenty of time to share a kitchen with a stranger. And Sadie, it seems, intends to come home every other weekend. And Mrs MacMahon might live for ever. Old women went on and on, especially bad-tempered ones. Look at Grammy Glick. No one knew how old she really was, but she had been sixty-nine for an awfully long time.

The lustre, Nora thinks, is draining from this beautiful marriage, this Maypole day of her life. What is she doing anyway? She is marrying a man her mother trusts. Nora suddenly feels bound and gagged. Somehow she must restore this seeping lustre. She will not allow them to rob her of her May dance. She will not be a demure little beige convert asking to be accepted despite her shortcomings, asking for verification of her existence, married in a chapel, married in November.

Nora and Lil visit the news shop where they inspect the latest fashion magazines. This time they buy one. They go to Mrs Pappas's Dress Salon, and Nora tries on several items, the seams of which Lil inspects in the dressing room. They tell Mrs Pappas's assistant the dresses are too large. Expressions of regret all round. Back on the street they head for J.C. Penny's and the patterns department. Lil finds two which she is sure she can chop and change to suit her sister's odd requirements.

"Remember, this is our secret, Lil." Not even Harry is aware of what's going on in Lil's room and Mama is far too busy to notice. She's cleaning houses and planning the wedding breakfast.

The next day Nora goes to the bank and withdraws half of Huntley Bates's wedding present. She doesn't take it all. She leaves them half their luck.

She boards a bus for Portsmouth where she visits the most exclusive department store in southern New Hampshire. There she buys seven yards of the finest silk chiffon which the salesgirl wraps carefully in tissue paper. Her next stop is Carbury's where she purchases a pair of satin pumps with not too high a heel (at five foot seven, Nora is considered tall for a woman.) At Suzette's millinery shop she finds a saucy hat of indeterminate fur. She buys two of them. Lastly she purchases a pair of silk stockings and some underwear. She is home in time to mash the potatoes, set the table and do a pile of ironing before she falls into bed beside Frannie who knows something's cooking and is burning to find out what.

Lil and Nora spend their evenings locked in Lil's room from which the sound of the sewing machine can be heard for hours at a stretch.

"I suppose you think this is bad of me, Lil."

But Lil is not the person to ask. She cares only for the dress as dress. Its moral implications are not her concern. Nora finds this comforting, how hard it will be to leave her sisters. She cannot imagine life without them and is suddenly afraid. She sits staring, the chiffon beautifully bunched in her lap.

"Get a move on, Norrie," prompts Lil. Nora threads her needle.

The wedding day. Nora wakes at 5 a.m. She lies in bed, something she never does, as if she were waiting for the sound of the motor cycle and her brother's curses. She feels as though she were flying apart, pieces of her hurtling off in all directions like iron filings, never again to be drawn together by the magnet of her self. She can just make out the dress, completed the night before, hanging on the back of the closet door.

At five-forty-five she makes a pot of tea. She would like to sit in the hammock on the front porch and drink it and eat a cold baked-bean sandwich, all alone. But Grammy Glick would be sure to see her and scurry round for a confrontation. She goes to the back steps instead, her coat over her bathrobe. She likes the morning and the bright cold. She sits and drinks her tea and looks at the littered driveway. Timmy and his friends have been drinking beer (not

123

allowed in the house), and the bottles still lie scattered where they left them. The cats have been at the trash can. No one remembered to take Skippy for a walk, and he is straining at his tether, having messed copiously by the garage door. Nora gets a paper bag and begins to tidy up. It is instinct, something she doesn't think about, a habitual reaction.

Jimmy emerges, monkey-wrench in hand, eager to attack his motor cycle. He sees Nora at work and starts to cry.

"Norrie," he sobs, putting his arms round her and burying his face in her neck. "How can you be getting married? You're just a kid."

Nora laughs and hugs him. "I'm two years older than you are." She will not cry, she will not, because if she starts she will never stop.

"You haven't even lived yet. You've just raised brats and gone to church and sung in that goddamn choir."

"Jimmy!"

"What'll we do without you, Norrie? Won't be the same here any more. What the hell will we do?"

Four automobiles are lined up outside 27 Harrison Avenue. Timmy's friends have come through and have begged, borrowed, and possibly stolen, sufficient transport to carry the entire family, minus Grammy Glick, to Great Falls.

The Winkles come out into the November sunshine. Here and there a few leaves the colour of dried blood still cling to the black trees. One of the Winkle boys wears his army uniform. Mama is very proud.

Uncle Brendan has been subdued lately, so they are risking it and he is allowed to come. He is not quite sure which of his nieces is getting married, but he is very happy. He beams, a carnation in the button-hole of his ancient overcoat and black rubbers over his shoes. His mother, whose face is pressed to the kitchen window, has insisted. She scowls at her ungrateful, disorganized family. She has been asked to the wedding but has refused, to the relief of all concerned. She would rather, she says, endure the fires of hell.

She is cursing them, Harry is certain. He averts his eyes as he gets into the car. He will be driving Nora and Mama and Frannie whom Nora has asked to be bridesmaid. She hopes this act of kindness and inclusion will somehow touch her sister and encourage her to reform. It doesn't. But she does like the dressing up. Harry will also give Nora away. Everyone is secretly sad that Papa is not here to do it. They know that he too is sad, but no one says anything about it.

The Winkles climb into the cars, arguing about who will sit where. They all get car sick on long journeys and want to be in the front seat. Even if they leave immediately, they will be half an hour late, but then no one really expects them to be on time.

They are now seated. They all lean forward, craning their necks for a glimpse of Nora who is coming down the front steps. No one speaks. She walks slowly towards the first car, giving the neighbours who are lined up across the street the opportunity for a good long look. She allows herself a quick glance in order to check their expressions. A few mouths, including Millie Flood's, hang open.

Finally Jimmy breaks the silence with a whistle.

"You look like a goddamn million, Norrie. But why the colour?"

"I like it," she says.

Mrs Winkle cries all the way to St Patrick's. She is remembering the times she slapped and spanked and shouted at Little Nora. (None but Sonny was spared her lightning corporal punishment.) Then she would hold them and cry, just as she is doing now. Frannie passes her Kleenex and keeps repeating, "Oh come *on*, Ma."

"I'm a damn fool, amn't I," blubbers Mrs Winkle who has barely noticed Nora's dress.

Harry holds Nora's hand and does not let go until they reach St Patrick's.

Yes, there they are: Lizzie and Sadie in dark-brown coats and identical felt cloches. Lizzie wears short, wool-trimmed boots on which she shifts her weight. They could have waited inside, Nora thinks. But they'd rather freeze and make her feel guilty for being late. Immediately she's sorry for being uncharitable. Why is it, she wonders, looking at the sisters, that in the family lottery of looks, brains and charm, one member should emerge such a clear winner? But Frank, she knows, has goodness as well. When she stands beside him in this dress of hers, she will look in his eyes and still see goodness. But she will see something else too, and that will be knowledge, a knowledge of her that has been hidden from him until today. And the knowledge will hurt him a little. And she will sense that and feel satisfied.

Everyone enters the church, the Catholics stopping at the holy water fonts to bless themselves. The youngest Winkles gape at the decor. Frannie gives a little snort and gets a quick kick from Harry. The brother and two sisters wait in the vestibule watching the others walk the long dim side-aisle to the chapel where there is barely enough room for them all and where they begin to get warm from the closeness of other bodies.

Nora refuses a coat. She wants to be exposed for as long as possible in her wedding dress, because she will never wear it again.

She stands at the chapel door, head up, straight back very straight. There is no music. She sees Frank, dapper but uneasy in a new three-piece suit. He is wearing his father's watch. Beside him is his best man, Toddy McVeigh, whom he has known since childhood and who is a fellow member of the Great Falls Chapter of the Knights of Columbus.

Everyone turns, expectant smiles on their faces, hankies at the ready. Then they see it: seven yards of deep-purple silk chiffon falling in five tiers over Nora's slender body. The tiers are cut on the bias, so that the bottom tier hangs longer on the right side, ending in a graceful point, while the left exposes Nora's black silk-stockinged leg as far as her knee. The sleeves are trimmed at the wrist in black fur, the same fur as the hat that adorns her head, tilted at a rakish angle and covering the top of her face with a black-net veil. The neckline is low and rounded, exposing her collarbones and the white, white skin of her chest. For the first time in her life she has made up her face.

She is a stunner, a million bucks, the classiest dame in the Tri-city area. She should be going to a night-club — Twenty-One, the Stork Club, El Morocco — those famous places they have read about but will never visit. She could be going to lunch on the arm of a congressman or modelling for a fashion magazine. She could be going to a funeral — the glamorous widow, the bereaved heiress. The one place she could not be going to is her own wedding.

She takes her best-loved brother's arm. They walk towards the small altar adorned with only two candles and two vases of red roses.

Father Happny's bushy eyebrows shoot up nearly to his white hair. He subdues them with difficulty and tries to smile and look benevolent, which he is.

Lil cannot stop studying her masterpiece.

Frannie thinks this the funniest thing she has ever seen.

Jimmy is embarrassed and can't think why.

Mrs Winkle is crying again.

Toddy McVeigh gives the bride a wink.

Lizzie and Sadie exchange looks.

Nora reaches Frank's side. She searches his eyes and finds there what she expects to find.

Uncle Brendan begins to sing "The Sash My Father Wore".

The wedding breakfast is over. Nora steps out of the purple dress and hangs it in the closet that is hers no longer. She removes the black pumps and unrolls the black-silk stockings. She takes from a hanger the simple, well-cut, inexpensive, dusty-rose going-away suit.

"You're not taking the wow-wee-wow dress?" asks Frannie who has been smoking a cigarette in the bathroom and Nora knows it. She sniffs but makes no comment.

"Why should I?"

"Won't you and Frank be stepping out in DC? Lots of night-clubs there, I bet."

"It's not really what we had in mind."

"You're a snit, Norrie. Marriage hasn't changed you. I feel sorry for Frank."

Nora doesn't tell her that their big Washington treat will be a visit to the Senate hearings.

"I'm not ever going to wear it again."

Frannie calculates that this is not the right moment to ask if she can have it. She'll just borrow it while Nora is away.

"That's stupid to let it rot in a trunk. It was expensive."

"I'm going to give it to my daughter."

"For her *wedding*?"

Nora closes the closet door firmly and slips into her coat.

"Don't be silly. To play with when she's little."

"Play? That beautiful — ?"

"Yes. To dress up in. What's a dress for?"

Nora leaves. Frannie locks the door to the room that will be hers alone until Jimmy brings his wife home to live. She kicks off her shoes, lies back on the bed and smokes another cigarette.

MRS TIGGYWINKLE
GOES TO TOWN

She'd brought supper — pasta salad, a cold chicken and a water-melon — insisting Clare would be too exhausted to cook after spending all afternoon at the hospital. They drank gin and tonics as the children, whom Alison had already fed, played rowdy games on the grass.

"This was good of you." Clare raised her glass. "Especially since you were meant to be my guest."

"Please. It's nothing. Is he better?"

"About the same."

"And his face?"

"Can't move the right side. Can't remember words. Can't — " Clare put her drink on the table and looked away.

"Where was it he fell?"

"Just there on the stairs. Mum found him."

"How awful." Alison pressed the arm of her friend who smiled weakly then pulled herself up straight, downed her gin and said she thought she'd have another. "What about you?"

"No, no." Alison covered the top of her glass with her hand.

"One is my limit. One of everything."

"Except kids."

Alison, mother of four, looked slightly confused. Was Clare blaming her, making a veiled reference to the overpopulated planet, the Third World, middle-class greed? She knew Clare read about these things. She never had time to read, so thankfully they were seldom discussed. Besides, she reasoned, she loved her family, was kind to her friends and neighbours. Wasn't that enough? How much could one life make room for?

Clare was in the kitchen slamming ice-cube trays while Alison stared at the garden. Here and there a flower pulsated colour into the solemn dusk. She sat entranced by the sound of the children's laughter, her favourite sound.

Alison and Clare had known each other for fifteen years, since university, though Alison had dropped out during her final year to marry Stanley. Clare had always been alternately bored with and grateful for Alison's friendship. In secret she had laughed at her: at her school committees and cooking classes, her volunteer work at the hospital flower shop, her classy, hyper-organized children's parties, her Jaeger clothes, her lousy haircut, her obsessive decorating, her collections of art deco crockery and original Fair Isle sweaters. *And* she embroidered cushion covers in William Morris patterns purchased from the V. & A. catalogue, since her extravagant domesticity allowed little time for such cultural activities as museum visiting. Besides, she and Stanley lived in deep green Richmond and never came "up to town", as she put it.

But usually Clare loved her. You are faithful, she thought, you are true. That is very old-fashioned. I hope that I will never be so stupid as to take it for granted.

Alison's homebody habits plus her sweet rather fussy good nature inspired Clare to christen her Mrs Tiggywinkle. She even dressed like her namesake and wore aprons and hats and full skirts in royal blue or bottle green to hide her hips, expensive baggy sweaters in contrasting shades, usually with an heraldic or floral appliqué, and pumps with very low heels, since she imagined she was too tall. (Clare, on the other hand, wore jeans with snappy lace-up boots or long straight skirts with the less ostentatious sort of slit but with big belts and tight tops to show off her waist and breasts. Her wardrobe was built on black.)

"Why don't you let Nicola stay?" She sat down with another gin. She was worried about her father. She was also irritated by the inconvenience of his collapse, and she held the two contradictory feelings side by side without much guilt.

"Clare, are you sure? No, really, that's kind of you, don't think I don't appreciate it, but you have more than enough to cope with. You don't need another child underfoot. And she's in a very demanding phase. Not as sensitive as your Evelyn, I'm afraid."

"Rubbish. All seven year olds are demanding. Besides, it will keep Mum occupied."

"And you."

"And me."

"Come, now, why don't I take Evelyn instead? You need rest."

Good old Alison, thought Clare. Always supportive. If only she'd turn a little of it on herself instead of propping up all the egos around her. She could do with a little selfishness, a little vanity.

"Nicola and Polly would love it, and I could return her on — goodness, what's happened to your mother's ceanothus?"

"Same as the last one. Killed it, didn't she? Mum's the Kali Durga of Clapton."

Alison was a dedicated and successful gardener, though where she found time to achieve such miracles Clare could not imagine. Thank God Mum was at the hospital, otherwise the rest of the evening would be spent in anxious botanical debate.

It was dark now, and they could barely see the children, though they could certainly hear them.

"Let's go inside," said Clare. "I'm chilly."

"It's because you're exhausted, I can tell. You work such long hours at that magazine, Clare. Not that you don't look wonderful," she hastened to add. "You always look wonderful, it's amazing really. I'm positively dumpy by comparison. You just eat what you like and it seems to make no difference."

"My arse is too big, Alison."

"Oh Clare, what nonsense. You're in proportion and that's all that matters. My bosom is too small and my hips are too large" (who but Alison would use the word "bosom" any more?) "and even my ankles — "

"We should go inside."

"You're right. Oh I'm sorry. I've been keeping you out here talking, haven't I? Now don't touch those dishes, darling. I'll do them."

Clare went to Alison's house at Christmas. Reluctantly she'd accepted an invitation for Boxing Day, knowing she'd feel suffocated by the crowd and the heat and the nappy-talk of Alison's friends, not to mention the loathsome presence of Stanley whom she'd always regarded as a stony-hearted prat in a suit who failed entirely to appreciate his wife and who scorned her accomplishments while being the chief beneficiary of them. But Evelyn was an Only, and being an Only at Christmas is hard to bear, so she'd said yes. There were times throughout the day when she thought she either might not be able to hold her tongue or keep awake. So she escaped the crowds and the screaming children and the whippets and spaniels and retrievers and the suffocating charm of Alison's overstuffed double sitting room and walked through the large garden which led down to the banks of the Thames. The clouds hung low over the water's opaque surface. It was unseasonably warm. She thought of her father in his wheelchair and of the way his face contorted as he struggled in anguish to pronounce the simplest word.

"Christ," she pitched a glowing cigarette at the water and addressed the river spirit, "get me outta this hell."

By ten-thirty everyone had gone and Alison had got the children and a noticeably tipsy Stanley tucked up in bed. The whole affair had been beautifully managed, Clare had to admit. She supposed a normal human being would actually have enjoyed it. Still, this bit was nice: sitting before Alison's marble fireplace feeling the fire's radiance and watching the soft crumbling of the cherrywood logs. Her mum had never bothered to open their flues, and so it was gas heaters backed up by a geriatric heating system, and the house exuded a permanent damp chill even in July. The dryness here was delicious. Clare basked in it. She was happy to be alone with her friend. She realized, and disliked admitting, that Alison made her feel secure.

She said she wondered if she would ever find a flat of her own. So far every one she'd inspected was either beyond her limited means or fit only for a squat. Ever since she and Richard had separated, she spent her days working at the consumer magazine, then set out evenings and weekends to look at property. As yet nothing suitable had turned up. And so she remained trapped in the house where she'd spent her childhood, along with her daughter, her invalid father and her air-head mother who went on as she always had, burning the supper and talking incessantly and killing more than half of what she planted in the dismal garden. No wonder Alison's house suddenly seemed a paradise.

Alison's news was quite different from Clare's. She was now on the board of governors at Polly's school. She talked of squabbling parents, officious officials and teachers whose theories of education seemed to her absurdly arcane. She talked of the children, her Thai cooking course, the bridge group, the children and the children. Meanwhile she was knitting. Her fingers flew.

"How's Stanley?"

"As you see him. He's under a great deal of pressure at work, and so he's often — what do you say? — stressed. And then he can be a bit severe. It becomes rather difficult to communicate with him. But I'm used to it. He's a very good husband."

"You always say that."

"It's always true. How is Richard?"

Clare made a face. Alison continued to worry about Clare's estranged husband, a concern Clare could neither understand nor share. Her fair-mindedness was irritating in a confidante, but Alison was the only one available, the only one she trusted. With whom else could she have analysed the disintegration of her marriage? Certainly not with her colleagues at the office. But what irked most was Alison's obvious hope that the marriage might still be saved.

"But I'm not suited to marriage," Clare protested. "So why waste any more time trying to change myself or change him? Why not give up and try to have a good time instead?"

"Is that your plan?" She sounded dubious.

"Yup. I want to be on my own, go out when I can, play what used to be called the field. No attachments."

"Well, you're brave."

"No, just tired. Of abusive men. They're tyrant babies who hate their own emotions and blame you for yours."

Alison considered it. "But that's the point. Men *do* have emotions. They suffer when they're rejected just like we do. They're afraid of the power women have over them, that's all, the way their mothers had power. That's what they remember, and that's what makes them afraid."

"Men don't fear us for our power," snapped Clare. "They despise us for our weakness. Our weakness being the need for their love and approval. As usual, the obvious is true."

"Well, I need Stanley. I'm a dependent sort of person, and I'm not ashamed to admit it. I don't want to be alone. I think dependency is the natural human state."

Moans and murmurs issued from the intercom. Alison jumped up. "Hang on, Edgar's crying." She stopped at the door.

"Clare?"

"Yes."

"You mustn't turn into a sourpuss, you know."

"Thank you, Tiggy. You're right, and I won't."

While Alison was attending to Edgar, Clare lazily inspected her lush surroundings. She'd never realized there were so many photographs — all of the family, naturally: grandparents on both sides, aunts and uncles, a childhood snap of Alison with brothers and sisters, happy on a beach somewhere long ago. Stanley at Oxford, wedding photos, anniversary and christening parties and, of course, the children. Alone or with each other at various stages of their adorable development, spontaneous expressions and poses caught at the fortuitous moment; or with their parents, mainly Alison. Clare noticed that in all these photographs, no matter what the time or location, Alison's gesture was always the same, either reaching for or touching or leaning towards a child. She never looked at the camera but always at a baby or a toddler or a group of youngsters.

It was touching, lovely. She looked a perfect mother. Then all of a sudden Clare could not bear the photographs. They made her feel smothered and sad and very lonely. She wished she could leave but it was too late. She chose one of the dozens of glossy mags that had been strewn about with such casual care. By the time Alison returned, Clare had gone to bed.

*

They shouldn't allow so many people on the ice," Alison fretted. "They really shouldn't. And just look. Do you see an attendant? I don't see one."

"They turn up whenever they feel like skating themselves. There isn't enough room to show off this morning." Clare's eyes followed Evelyn who looked like a little chocolate bear in her brown, loose-fitting one-piece skating suit. She went cautiously, but she was graceful. She was getting better. Clare smiled, unaware that she was doing so.

"And those puddles. Oh God! Watch out, Sebastian! Clare, is this wise?"

The women alternated Sunday mornings at the Broadgate and Richmond rinks. Alison disapproved of Broadgate because it was not supervised to her high standards. Besides, she hated coming into the city and felt ill-at-ease outside Lib-Dem territory. On the other hand, she did not want to inconvenience Clare who didn't own a car and for whom Broadgate was only a short bus trip.

Clare shrugged. "They don't mind about puddles."

"Well, I do. Nicola, please be careful!"

"Children are resilient. But clearly this isn't for us. Let's have a *cappuccino*. We can sit outside and keep an eye on them."

"But will we be able to see them properly from over there?"

"Don't *fuss*, Alison."

"I'm sorry. I'll stop. I promise."

At the outdoor café they found a seat in the sunshine. Alison kept eyeing the rink, anticipating disaster. She was fidgety and Clare found it annoying.

"Why do you always expect the worst?" she asked.

"That's the point. I don't expect the worst. As long as I'm watchful I assume the worst won't happen. As long as I keep my guard up — oh dear, that sounds awful, doesn't it? Makes me seem a really paranoid and anal sort of person."

"You're all right, Tiggy." Clare patted her hand. "You're just a better mum than I am."

"Oh Clare, what nonsense!"

She'd sparked another string of indignant protestations. Clare waited as they spent themselves, gazing up at the towering stories of glass, the ivy that cascaded from every balcony, the second-floor bar where the well-heeled sipped their pre-prandial drinks and watched the spectacle on the ice below, and at the bright winter sky above the huge concrete circle that enclosed them. Alison caught her at it and guessed she wasn't listening.

"I'm not sure I like Broadgate," she said.

She looks frayed, observed Clare. Wispy and frayed despite her plumpness. She's doing too much, always rushing about, ferrying those kids, going to meetings, walking the damned dogs. And when her hundreds of obligations are finally fulfilled, she initiates new ones. What for? And her hair's gone silver. It's becoming like angel's hair. She is an angel, a worn-out, repressed angel. There are rings under her eyes. Something's wrong. What isn't she telling me? But the idea of Tiggywinkles having secrets was patently absurd.

"I've found a flat," Clare announced.

"No! Oh Clare, how marvellous — and after all this time."

She noted the genuine pleasure in Alison's eyes. "Well, if I can fiddle the mortgage —"

"Perhaps Stanley and I can help in some way."

"That's lovely of you, sweetheart. Really kind. But I wonder if Stanley will be so enthusiastic."

"Why, Stanley adores you."

"Sure he does. Anyway, I can manage, provided the sale of our old house goes through." She was imagining Stanley's horrified reaction to any requests for financial assistance. They had never liked each other, and antipathy had deepened over the years. He was one of those husbands who is permanently suspicious of his wife's best friend.

"Won't you feel strange being in a flat, being off the ground?"

"Not all flats are off the ground, Alison. This one happens to be a basement."

"Oh. Awfully dark, but easy to heat I suppose. Where is it?"

"Dalston."

"*Dalston*? A basement flat in *Dalston*? But the crime rate's terrible there. And isn't it where all that police corruption is going on? I hear it's full of, excuse me but — foreigners, and that it's virtually a slum. You'll have to get window bars right away. And what about coming home late at night? The muggings, the drugs, oh darling, some of them are *armed*. Are you sure about this?"

"Alison, I can hardly afford Eaton Square. Anyway, it's an interesting area. The flat's nice, or I can make it nice. There's a tiny garden, a bit dark, but — "

"Ferns." Alison interrupted, something she seldom did. "You want ferns. And hellebores, they're lovely, and *Anemone nemerosa*. Let's see, geum does well in semi-shade, and you might even have a climber. Hostas for the summer, of course, though you'll have to be ceaselessly vigilant. The snails love them."

"Well, now that we've landscaped the place, would you like to hear about the interior?"

"Sorry, Clare. I'm a plant bore."

Alison listened attentively to Clare, repressing the urge to spout decorating tips. But when Clare had come to the end, she couldn't help herself.

"Get one of those screamers, darling. Promise me you will. Is mace still illegal?"

"Alison, please. Fear of disaster invokes disaster. I know that's not your philosophy, but — "

"There's nothing neurotic about a bit of caution, surely. Oh I suppose I'm timid and that I've led a sheltered life."

"Well, I'm not quite the raver you like to make me out, either. Another *cappuccino*?"

"No thanks. You've yet to witness the terrible truth about my waistline. Besides, I only have — "

"One of everything. I know." She did not refer to the renowned crockery collection. Alison was considering building an extension to the kitchen to house it. What was she compensating for?

When Clare returned she found that Alison had been turning matters over in her mind because she launched into a by now familiar theme.

"Well, Evelyn will need a father, sooner or later, I mean."

"Alison, I know Tiggies feel obliged to play advocate for family values, but in a word, lay off."

The corners of Alison's mouth turned down.

"Anyway," Clare went on, "she and Richard see each other whenever they want. I've made no stipulations or restrictions. Absolutely none. And speaking of family values, no one has yet provided a satisfactory explanation of the whereabouts of *Mr* Tiggywinkle."

Alison did not laugh.

"But won't you be lonely?" she asked.

"I like being with Evelyn, just the two of us. In some ways it's harder alone, but I'm so happy he's gone that nothing else matters." She signalled for the waiter. "I like living without a man."

"You keep saying that, and I'm not sure why I don't believe you."

"I don't require your belief. Oh I'm sorry. I'm not suggesting everyone should be like me."

"You are, you know. It makes me feel quite separated from you."

"Please don't." She touched Alison's arm. "All I'm saying is that men take everything. They can't help it. It's habitual, part of their training. Haven't you noticed this? Don't you feel it?"

"Do you mean me personally?"

"I mean you, me, all of us."

"I see."

Clare couldn't halt the diatribe. She was into it now.

"After you've been with a man for a while all your energy seems to drain away and you become self-conscious, even scared. Because he's got power by taking all of yours and suddenly you're weak. He grows as you shrink. It's like he's eating you. He takes your secret. They all do, it's their special little trick, Stanley included, Stanley especially, and don't pout. And the awful thing is that you let him. You give it to him or help him steal it. And all the time you tell yourself it isn't really happening."

"Please stop saying you. It makes me feel terribly nervous and inadequate."

"I apologize. You're anything but inadequate."

"It seems crude, what you said."

"Truth is crude. Anyway, here come the kiddies. They know all about crude truth."

They were rowdy and over-excited and demanded ice-creams and crisps and fizzy drinks and got everything they wanted, consuming it in seconds before racing back to the chaotic rink. Chaos was their element.

In April Clare met Ben. He taught history at a North London university, was amusing, intelligent, not especially ambitious and a little shabby. He wasn't quite the fiery fling she'd had in mind, but she liked him. Once in a while he made genuine efforts to reach her mind and body and as a result got gradually under her skin. Besides,

all those other men — the ones she'd intended to gaily love and
leave — had not materialized. The brief was that she was taking the
affair slowly, not getting too involved, revelling still in her new flat,
her independence, the single-parenthood she heard government
ministers insisting was the scourge of the nation.

It was a Tuesday afternoon and she was in a rush. She'd caught
the Tube at Liverpool Street, and it had broken down. Clare sat in
the dark tunnel checking her watch. She must be home by five-thirty
when Evelyn returned from Effie's house. For a small fee, Effie's
Mum collected Evelyn from school and drove her home after Clare
had returned from the office. They'd be sitting outside in the car, she
fretted, it would be getting dark, she probably wasn't paying Betty
Clayton anywhere near enough . . .

And yes it was dark when she finally reached the flat, and yes they
were sitting outside in the car. The girls were bouncing on the back
seat, made manic by an afternoon of Coca-Cola and children's telly
programmes, and chanting "Prizes and sur-prises, prizes and sur-
prises" as though they could never tire. They had been waiting, said
Betty, but not to worry, it didn't matter. She was amiable and
understanding and referred as usual to the "heavy burden" that
Clare was carrying. And Clare wanted to say no, no, it's not in the
least heavy. In fact it's a pleasure, one you can't or won't imagine.
But she thought better of it.

There was a message from Alison on the answering machine. She
had to play it twice because Alison was speaking so softly and
Evelyn was marching up and down the tiny bare sitting room
singing tonelessly "Prizes and sur-prises." She asked Clare to ring
back, as soon as possible. She sounded peculiar.

"Oh no, not now," Clare said aloud. She still had to get Evelyn's
tea before her mother arrived to babysit. And she must bath and
change. And she was waiting for the call from Ben to say where and

at what time they would meet. He was meant to call at six. It was now six-thirty. And suddenly Clare wanted that call. Very much. What could have happened? Why hadn't she heard from him? She felt anxious. Anxious. For the first time in many weeks, despite chronic cash-flow problems. What was going on here? She'd ring Alison tomorrow. She didn't want the line engaged when Alison probably wanted to discuss curtains. What was going on?

"Prizes and sur-prises."

"Evelyn, please be quiet."

"But I can't stop."

The telephone rang. Finally.

"Clare, I'm sorry. You're probably busy."

Oh God.

"Is it a bad moment?"

"Well . . . did you want something in particular?"

Alison hesitated. "Just to see you, Clare."

"Fine. When?" Clare glanced at her watch.

"I — well — perhaps now."

"Now?" Alison who arranged her life and everyone else's six weeks in advance? Who couldn't make a move without consulting her Royal Horticultural Society Diary?

"I'm sorry . . . I didn't mean . . . oh, it was a silly idea. You're absolutely right."

"Hang on. I didn't say — "

"We could speak tomorrow, I suppose, or whenever you're not busy. Not that you have an abundance of leisure time, quality time, isn't that what they call it?"

"Alison, are you all right?"

"Me? I'm — as I always am. Maybe a little more so. How do I sound?"

"In a flap."

"Perhaps. Yes, perhaps a bit. Oh dear, is that how I really sound? Couldn't we meet? No, you're busy. Of course you're busy. You work so hard, Clare."

"Alison, I will see you any time but this evening. Any time."

There was silence at Alison's end of the line. "I'll ring back."

Clare stared at the receiver. She'd hung up.

"Alison is stressed," pronounced Evelyn who'd been standing beside her mother throughout the last part of the conversation. "She needs prizes and sur-prises."

"I'm not sure. Do you think so?" She stroked Evelyn's hair. "What do Alisons really need?"

The phone went. She made herself wait until it had rung four times then lifted the receiver.

"It's me," said the voice she most wanted to hear. "Can you come out and play?"

When the police rang, Clare asked Sam if she might leave the office early, saying it was a family emergency, and he did not question her further but kindly let her go. She wondered, as she waited for the lift, if she was blotting her copybook. She'd had to leave mid-morning three weeks ago to rescue Evelyn who'd been ill at school and thrown up all over her desk, prelude to a bout of flu. That's what happens with working mothers, they'd say. And she had to look after her father tonight so her mum could go to the Bingo.

But how can I be worrying about my job or Bingo at a time like this, she berated herself as she hailed a taxi she could not afford. What kind of friend am I?

Clare waited a long time before they let her see Alison. She sat on a bench — how could she have forgotten to bring a book? — her back against the wall, watching a parade of felons: the misjudged, the misguided, the misunderstood, none of them looking particularly dangerous. All were male and most were black or Asian. What could Alison be doing among them? What could have precipitated such a reversal? Well, she would know soon enough because here came the sergeant on duty, having just dispatched a self-confessed beggar to a waiting cell. The beggar kept asking about his dog.

"Come this way," the policeman said, and she followed him along a cold corridor, feeling unsteady and fearing she might lose her balance and crash into the wall, as though she were attempting to ride a bicycle for the first time. It was that kind of panic. She waited as he unlocked the grey metal door with its sinister viewing window, thinking she would rather be anywhere than here.

Alison was now before her, a person utterly familar but in a new guise — the guise of grief. Perhaps it was only a costume that would shortly be removed and her friend would then reappear: benign, sweet-tempered, too altruistic for her own good. Then Clare knew in a kind of rush like a sudden wind that what she was seeing was not a mask but the real Alison, the real, true Alison who had been living all this while beneath her quotidian self. The Alison she knew had been the costume, the fake. What sat hunched before her was the genuine article. The realization made her catch her breath, and at the sound Alison raised her head.

"I look awful, don't I?" she murmured. The emotion emanating from her eyes and body did not translate itself into her voice which was flat, dry and barely audible.

"Ten minutes," the sergeant said and left them alone. Clare nodded and stared at Alison, unable to answer her, hoping for some impulse that would allow or compel her to respond. The walls of the cell were a smooth, shiny off-white, recently painted to expunge the graffiti which had nevertheless begun to effloresce here and there like an eczema.

"You look all right under the circumstances," she finally said. She could not yet approach Alison but remained where she was, in a patch of light that came from the mean window high above. The sun was western, inappropriately gentle.

"What are the circumstances?" Alison lowered her head again and slowly shook it from side to side, so that her silver-blonde hair flapped against her cheeks and ears.

"You tell me. That's what I'm here for — and to do whatever I can to help you, of course." She was not handling this well.

"Are you angry with me? What did they tell you?"

"Hardly anything. And I'm not angry with you, whatever it was you did."

"Thank you." At least she was not apologizing.

"They told me you assaulted someone." She sat down beside her and took her hand. "Is this true?"

"I can hardly remember. It might be true. I think it is true."

"Who did you — assault?"

Alison sighed and looked up at Clare, her large eyes brimming. "A child. And her mother too, it seems. I'm told they're somewhere in the building. Have you seen them?"

"No. Can I get you out of here? What do I have to do?"

"I have no idea, Clare. Did I thank you for coming?"

Her torpor made Clare think she had been given a sedative. "Have you talked to anyone? A lawyer? A doctor?"

"A lawyer. I suppose that's what she was. I'm not sure."

"What about Stanley? Have you called him? Do you want me to call him?"

"Oh I don't know . . . no."

"Please, Alison, what should I do?"

"I hoped you might already have done it."

"Look, if you won't tell me, I'll have to ask them, the people who brought you to this place. Where were you when this happened?"

Dully Alison scanned the cell. "On a bus. I can't remember the number. It was the wrong bus, you see. The car was in the garage, the exhaust, I think, and I had to go into the West End on an errand, to a shop, what shop was it? I got a bit lost and I was late so I took a bus. The Underground terrifies me. I never go on buses, I never go to the West End. Such a bad combination. It was the wrong bus, I said that, didn't I? I had no idea where I was going and no one would tell me our destination. I asked and asked. I got so agitated, and now I can't remember. What's wrong with me, Clare?"

"I can't say. I can only try to get you out of here. You struck a child."

"I did. I hit her and hit her. And then I hit the mother. At least that's what they said I did."

"My God. But why?"

"I'm not sure. The sequence is all confused. When I try to remember exactly what happened, events sort of shuffle themselves. It's so frustrating. Perhaps it was the child's voice or the colours she was wearing. They were so intense and all wrong together, clashing, nerve-wracking, and she wouldn't stop talking and repeating the same words I couldn't understand, a kind of sing-song chant in a foreign language, or maybe it wasn't foreign, how could I tell. She was so little, so very young, and her mother couldn't control her or she just couldn't be bothered, and the child went on and on in that voice like a chipmunk or a computer game, and no one would tell me where we were going or what our desination was, and I was so awfully, awfully late. I never go on buses, you see, and there would be Nicola waiting at school, all alone, the last one. I could see the expression in her eyes and then the teachers so annoyed with me, so annoyed —"

"Alison —"

"What kind of mother would they think I was? A mother who

forgets her child, abandons her daughter, leaves her daughter alone at school to the tender mercies of . . . when all the other mothers . . . and she'd be waiting, waiting, waiting, and no one comes, she'll never forgive me, no one will ever come. I'm here forever, that's what she'll think."

"Alison, *was* Nicola collected from school?"

She gave Clare a horrified look. "Whoever would or could collect her? Who if not me?"

"Christ, Alison, what's Stanley's number at the office? Do you have it? Do you have the number of the school? I'll call them." She knelt beside Alison and rubbed both her hands which were cold and damp. "Alison." She pressed them hard but there was no response. "Alison, I'll come back. I'll make them give me more than ten minutes. I want to make sure Nicola's OK. I want to tell Stanley what's happened."

"What *has* happened? Oh Clare, do you know what I wonder now? I wonder if I ever actually asked anyone which way the bus was going. Maybe I only dreamed I asked. If it's true that I didn't ask anyone after all, and got so frustrated and annoyed, then that means I'm, it means . . ."

Clare left to find the telephone. It was as she stood dialling the school number that she saw the mother and child.

"They're Bangladeshi," she told Richard. She was telling him everything because she had to tell someone and Ben was unobtainable and, ironically, Richard had called. "They barely speak English. The attack was completely unprovoked."

"So what happens next?"

"They've been advised by their lawyer to prosecute, and everyone on the bus wants to testify. The family's from Tower Hamlets. There's been a rash of racist attacks there lately and very little response from the police. Naturally the Asian community is upset."

"Well, if anyone will have a good lawyer Stanley will. God, this is unbelievable."

"Yes."

"It won't come to anything, though. They'll never get it into court. Alison's clearly barmy. I never did think she was quite the ticket."

"Didn't you?"

"All that angst under all that icing sugar."

He was a pillock.

"They were so shocked. They couldn't understand what had happened. The child has a black eye and bruises on her shoulders and a hairline fracture of her nose. The mother's all right now, though she was completely hysterical. She's baffled, you could see it in her eyes. Everyone's baffled."

"It's a nightmare, but these things happen."

"Do they? To whom do they happen, please tell me."

Clare paused, sighed.

"I went to see them. I went to Tower Hamlets. I tried to tell them how sorry Alison is. That she has no excuses, only remorse."

"You did *that*?"

"Think Stanley would?"

"What did they say?"

"They were very polite, though the husband seemed angry, and who can blame him? The mother actually thanked me for coming. Does the woman have children, she wanted to know, and how many does she have? When I told her she stared at me in disbelief. You could tell she thought it was impossible for a woman with children to behave like this. Then she asked how many I had. The little girl was hiding in the other room. She'd peek at me when she thought I wasn't looking. I'm not sure whether she was frightened of me or whether she thought I was mad. Perhaps I am mad."

"You're not mad, you're just tired." He was about to remind her, and at length, of how much easier and more pleasant her life had been when she was married to him.

"I've never been more awake."

"That is a symptom of your tiredness."

"Richard," Clare answered, "you are absolutely right. And so I am going to bed this instant, and I suggest you do likewise. Goodnight."

"I've expressed myself at last, and it was a mistake. Some people are better off repressed and I'm one of them. Repression is terrible, but look what happens when law and order break down. Which is worse, Clare? Please tell me. Then I might be able to understand."

"Don't try to understand. Not yet, anyway. Just rest," said Clare, feeling stupid and desperate to go home. There was Evelyn's tea to get, and the laundry to do and then some work she'd brought back from the office. Yet she sat in the darkened room, forcing herself to remain, expending all her energy on just remaining.

"Tiggy, I'm here," she'd say. "I'm still here."

The light through the tilted blinds threw soft bars across the Turkish rug. The room was filled with the scent of a woodland pot-pourri. It was an attractive, even desirable prison. Clare thought of another bedroom — that of the Bangladeshi woman. Six people slept in it.

She leaned towards Alison, trying to see her eyes in the gloom. She wanted to look into them, to compare them to the eyes of the smiling plump blonde child in the photograph. She wanted to see if they still bore any resemblance to those eyes full of hesitation and hope.

Suddenly Alison's head fell forward so that her eyes were covered by her hair. Clare reached out to touch her but withdrew her hand. Still here. Still here.

"Hi. Sorry. Can't sleep."

"Why is that?"

"Keep thinking about her."

"Why shouldn't you think about her?" It was 2 a.m. and she had woken Ben up.

"Because I reach no conclusions. Why she did it. What I should do."

"Conclusions are a luxury and usually not very reliable. You can't possibly amass all the facts that would enable you to conclude. Therefore, most conclusions are erroneous."

"Stop being academic."

Ben laughed. "Why ring me up, then? You know how I'll be. I can't be any different."

"But she's ruined her life."

"Maybe."

"I can understanding her cracking — the domestic pressures, the self-effacement, the disintegration of her personality. But why crack *in that way*? Was she trying to kill the thing she loves? Symbolically, I mean."

"Maybe."

"Stop saying maybe."

"I'll try."

"I think about them too," Clare said. "All the time."

"The child and the mother?"

"Yes. I see their eyes, their hands, their clothes. It turns out the mother works in one of the local sweat shops. She makes fake leather mini-skirts. She has three other children and an unemployed husband. Then there's the husband's aged half-blind father. She deserves compensation, the price of which will be Alison's freedom."

"I don't think so," he said gently. "The price will be money. It usually is."

"True, but Stanley's mean. I think he'd almost rather lock Alison away if it weren't for the personal inconvenience of being without an unpaid domestic."

"He'll pay," Ben chuckled. "Not enough, but he'll pay." He was obviously tired. "Just do your best, love, and I'll support you."

"That's very nice. Thank you."

"It's nothing. I like you. I'm going now."

"OK."

"A man was here this morning." Alison was wearing the same crumpled dressing gown. Clare wondered if she had changed it since she'd last seen her.

"Which man?"

"Perhaps it was yesterday morning. I can't remember."

"It doesn't matter."

"It matters a lot. A very great deal." She spoke slowly and heavily, emphasizing each syllable. Her voice was grainy and thick.

"What did the man want? Was it about your case?"

"Yes. But I can't talk about it."

"Try, Alison."

"I'm too ashamed to talk. Since that afternoon I'm ashamed all the time."

That afternoon. And if I'd cancelled my date the evening before, Clare reflected. If I'd been to see you. If I'd let you come to see me. If I'd returned your phone call . . .

"Unless I've just taken the medication. Then I stop feeling ashamed for a while."

"Alison, this man."

"But that's wrong, isn't it? I mean, I *should* feel ashamed."

Clare didn't answer.

"Clare, you're my friend. Shouldn't I feel shame?"

"Yes."

The smile Alison gave her was terrible.

From then on, Clare felt that a chasm had opened between her and Alison and that there no longer existed even a fragile rope bridge by which her friend might cross giddily but safely to the other side. And though she went on waving and calling, "come back, come back," Mrs Tiggywinkle stood on the cliff opposite and stared straight ahead as if she did not see or hear her.

Still, Clare continued to visit even after Alison had been put in the clinic. The establishment was not satisfactory, and the administration of her medication, which had caused her to gain an alarming amount of weight, seemed based on an arbitrary schedule, so that she sometimes suffered moments of agitated lucidity which were crueller by far than her usual torpor.

"When can I go home? I ask the nurses, the doctor, the other patients. I think I even asked the ladies in the cafeteria. But no one will tell me. It was supposed to be a short stay, just a while until I recovered, just to have a rest, that's what they said. But it's been nearly two months. You see, I keep track of time. I'm aware of the passage of time and aware of my surroundings. I know who comes and who goes and when, I understand the routine, I recognize everyone, I keep track of time. I keep it separated into segments and compartments and don't allow it to run all together like a bad water-colour, like soup. I keep time neat. I'm not a prisoner of my own world like some of the people in here. I'm a responsible adult, I have important matters to attend to. Why won't they tell me anything at all?

"Stanley doesn't answer my questions. He thinks I'm in some kind of terrible trouble, whatever gave him that idea? He's told the children not to say certain things to me, not to answer my questions. They treat me like a stranger, it's unbearable. Except for my little one, except for my Edgar. With Stanley it doesn't matter, he's treated me like a stranger for years. I'm used to it. But why are the children this way, why should they suddenly be like their father, so secret, so controlled? I don't know, Clare, maybe it's better to be like that. Stanley's never assaulted a woman and a child on a bus."

Stanley also paid, just as Ben said he would.

Clare's father suffered a second stroke and died two months later. At the same time, Alison was transferred to another clinic where she received good care without making great progress towards recovery. She had entered a melancholy country where she seemed determined to reside for a very long time, perhaps for good. While she was in the clinic, Stanley sold the collection of art deco crockery to cover what he regarded as the exorbitant cost of her catastrophe, and when Alison came home on a visit she hardly noticed its absence.

Clare's divorce became final, in the end uncontested by Richard, and she was free. On a windy November morning the following year, pleased but sensing the loss of something she had barely tasted, she married Ben.

END OF TERRACE

"He's gone!"

"Who?"

"The plumber. I mean Mr Phebey. Mr Phebey the plumber."

"My dear, I'm so sorry. Are you all right?"

"Yes, yes." Fiona looked hectic but not unhappy. "Don't stand in the doorway. I've made a pitcher of Martinis."

By nine o'clock they were both quite drunk. Fiona could not keep off the subject of Mr Phebey.

"What did you think, Dorrie? Really."

"I envied you. That crop of curls, albeit grey. And carrying in the coalite and calling you my lady."

"He was a wag." She stopped. "But you were meant to be reading me your talk on alpine clematis. Oh God, you've even brought the slides."

"Never mind."

"It was because of the carpet," Fiona went on. "The carpet and the house."

The houses on Hellebore Grove were built in 1840, flat-fronted and in sets of four. A year ago Fiona had purchased one of them. She had little money and a large mortgage, but her nesting instinct was strong, and she was impatient to conceal the concrete ground floor beneath a dusty-rose carpet on sale on the Balls Pond Road for £6.95 a yard. Fitters from Stiletto Carpets arrived early on a Friday morning and had finished their work by noon. Not surprising, as there was no furniture to shift other than one table and one wicker chair. (She was starting from scratch, making a new life.) At five she noticed the damp patch. At five-fifteen she noticed the damp patch inching like lava across the dusty-rose carpet.

"They hammered a nail straight through an underfloor pipe, the devils. I didn't know the neighbours. I didn't know a plumber. Besides, who'd come winging his way for my sake to the borders of N1 at six on a Friday night?"

"Who indeed?"

She found "London's Leading Central Heating, Guttering and Washing Machine Installation Expert" in *Thompson's Directory*. He'd had difficulty locating her house as there was no number on the door, but then he'd remembered the "Nuclear Free" sign on the corner and that she was end of terrace.

"The problem, he said, was not so much the pipe as the whereabouts of the pipe which lay embedded in concrete just inside the broom cupboard. He promised to do what he could and not abandon me, only next time would I please employ reputable workmen. (He was fifty, you see, and had served a proper apprenticeship and was snotty as hell about anyone who hadn't. Anyone under fifty.) Meanwhile, as the situation was critical, could he ring his mate or rather his girlfriend who would collect his mate who couldn't drive. Then he strode like a lord to the end of the walk and switched off a mains I didn't know existed.

"My impression was that Norman Phebey was no ordinary plumber. He was six foot five with a magisterial voice and a back like a Rodin sculpture, and he took two and a quarter spoons of sugar in his tea. Jane was afraid of him. I'd forgotten Jane was coming to dinner. She arrived, followed shortly by Maggie the girlfriend and Albie the mate. Maggie was pale and pretty and Albie wore a tired blue suit. Mr Phebey whispered to me that Albie was once the greatest of them all, but it didn't take me long to work out why he couldn't drive. I brought an armful of towels to mop up the emissions of the pipe which was being gradually exposed in its grey puddle. Maggie appropriated the wicker chair and opened a bottle of McKinley's.

"The banging was terrific, so Jane and I went upstairs to sit in the empty sitting room. Hours later we found Mr Phebey, acetylene torch blazing, sprawled on the sodden bath towels, his magisterial body half in and half out of the broom cupboard. Albie swayed over him with goggles and spanners, looking the worse for the whisky he and Maggie had finished off."

" 'Don't worry, Fiona,' she smiled. 'Norman's saved your carpet.' "

"Norman was my hero. I opened a bottle of gin (they didn't seem interested in wine) and divided the fillets of sole stuffed with asparagus among the five of us. In our relief-generated hysteria, we carried on until 3 a.m. while the towels went round and round in the Zanussi. Then they left to put Albie to bed.

"Mr Phebey soon returned on the pretext of making out a false invoice for me to use in my suit against Stiletto Carpets. He suggested a drive, so off we went in his big white van which was full of washing-machine parts and tools, the uses for which I could not imagine. He took me to the street in E8 where he was born and told me he was falling in love with me."

"He was unhappy at home," offered Dorrie.

"Maggie's dipsomania was having a depressing effect on him."

Fiona could not prevent it. Mr Phebey arrived one morning with a red suitcase and asked could he have a shelf — just a tiny shelf — to call his own. His flat was so bad that the mice were walking around on stilts.

"I did wonder what the neighbours thought. They hardly knew me. Would they interpret Mr Phebey's presence as the beginning of a trend? Were eyebrows being raised behind my back? It's hard not to notice Mr Phebey."

No eyebrows were raised, not even when Fiona took him to the monthly garden-club meeting in the crypt of St Ambrose and he dropped off in the middle of "Orchids of Northern Thailand". Of course neighbours could not see the interior of Number 50, which looked increasingly like the back of Mr Phebey's van. He stored machinery parts in the bedroom and brought Fiona superfluous presents such as ten rolls of radiator backing and two broken Hoovers and his Magimix. The Magimix made her particularly nervous. Still, he was no ordinary plumber. Not only did he have a back like a Rodin sculpture, but he was an accomplished mimic. They dined every night in a different accent. He opened new worlds, taking her to Tony Bennett and Shirley MacLaine concerts and encouraging her to wear stretch jeans. They would get drunk at the Merry Monarch, dance sambas and tangos and fall down the stairs. It was divine, though he did insist on drying his laundry in the sitting room.

"But it's all empty, your ladyship," he reasoned.

"It's still the sitting room."

On the night she cooked him a rabbit chasseur, he was three hours late for dinner.

"I've been locked in the bloody flat since noon," he announced.

"You went home?"

"She begged me. I was worried."

"And she locked you in."

"She said she was saving me from you." He put his arms around Fiona. "Why didn't you tell me about the letters?"

"What letters?"

"You are a kind, good little person, but she's confessed."

"What letters?" Dorrie perked up.

"She'd written me dozens, very abusive. She'd get looped and slip them through the letterbox in the middle of the night."

"And you never received them?"

"*I* didn't. But someone did."

The houses on Hellebore Grove were built in 1840, flat-fronted and in sets of four. One is not so different from another. Being end of terrace is a minimally distinguishing feature, and 50 is much the same as 42.

"She'd put the letters through the wrong door!"

Fiona nodded, the corner of her mouth upturned and wry.

"What could I do? Go and claim my letters? *My* letters? The people in 42 were a young couple, rather reserved except on Sunday afternoons when he'd push her on a swing in the back garden and she'd scream. Sweet. But I had begun to sense a change in their manner. Naturally there were no specific references to the post, and when we met they'd nod and smile as usual. But something was in the air and it wasn't spring. Was I mistaken or did an atmosphere of strain surround them? Maggie had not addressed the letters to me personally. Had the wife read them and not told the husband, or was it the other way round? Who was keeping dark secrets, who suspected of adultery? Had there been confrontations, tears, accusations, detectives hired? Were lawyers already draughting documents? Or had they, with unsuspected urbanity, laughed together over the letters before tossing them into the dustbin? Perhaps they had tossed them in the dustbin *without* reading them. This is England. All that's certain is that I'll never know."

"Why not?"

"They're moving out. Rumours of Mortlake."

"And Mr Phebey just — "

"Bolted. He loved Maggie, I guess." Fiona drained her glass.

"After the letters things deteriorated. He spent every morning with a pack of cigarettes and the *Telegraph*. Asked why he no longer went to work he replied, 'When I'm 'umpty I'm 'umpty.' Meanwhile I was being smothered by the Magimix and the laundry 'forever drying in the sitting room."

"But you were fond of Mr Phebey?"

"He was my hero."

"Well, I suppose he did save your rug." Dorrie eyed the empty pitcher and the box of slides. "What about Stiletto Carpets?"

"We settled out of court."

THE OCTOPUS VASE

We came to the island in 1973. Neither Jack nor I had ever been to Greece, and we chose a spot by covering our eyes, swirling a pencil above a map of the archipelago and stabbing blindly at the paper. Then we looked. Andros, a big one where it should be easy to find seclusion. Escape into Arcadia — that was what we were after. We hitched the length of Italy, boarded a boat at Brindisi, disembarked at Patras, shared a taxi to Piraeus with some Austrians, stayed up until dawn, left on the *Zeus* at 6 a.m., sat exposed in the ship's prow listening, rapt, to a man playing the bouzouki, gathered up our packs and our snacks and got off at the wrong island.

It took us about an hour to realize we were not on Andros. We'd been paying too much attention to the bouzouki and to each other and had lost track of the stops. (We'd just finished our theses and were still tired to the bone and light-headed with freedom.) We laughed, but we felt also dismayed and a little vulnerable. We needed to get our bearings. We went to a wind-lashed café that faced the choppy sea, and there we drank Greek coffee and ate cheese pies while the shadow of a blue awning crept across our table. In the end we decided to stay. It was fate, we gaily declared, meant to be; a sweet and just-safe-enough adventure. An adventure that was to repeat itself every summer for the next sixteen years. We checked into the cheapest available hotel.

It was July and the port was crowded. It was also prosperous and perfectly preserved.

"In an awful way," mused Jack, "this place has been saved by the tourists. The islanders could never have afforded to keep these buildings in such mint condition." He'd studied architecture and cast an appraising eye over every structure. "They'd rot with the salt wind." It was true. The streets, wide enough for two donkeys to pass, were scrubbed and immaculate. Shutters and balconies gleamed with yellow and blue gloss paint. Geraniums, basil and bougainvillaea decked every door and stairway.

"It's like a Greek theme-park," he said. Nevertheless it was charming.

We wanted something wilder, though; more authentic and less expensive. But the island was large and we had no idea where to go. At sunset we wandered back towards the harbour, losing our way several times in the maze of little streets. We stood on the quayside and took the place in: the lights strung as far as the harbour's curve, the islands rising darkly from the water beyond, and the disturbing rosy light that prefaced night and made the whole unreal.

"It's beautiful," I said, "and somehow scary."

We turned back towards the clutter of cafés, restaurants and shops.

"Well." Jack gave me an uneasy smile. "What shall we do?"

At a nearby table a group of people rose to leave, conspicuous by their laughter and their handsomeness. They had a subdued chic that seemed unrelated to money. A tall woman in black tights, a billowing white shirt and large dangling ear-rings was laughing louder than the rest. It was a thundering laugh, unselfconscious, uninhibited, the like of which I'd never heard from a woman. She wore her hair severely back in a French twist and her profile was striking. I could not help staring at her. She caught my eye and smiled. That was the first time I saw Veronica Beattie.

"Let's ask *her*," I said.

She was kind, even seemed eager to please. She liked directness, she said in her American accent, and was surprised to find it in English people.

"What good instincts you must have," said the man beside her, a Frenchman, "to choose Veronica. Out of all these — " He gestured dismissively at the diners, but the wind blew away his insult.

She knew exactly where to send us: a beach further along the coast where there was a small taverna that had rooms to let — very basic, cement boxes, she warned, but we would only sleep there after all and they were cheap. She told us the right bus, the right boat. She wrote a note in Greek to the proprietors. She wished us good luck and a happy stay and said she would probably see us on the beach. She lived just up the hill.

She took a silk shawl from the back of the chair and draped it deftly around her shoulders. She and her retinue were leaving, expected at some delightful destination, I had no doubt.

"Thank you so much for your help," I said, reluctant to let her go. "Sorry to accost you like this."

"My dear," she pressed my arm with a warm hand, "it was divine of you."

As they walked away I saw that she was barefoot. They looked, from a distance, like a band of exquisites, the sort that trouped across the Mediterranean every summer, their diaphanous garments fluttering, living out of *one* bag, wearing *one* item of exotic, stunning jewellery. Yet I knew they were more than that, certainly that she was more. I turned to Jack but he was still staring after them.

"What a wonderful woman," he breathed.

We spent two happy weeks at Karaki. We swam, read, ate, made love and mastered rudimentary Greek. We met a couple from Cambridge, friends of friends, and passed gay sozzled evenings in the taverna under the brilliant stars. Every day I looked out for Veronica Beattie, but she did not appear. I peered through squinted eyes at the little white houses on the mountains and wondered which was hers. Because I had not met her again my happiness was curiously incomplete. I wondered if Jack felt the same, but his only comment was that she seemed like a character out of Somerset Maugham.

Then I saw her. It was late in the day. I had fallen asleep with my head against the sand. Suddenly I woke up. People were collecting their towels and bags and snorkels and climbing into the blue-and-green caiques that would take them back to the port. Far off, at the furthest end of the beach among diverse bodies, she stood by the water's edge. She wore a pink-striped sarong which she shed and left lying on the sand as she walked naked into the sea. She swam slowly, with great economy of movement. I watched her emerge, wring out her wet hair and wrap herself in the sarong without drying off. I willed her to walk our way, but she sat down and stared for a while at the sea. Then she rose and came towards us. I waved. She didn't recognize me and walked on at a stately pace. She was so elegant I felt suddenly shy. Then she recognized me.

"Oh," she cried, "it's you!" and came smiling towards us.

She seemed genuinely pleased at the encounter. She wanted to know all that we'd been doing, where we'd been, if we'd met anyone interesting.

"Not interesting like you, if that's what you mean," Jack said and she laughed her loud laugh. I suddenly realized that she was a good deal older than we were. I don't know how long we sat there talking. When the time did occur to me I noticed that all around us the little craters made by our human footprints had filled up with shadow.

"Come to my house," she said impulsively. "No. Eat supper with me first, then come. My cupboard is bare. I haven't been into town for a week. That's why I came down to the beach — to eat supper and charge it. Normally I don't swim here. Too many people. I have a little place where I go — off the rocks. Back there," she pointed. "Me and the old Greek ladies. I come here again in October when the tourists have gone."

She's thirty-five, I thought. Maybe more. Ten years older than I, five inches taller, and ten times more attractive.

At the taverna they offered us octopus and ouzo. I had seen the octopuses drying on lines outside the restaurants, but I had never tried them. She encouraged us to sample but said that she herself was unable to eat it. She said she loved octopuses, that they were gentle and shy and lived in gardens made of green-and-mauve urchin shells and when you uncovered them there they gazed at you with big sad eyes that looked even bigger through a diving mask. She'd heard they could be tamed and that they stroked divers' faces with their tentacles. It was even said that having lost a leg the miraculous creatures could grow a new one.

We ate kalamari, chicken, watermelon and a plate of bitter cooked greens over which she squeezed a lemon, telling us the Greek names for everything. She laughed and talked with the proprietor's family, exchanging local gossip, and knew every one of the resident cats. How pleasant, I thought — I've never known anything so pleasant. I was entranced, bewitched. I never wanted to leave. But this was only the beginning.

"We'll go now," she said, raising her eyebrows to make a question out of a command. She didn't have to persuade us. We rose to leave.

"The bill," exclaimed Jack.

"Please don't worry, darling. I settle with Nicola at the end of every month."

She would not take our money. She could be stubborn, I could tell. Jack was flustered. Deep inside he still thought women ought to be paid for, strange women, at least. "You're really kind to us," I wanted to say, but I knew she didn't like too much gratitude. Gratitude implied returns, and kindness was something done for its own sake, something to be taken for granted.

It was dark and the moon had not yet risen. Walking along the dirt road we could see by the light of the stars. But at the top of the hill we turned right through a broken gate and into a rocky path that was treacherous and almost invisible. She tripped along as though her bare feet were hooves, but when we began to stumble and cry out she turned back.

"I'm sorry," she said. "I forgot what a bitch this path is. I'm so used to it. I can't tell you how many drunken friends have cut their feet. I have to keep the first-aid kit well stocked. Here, take my hand."

I clung to her as she guided us painstakingly among the stones. "Step *down* here . . . now we're turning left . . . watch out for the prickly pear . . ." We'd have been helpless without her. English people confounded by paradise.

"I've never been so aware of my feet," said Jack. "All my life I was under the impression that they were controlled by my head."

We passed a one-roomed house that was dwarfed by an enormous fig tree. Through a window that was barely a foot square I could see a candle flickering.

"No electricity out here," she called cheerfully as though reading my thoughts. "No plumbing either." Just for a moment I wondered what we were getting into.

Then all of a sudden the path changed to flat packed earth. Bamboo clattered softly on either side.

"This is the beginning of my property," she announced. "Though

Yorgos and I are still fighting over the boundaries. It's been in court for a year. Litigation — they love it."

We proceeded up a little hill then into an open space where the wind whipped our clothes. Then up three white steps to a white patio spread like a proscenium before the white house. Below us was the sea, above the Milky Way that covered a third of the sky.

"Wait here," she said. "Look at the stars while I do the lamps."

We sat on the low wall. There was a glow above the next hill where the moon was about to make her entrance. Sounds came out of the night: the wind in the eucalyptus, the barking of dogs, the crowing of cockerels, music from the beach and from another house. Nothing was ever quiet here. All of life was off the lead.

She called from the doorway. Her tall slender form was lit from behind by the soft glow of the oil lamps. She beckoned. "Let me show you," she said. I felt privileged, as though I were about to see a newborn baby or enter a temple.

None of the three rooms was connected. If you wished to change venue it was necessary to go outside and re-enter. There was a small kitchen with a gas hotplate, a rickety table and chair, walls lined with ancient battered pots, a clay water jug, staples in jars and sacks, figs and plums in baskets and an oval fireplace at chest-level. In a second room was a mattress covered with a white cotton counterpane and an overflowing bookcase. She lived and slept in the largest room, the walls of which were equally bare except for some sconces of old silver. Two sheep skulls were adorned with a little jewellery, there were a couple of small statues which looked old and genuine and a collection of rocks and shells. Some were arranged to form small altars. A crude but comfortable bed was covered by an intricately patterned piece of fabric. A black transparent cloth concealed the dressing area. There were no angles anywhere, every door and window frame and corner having been rounded

175

by hundreds of whitewashings. Oil lamps and candles flickered and dripped in the breeze. It was so clean, so serene. I had never felt so enfolded by a place.

"It's beautiful," I whispered. "How old is it?"

"A hundred years."

She poured us red retsina from large plastic bottles which she had carried herself all the way from town. She told us about the seaweed that insulated the ceiling and about the little orange lizards who lived in it; how the seaweed must be fetched by boat from another island and the bamboo cut from her grove to hold it in place; about the nightmare of getting the original fireplaces to work (if one did, the other didn't — no one knew why).

"How do you survive the winters?" asked Jack.

"With difficulty. Sometimes I run away to Athens or Paris. If I'm here I wear a lot of sweaters and keep moving. Pretty soon I'll have to be here all the time because I'm starting a vegetable garden. A big one." She poured us more retsina. I think we were all pretty high. "I like it basic," she explained. "I love the candles and carrying water. I love shitting outside. I love going down to the well and pouring a bucket of water over myself. I love it. Choices are limited. Everything is simple. Everything is free."

"You live here alone?" Jack asked.

"Mostly. I have a lot of visitors. In the summer too many. I was just having a day away from them all." She smiled. I felt slightly guilty. "In the winter I see no one but the Greeks."

"And the house is yours? You don't rent it?"

"It's mine." She did not elaborate. "It's the only place I've ever been happy."

"I can understand that."

Of course. Americans were pioneers, physically and culturally. They needed to press to the extremest edge then live on it. She was a

176

daughter of the New Frontier, after all — and high priestess of simplicity.

"I don't like owning things. I'm a communist really," she declared in all innocence.

"It must be hard being a communist by yourself." I didn't think that was called for.

"Boy, is it," she laughed. It was remarkable the way she could laugh at herself. "But on the other hand, nothing takes place in isolation. One good life can radiate out and affect the entire universe."

"The island as metaphor for society — " Shut up, Jack, I thought. But she went right on.

"That's why we have to do the best we can. Make our life our art. Each in his own way. I really believe that it makes a difference. That's why I want to spend more and more time here."

She and Jack talked on while my eyes wandered over the white womb from which everything contemporary seemed to have been excluded, banished. I inhaled the incense that she burned in a little chipped clay vessel and which she said came from the shrine of the Black Virgin on Tinos. I watched her. She seemed totally at one with her chaste environment, yet uniquely herself. In her presence I felt awkward and stiffly cerebral. She made me aware of my ordinariness, but I did not dislike her for this. I loved her.

"Haven't you ever wanted to own *anything?*"

"Art. Ancient art. But I wouldn't. Art like that belongs to everyone. No one should be allowed to drool over it in private. Just once I felt what I suppose greedy collectors must feel. I was in the museum in Heraklion — my favourite museum — and I saw these exquisite vases. Minoan, the most beautiful of all. They were round and flat and had octopuses painted on them. Have you ever seen them? They're about this big with two little handles at the top like ears and

177

the octopus's head in the centre and its tentacles radiating all round to the circumference. Every vase is different, like snowflakes. Well, there was one, it was just so wonderful, and I stood looking at it in rapture. It seemed the most divine thing I ever saw. I just wanted to worship it. Then I was seized with a desire to possess it, and I was terrified of it, of its beauty, and terrified of myself, afraid I'd smash through the glass to get it. I was capable. At that moment I swear I was. I had to ask my friend to take me out of the building." She sighed. "You've never seen them? Never been to the Heraklion museum? You'd adore it. Go sometime. You must go."

Jack remarked that we should first be going to bed.

"Stay here," she offered and we agreed.

As she was making up the mattress a grey-and-white cat wandered in and fussed around her ankles.

"I know this one," she said, picking him up by the back of the neck and kissing him. "He'll sleep with me and be gone in the morning. Greek cats tend to be one-night stands."

She blew us a kiss and left. I am certain it was on that night that Virginia was conceived.

It was the island where the gods came to play. Every stone held a memory of their revels. How could we not return?

The following summer the port was even more crowded. In the August evenings one could barely push one's way along the little streets, some of which were now lined with leather and jewellery shops. But out at Karaki things were unchanged. There was still the one taverna set back from the beach among the bamboo groves, still the clean white sand unobstructed by any building, still the same donkey tethered by the same small church beside the road, still the tangerine starfish under the blue water, still the mountains dotted with white houses in one of which Veronica Beattie was burning candles and incense and cultivating a vegetable garden.

On the second day I walked up the hill to see her, carrying Virginia in my arms. It was our first trip with our five-month-old daughter whom I was anxious to present to Veronica. I wanted her to hold my baby, as if, like a fairy godmother's, her touch might exert some benign influence over Virginia's future. I was a new mother, believing, in the face of all evidence to the contrary, that I might protect my offspring from trouble.

Her arrival had changed our life, speeding up its action as in an old movie. We had married, moved in together, and acquired basic furnishings with the help of Jack's father. Jack worked hard. We were getting by. It was good to be back in Greece with a promising future.

As I approached the house, I noted the young olive trees, the pomegranates and the Easter tree. They were alive but looking shaky. An enormous canvas hosepipe ran from the well to the back of the house where yellowed stalks bent under the weight of a few blood-red tomatoes and the aubergine plants withered. A lone sunflower was barely three feet high. The garden had failed. In the field beyond, however, some vines bore grapes and there was fruit on a plum tree.

I called but no one answered. Her doors were never locked. Indeed, one was permanently open. But I was reluctant to enter unannounced. A man appeared on the terrace. He had a high forehead, slicked-back hair and seemed well-groomed even in the dhoti-like garment which was all he wore. I recognized him as Veronica's French companion of the previous summer.

"Veronica's not here. She's in town. Oh, what a heavenly baby! May I take her? And the T-shirt. So chic. Come in and I'll make you some tea."

Émile turned out to be almost as nice as Veronica. We sat in the little room where he was drawing, volumes of *The Duino Elegies* and Paul Bowles on the bed beside him. He came here to work, he said, when Veronica was at the shop. It was so chaotic in town, so distracting. Here there was peace. Wasn't it bliss?

"Wonderful. What shop?"

"She works in the boutique of a friend. She hates it, but she must. Unfortunately she is broke." He nuzzled Virginia. "Like all of us." It was hard to imagine, cosmopolitan and sleek as he was.

"I wondered how she lived." I could not restrain my curiosity. And Émile seemed to like talking. People had so much time here.

"She doesn't make a lot, but she'll now get through the winter. Last year she took an acting job — "

"She's an actress?"

He flicked his splayed fingers from side to side, pursing his lips. "You could say. Now and then she gets film work — very small parts — you know. She says she's finished with it." He sighed. "It's so terrible for her, serving those vulgar tourists. And when I think why she came here . . ."

"Why *did* she come here?"

"To escape corruption."

"I don't understand."

"Veronica is very pure, you may have noticed. She won't prostitute herself. She won't compete. Of course you and I know this is impossible. I tell her, darling, all of us must compromise a little to survive. But no, no, *she* must live on a higher plane."

"I admire her very much."

"Admire? My dear, she's completely divine."

And she'd had a frivolous existence, as I'd suspected, before her love affair with Greece. I asked if she'd always lived alone.

"Off and on. Her liaisons don't last. Something is always wrong. Maybe because she is addicted to beautiful monsters. There was a husband once — long, long time ago. Not a person she likes to discuss." I vowed to myself I would never mention this brute, whoever he was.

Virginia was restless, so I wrote a note with an announcement of our arrival and whereabouts and left. At the door, Émile kissed us both. His lips were soft and warm, and he smelled of limes. I saw that his eyelashes were mascaraed.

"Give her my love," I said.

The following evening she appeared at the taverna with Émile. She was so excited to see us again, she said, and enthused over Virginia whom she insisted on holding even after she'd vomited down the front of her dress.

"It's just a friendly little puke," she laughed.

"Such an earth mother," Émile teased.

I could tell he made Jack slightly uncomfortable, but I ignored this. I wanted to have a good time.

I had one. I visited Veronica as often as I dared. (The closer we became, the more in awe of her I was, and yet not uncomfortable, never that.) She insisted on babysitting so that we could have a night in town. We returned at four in the morning (cutting our feet on the path) to find her bent over the little body.

"I think it was bad dreams," she said. "She's fine now." Veronica hadn't slept a bit. We decided to sit on the terrace and watch the sun come up. It rose on us like the beginning of the world, giving us back our lives all new. The night had been uncommonly still, and the sea below us was like blue glass, unmarred by whitecaps. We watched a herd of goats crossing the opposite hill, the sweet anarchy of their bells playing an accompaniment to their progress. The cries of the goatherd were like arias from a primal opera.

"Do you know any places for rent?" asked Jack. This was the first I'd heard of such a plan.

"No, but I know who would. You want to be out here, right? I'll ask my neighbour." She pointed to a house halfway down the mountain from which an antiphonal chorus of chickens arose. "He's my great friend who helps me sometimes with the garden and when the pump breaks down. We've had our fights, but it's a good relationship. In fact," she studied two forms approaching from below, "here come his nephews. They worship him, won't leave him alone. He takes them shooting. Yannis! Dmitri!" she shouted at them and they waved. She beckoned and they turned into the broken gate. They were about eleven, and I marvelled as always at the beauty of Greek children. They listened with serious faces to the American woman who babbled to such effect in their difficult language.

That's how it happened. By the time we left for London we had met Alekos, the neighbour, and arranged to rent for a month the following summer a house on the hill where we'd seen the goats pass by. It was not as old as Veronica's, nor as pretty, but it was larger and the rent was modest. The house belonged to an uncle of Alekos who owned much land and property on the island, was very enterprising, and, we all suspected, a bit of a gangster, though this possibility only seemed to enhance his already dazzling charm. Greek men, I had noticed, age very well, retaining their hair and their looks well past middle age. Veronica said it was their splendid immune systems. I felt attracted to them and a little frightened.

We were paid a few visits by the nephews who came to the beach to catch octopus and watch foreigners.

"What are they doing?" I asked Veronica late in the afternoon of our last day.

She turned. "Oh God, they're beating the octopus." She covered her face with her hands and shuddered.

"But why?" I watched, fascinated, as they whacked the unfortunate creature over and over again against a stone.

"To tenderize it. Oh I can't bear it."

"Is it dead?" I could not tear my eyes away.

"By *now* I suppose."

Even Jack was disgusted. "Is it true that to kill it they — "

"Stop!" she screamed and put her hands over her ears.

" — bite its eyes?" he finished.

She shook her head and wouldn't speak. Her hair fell loose from the sleek knot into which she'd pinned it.

Émile slipped his arm round her. "I've heard this."

She looked up, her eyes moist. "I love the Greeks," she said, "but sometimes I just can't — I just don't — "

Émile raised his eyes to heaven. Suddenly she laughed.

"Isn't it stupid?" she cried. "Aren't I crazy?"

She said she would write to us in London, but she never did.

"Veronica has too much time to write letters," Émile explained.

Consequently we did not hear from her from one summer to the next. The gap made seeing her again all the more exciting. Not that we lacked news of our own. Our fortunes, accelerated by the coming of Virginia, were further improved once I was pregnant with Paul. Babies brought us luck, Veronica said. It was true. Life had picked us up like a wave and carried us forward. Jack was a rising star. He was clever and energetic and made money, which for a while we were careful not to spend too lavishly. We kept the same flat. And we always saved enough for three weeks on the island. We were prospering. That has an unpleasant sound, somehow, but we couldn't help it. Sometimes I wondered why it should be so easy for us.

From my kitchen window (we had plumbing) I could look out towards Veronica's house on the opposite hill and see her sweeping the terrace or whitewashing the wall or dragging the hosepipe about or hanging out the linen which she washed by hand at the outdoor sink (fed by a tank on the roof — a great and much discussed concession). I could hear her arguing with Alekos, often screaming at the top of her voice, usually when one of his pigs escaped and ransacked her kitchen. They seemed almost to enjoy these conflicts, and she fitted happily into the disputatious culture of the island.

In the late afternoon the sound of the pump would begin, continuing sometimes until long after dark. She had been given a portable radio, but usually kept the volume low. Even so, acoustics in the valley were such that I always knew when she had it on. One morning it was unusually loud, the music coming, it seemed, from some Arab country, maybe Egypt. I looked out. She was standing on the terrace with her arms raised above her head, facing the newly risen sun. As I watched she began to sway and turn, losing herself in the music and in the elaborations of her private choreography. Jack came in to ask me a question, but stopped when he saw the performance that held me spellbound. Together we observed the solitary dance until she vanished suddenly into the house. Then we left the window, neither of us having said a word.

Occasionally I caught a glimpse of a young man. For about a fortnight he appeared on the terrace. Sometimes he was naked. Then he stopped coming.

Mainly I saw her in her garden, to which she was fiercely devoted and to which she gave her best energies, saying she didn't want to be just another colonialist. It had begun to take shape at last. In June her sweetcorn was already high. She had cleared a field to the rear of the house, removing stones (some of which were very large) almost unassisted. New olive and plum trees replaced the ones that had died. She would have a bumper crop of black-eyed peas. Only the melon patch was desolate.

"Got to rethink it," she said, frowning. "I gave them loads of

184

manure. I talked to them. I planted at a good time, when the moon was in just the right position. Perhaps they're in the wrong place."

We were drinking wine under the eucalyptus tree, joined by an American girl from Boston who had just bought a house near the port. (Foreigners had recently begun buying property on the island.) Overhead the cicadas droned.

"What happened to them?" she asked, not all that interested.

"I didn't spray, darling. At least Alekos says that's the reason. I'm one of the few remaining people in the valley to hold out against chemicals. All the others have been seduced. They're pouring on the nitrates and pumping out the pesticides."

"Well, I guess it works for them." The American eyed the devasted plot.

"In the short term." Veronica snapped uncharacteristically. "Alekos told me his father had the most famous melon patch on the island — practically in the whole Cyclades — and that he never sprayed and hardly watered. The melons get used to bugs and dryness if you leave them alone. They get tough. Like the Greeks. Like me."

She had not become tough, she could never be that. But she had roughened, albeit attractively. The sun had etched little lines across her face, and the skin on her arms and legs was dryer and beginning to crinkle at the joints. Her hands were those of a peasant. But she remained the long-legged American archetype whom everybody teased about looking like Jackie Kennedy. She was still *soignée* even in torn shorts and a stained T-shirt with dirt under her nails. The old straw hat that she wore in the garden and which now lay beside her, its brim rolled over and fastened at a rakish angle with a few sprigs of corn, might have been some *faux-naïf* masterpiece from a little Paris shop.

"I try to talk to people about the chemicals. Whenever I can. I try to tell them."

Her crusade was touching. I was impressed all over again. But to my esteem was added some new element, one I could not quite understand and which seemed inappropriate for a woman like her. I realized with a start that it was sympathy.

The beach was particularly crowded that summer and we often took boats to more remote places Veronica had told us about that were further along the coast. (The following year we hired a car. It was horribly expensive, but I was pregnant again and Paul and Virginia were active two and four year olds who became over-excited on the water.) But even at these more esoteric spots the odd villa was under construction, and soon the inevitable beach umbrellas appeared, for rent at an exorbitant price. The fact was that the island was being invaded. It had always been popular but now from June to mid-September tourists swarmed over it like an army of ants on a cake. There were several hotels at the beach just down from Karaki, a villa had sprung up on the hill behind Veronica along with a small new house at the bottom of the valley, and Alekos's uncle was said to be negotiating the sale of some land just back from our beach. Rumours flew. Veronica's response was to shrug philosophically or wave a dismissive hand.

We arrived very late in the season that summer Camille was one. For the first time I felt worn out and irritable after my pregnancy. Labour had been long and delivery terrible, completely unlike the first two. I'd been unable to lose the weight I'd gained. I told myself I'd had enough. I did not want any more children. We had an au pair now (we'd finally bought a house and were renovating it), but she was unable to join us on the island. Then came the last straw. Jack was called away. There had been trouble over an important commission, and it was imperative that he return and set matters straight. I chose to stay and manage the final week by myself.

Jack had scarcely been gone an hour when Camille began to

exhibit the symptoms which by the next morning had me completely panicked.

A three-hour wait in the doctor's surgery was rewarded by a diagnosis of tummy bug, which he casually regretted; there was little I could do but wait it out and give her the pink medicine, to which at first she did appear to be responding. But during the night she relapsed, and at first light I sent Virginia to fetch Veronica. I was exhausted after two nights without sleep. I was also frightened.

She came at once and managed everything. She fed the children, washed the dishes, changed Camille's linen — often — and made me go to bed. I surrendered to her benign authority.

"Greek doctors are all horrible," she said.

I listened, from a great mental distance, to the sounds of my everyday life. I heard it proceeding without me, and didn't care at all. Gently I drifted away into my fever.

It went on for three days. She told me that Camille got better as I got worse. Then I rallied and just as matters seemed to be reaching a kind of equilibrium, Paul vomited his lunch all over the table and the nightmare resumed. Only she and Virginia, 'the tough ones', were spared. I don't know when she slept, if she ever did. She claimed she could cat-nap and snatch back her energy from the briefest immersions in her unconscious. At the end of four days she still had three feeble invalids on her hands. We were nevertheless on the mend, and by the evening of the fifth day I was able to join her on the terrace to watch the sunset. I was still shaky, and she insisted I stay wrapped in a blanket.

I tried to thank her. Insensitively perhaps, I let slip my surprise at her proficiency with children. She was unoffended.

"Oh darling," she laughed, "I'm practically the local midwife. You know now what the doctors are like. No one will come all the way out here. And anyway, who needs them? Last year Yanna's baby was three weeks early. They called me and I came. I knew nothing, believe me, but I managed to hold the fort until the mother-in-law arrived. By then I was hooked. I stayed and watched. A few months later I delivered Irini's — by myself. I was scared to death, sweating like a pig, but I did it."

"You're amazing."

"I just like all that."

Why, I burned to ask, did she not like it for herself?

"Children love you. I always remember Yannis and Dmitri trailing after you."

"Hmmm . . ." she smiled. "I'll tell you a story, but don't mention it to anyone."

"I promise."

"Well, last spring I was sitting on the bed reading when the two of them came to the door. I was a little surprised. I mean they're fourteen/fifteen now. They don't trail after me so much any more. Anyway, you'll never guess why they'd come."

"Why?"

"To proposition me. They were very straightforward about it, said they didn't mean to offend me. All serious. They were sick of being virgins and wanted to get laid. The local girls, believe it or not, are virtuous, and the married women all have big angry husbands, so the only alternative was the whores and they didn't want that. So they asked would I help them out."

"What did you say?" My eyes must have been like saucers.

"I said I'd have to think about it. I told them to go away and come back in two days."

"And?" Actress that she was, she made me wait.

"I said no. I said it was just too close. I know everyone in their families, and it just wouldn't be right. I told them I was very flattered, which I was, and I wished them the best of luck. They said they were disappointed but that they understood completely. We drank a couple of beers and that was that."

"Weren't you tempted?"

"Are you *kidding*?"

"You're very proper, really."

"Yeah." She considered it. "I guess I am."

We were quiet for a moment. Again I wanted to ask her about the naked young man on the terrace, but I knew this was territory into which I must not stray. She had boundaries, not apparent at first, but nonetheless real. I studied her profile in the fading rosy light.

"Are you ever going to do something of your own?" she suddenly asked.

"I don't know what you mean."

"You have a degree, don't you? A good one from a fancy college. Aren't you going to use all that knowledge?" This was very out of character. Her voice was almost sharp. "I never learned anything. Just *had* to go to drama school, didn't I? Stormed and raged until they let me. Consequently I'm a bimbo."

"That's ridiculous!"

"Sometimes I write," she confessed.

"Really?"

"Try it. You ought to. Clarifies things amazingly."

"What do you write?"

"Oh little things. About my life. What I see around me. Nothing with any pretensions. I hate big sprawling egotistical tomes, don't you?"

"Can I read these little things?"

"Oh no one *reads* them. They're not ready to be shown to anyone yet."

"How long do you work on them?"

"Oh . . . years . . ."

189

That's when I saw it: her secret vice. I suddenly put the boys and the young man and his absence and the writing all together. I saw her pristine house, the dramatic simplicity with which she dressed. I saw why she had not married again. She was a perfectionist — that was the secret vice to which she never admitted and probably didn't even know she had. But she was not a cold perfectionist, and she did not demand perfection in others. She was a perfectionist of atmospheres and combinations and, yes, appearances. "It's not the right time," she'd say. "It just wasn't quite right." "I wanted it to be just right, but somehow . . ." Perhaps it was my weakened state but I felt very sad.

We decided to go to Crete. I'd persuaded Jack that it was actually fun to drag three children and a nanny around with us at vast expense. Not only fun but necessary.

On a hot noisy afternoon we sought shelter from the chaos of Heraklion in the dim, low-ceilinged museum. We were all entranced, even two-year-old Camille. I found her with her nose pressed to a glass case which she could not be persuaded to leave.

"Octoputh, Mummy," she said. "Octoputh."

There they were, the vases Veronica had described to us on that first night. And they were as charming as she'd said, with that seductive grace mixed with a hint of humour that makes Minoan art so appealing. They were a perfect marriage of form and design, and in their archaic beauty lay the germ of a puzzling modernity.

"I saw them in a shop," the observant Virginia informed us. "Didn't you see them? They were copies of these, exactly the same."

Her father pointed out that they could not be copies and "exactly the same".

"Can we buy one?" asked Paul.

"I think we should buy two," said Virginia. "And give one to Veronica."

"Because she looked after us last summer," said Paul.

Not only was I proud of my thoughtful children, I was amazed at the synchronicity of the event. Their little intuitions seemed to be operating at full blast.

We purchased the vases. Of course they were nothing like the originals. Mere trinkets, hastily and crudely produced. I felt slightly embarrassed presenting Veronica with such a travesty, but somehow I thought she'd see the point.

"Oh," she squealed, "it's too perfect!" and covered the children with lavish kisses. "I'm going to put it right here," she announced, placing it on the kitchen mantelpiece. "And whenever I see it, I'll remember the real vase. And I'll remember all of you."

"We liked Crete," Paul told her. "Do you like Crete?"

"Love it."

"Why don't you ever go there?"

She roared with laughter. "Sweetie, I never go anywhere."

It was true. More than two years had passed since she'd left the island. There was always a good reason: the garden required constant attention, and she tended it with dedication, squandering her best energies on it from February to September. The house needed repairs which she must personally oversee. Émile was ill and she must nurse him. She was directing the school play. All summer there were visitors in her house, and I seldom saw her alone. In fact I seldom saw her, except from my terrace or my kitchen window as she hoed and watered and whitewashed. The pump throbbed away until after dark, and her raucous laugh echoed across the valley.

The year we came for the whole summer, I hardly saw saw her, though when I did it was delightful. Otherwise she was a figure in a landscape, a landscape that was changing. Alekos's uncle had behaved as we'd predicted and sold his seafront property to the

191

developers for a handsome profit. He then went on holiday to the Seychelles, much to everyone's amusement. The hotel, however, was no joke. It was real and it was rising fast — straight up into Veronica's pristine view. Shortly after our arrival at the end of June we commiserated with her over dinner at the taverna, which was no longer a quiet little restaurant, but rang with the laughter of Australians, Germans, Americans, Italians and even Japanese.

"Well, it's happened," she said. "Karaki's been discovered." She confided that the infamous uncle had recently made an offer on her house, his third that year. "I told him to piss off, nicely of course." She surveyed the general hilarity. "It's like a war," she grimly observed. As she turned, I noticed the muscles and tendons in her neck. She was even thinner than last year. I was made aware of the weight I had still failed to lose. "And the sea's getting polluted."

"Looks fine to me," said Jack.

"When I go snorkelling I see fewer sponges and anemones. They're always the first to go when the shit starts seeping in."

"What about the octopuses?" he teased.

"Oh they're out there," she smiled, "hiding or trying to hide. I don't know how long they'll last with all these new chemicals being washed from the farms down into the ocean. You know I'm *the* last person in the valley to be organic? Everyone sprays now. They think it's great and that I'm crazy."

An associate of Jack's who'd come out for a week on the plane that now flew direct from London to the island suddenly spoke up. He was a brash young man and I didn't particularly like him or want him there.

"You can't hold back the change," he told her. "These people want a better life and they deserve it."

"What makes you think you know what they want?" she responded.

"It's selfish to expect them to remain picturesque just to gratify your aesthetics."

"Veronica's been here a very long time," I began.

"The better class of tourist, as they like to think of themselves, always complain that the indigenous culture is being ruined. Yet they rent the villas, shop in the boutiques, hang out in the discos, leave their rubbish to be dumped somewhere beautiful. It's not only inconsistent, it's hypocritical. If they're so worried about what's happening to Greece why don't they do the decent thing and stay away?" He enjoyed being difficult and was clearly excited by his own rhetoric. "Because if Greece is dying, they're its murderers, not the peasants who put fertilizers on the fields."

We all went very quiet. Veronica rose with dignity. She said goodnight, put some money on the table for her untouched food and left. I started after her, but Jack restrained me. I hardly said anything for the rest of the meal. All I could think of was Veronica walking barefoot over the rocky path, alone in the dark.

I suppose that was the reason we saw so little of her. The children would visit her to beg for cookies and she would wave to us from across the valley. But that was all. I was sad and wanted to see her but felt embarrassed, somehow. I stayed away. I was not the only one. She had stopped entertaining and seemed to associate almost exclusively with the Greeks. (They may have thought she was crazy, but they still adored her. Their eyes lit up when they saw her coming.) No one knew how she managed, what she lived on — besides the garden, that is. She did not buy or sell. She did not consume.

We, on the other hand, had made friends with a few couples our own age who, like us, had come to the island and loved it and stayed whenever they could as long as they could. Of course Jack couldn't spend all summer with us, but would fly out from London when work permitted. It was an exhausting schedule but it suited his restless energy. And I? I grew fatter in my contentment. But I did have a bit more time to myself. So belatedly I took Veronica's advice and tried writing. Just now and then. Whenever I got the chance or the spirit moved me.

Then the inevitable happened. Alekos's uncle sold yet another piece of land for yet another handsome profit and construction work on another new villa was soon underway, only this time within a few yards of our house. This was the end, Jack declared. Karaki would become nearly as overrun as the port with none of its conveniences. We would have to look for a place further down the coast. Or . . . He gave me a significant smile.

There is a point of land along the road that runs eastward out of town. It faces south and affords a view of Paros when the island is not hidden in its customary haze. A beautiful white house trimmed with blue, the next to the last from the port, is built into the side of the hill on the sea's edge. It has three and a half levels that follow the rise and fall of the land. The rooms, which are always immaculately whitewashed, lie at odd angles to each other, and this increases their sense of privacy and protection. It is simply but comfortably furnished with Greek and Turkish rugs and furniture built by local craftsmen, although some has been sent from England. The fireplaces are as near to authentic as it was possible to make them. The kitchen, however, has every modern convenience, and the bathroom shower is excellent, all things considered. Everyone says it is the most wonderful house. It is ours. Jack designed it, and it was built over three years at great trouble and expense. (We had to take out a second mortgage to complete it.) But of course it was the only thing to do, the only thing that really made sense. We love the island and we'll always come here. Our children (there are four now) will come as well, we hope, and it will remain in the family for generations, provided the Greek government doesn't turn funny again. And naturally we enjoy the convenience and gaiety of the port. It is lovely, after an evening at our favourite restaurant, to walk home under the starry sky, the children running ahead of us, the sea lapping on our right, and return to the quiet and comfort of this beautiful place. (Motor bikes are a bit of a nuisance.) Some people from a colour supplement came to take pictures of it. Jack was very proud. In so many ways it is a symbol of all he's achieved.

When it was finished at last I decided to give a party. We now had many friends on the island — Greeks, Europeans, Americans — and it would be fun, I thought, to bring them all together, representing as they did our progress here since that inauspicious arrival so many years ago. When I sat down to compose the guest list, Veronica's name was the first I wrote.

Jack predicted she wouldn't come. The party girl, he maintained, had become an anchorite. But I felt certain she'd accept. Just to make sure, I decided to deliver the invitation myself. I'd make an occasion of it, I said. I'd take a caique out to Karaki and walk all the way up the mountain to find her. The prospect excited me, I don't know why.

I'd seen her only once that year at a shop in town where she was buying candles and tahini. We'd embraced. I'd told her about the house and she'd seemed enthusiastic. We'd agreed to meet but we hadn't. I thought with a pang that an entire summer had passed and I'd hardly spoken to her. As I disembarked and picked my way among the bodies on the beach I remembered the first time we'd eaten at the taverna, the first time I'd carried Virginia up the narrow dusty road. Now, as then, I was coming to ask her blessing. Just as I had wanted her to hold my child, I wanted her to see my house, to give it her acknowledgement, her approval; to verify it and, by extension, to verify me.

I turned with disgust from the new villas to rest my eyes on the bamboo groves and giant prickly pears that surrounded her land like guardians of a benign fortress. I thought how heroic she was, holding out against the future, preventing, all alone, its absolute triumph. The sense of siege was enhanced when I saw the garden. It had been ravaged. Only the larger trees were left.

"Bugs," she said. "Don't ask me what kind. Then the pump broke and no one had the right parts and by the time they arrived ten days later it was too late."

"But the rest — " I glanced at patches of green on the otherwise grizzled valley.

"They spray, darling. Want some tea?"

She looked haggard. Her cheekbones, forehead and collarbone were too prominent and her brown eyes were too large. In their expression was something both driven and distant, some powerful emotion held too long in check. Behind her the congested villas spread over the hillside like a white contagion. I wanted to cry.

She had preceded me into the kitchen, so I had a moment to collect myself. When I stepped into the dim interior I could barely see. Then the room came into focus. It was as before, only cleaner and more orderly, if that was possible, and permeated by the smell of incense mixed with basil and wood-smoke. The steps appeared to be made of some spongy material and not stone at all. Everything was rounded, inviting, soft yet bare. On the mantelpiece was the octopus vase.

"Oh!" I touched it gently. She had placed a few dried flowers in it.

"Still got it," she sang over the sound of the hissing kettle.

"I'm surprised."

"Why?"

"It's hardly pure. A piece of junk, really. A fake."

"Every home needs a touch of madness," she chirped and carried the tea tray out to the eucalyptus. I noticed how thin her legs were.

"What will you do?" I asked, indicating the garden.

"Start again. What else?"

"Do you need help?"

"The boys help sometimes. They're angels." I assumed she meant Yannis and Dmitri.

"Do you need — money?"

"Oh darling." She laughed, but her eyes were sad. She seemed embattled, surrounded, doomed. "I'm fine."

I'd forgotten how stubborn she was. I did not pursue the matter. I told her about the party and she said she'd come.

I told Jack how worried I was about her.

"She could always sell."

"*Sell?*"

"That place would fetch a small fortune now, if she put in some plumbing. Why don't you believe her? She's fine."

She came alone, dressed as she used to in a wide swirling skirt, black sweater cut low at the back, ballet slippers and dangling earrings. Her brown sun-streaked hair fell over her shoulders, and for the first hour or so she smiled a lot and even laughed her loud laugh. Then she seemed to retreat, conversing only with some of the Greeks who were present or with the children. Once, I thought, she would have been the life of the party.

Yannis and Dmitri arrived with their respective girlfriends, and she stood for a while with them. What does she think, I wondered, when she sees them now? Does she regret anything or has she forgotten completely?

I did not have time to contemplate the matter further, as I was swept away by the tide of guests that came through my door all evening. The house was magnificent, they said. Had I made all the food myself? (I had.) Then they drifted into several large groups all of whom were complaining about the tourists, as though they had become self-appointed Greeks.

"They're going to build a camping site right on the beach at Karaki," an Englishwoman announced.

"You're not serious."

"It's true, I promise you. Ask Veronica," said Jack who was among them.

Just as she was summoned I approached with a tray of canapés. Wonderful, I thought, she's circulating. I had begun to worry that she did not completely approve of my house or my guests. Were we "not quite right" after all? I watched her smile as they questioned her. I watched her eyes. I offered everyone the tray, but she refused.

"None for you, Veronica? You can't be on a diet."

"I don't eat octopus," she said.

"Sorry. I forgot."

"That's all right, darling."

"I heard something really grizzly about octopuses. Shocking stuff." Jack addressed her, making sure the others were all listening. "The chap we buy our crayfish from told me. He said octopuses aren't harmless after all. In fact they can be deadly. It seems they have a kind of proboscis like a very fine needle. Once they've got the poor old crayfish locked in their talons, they insert this device under the shell and suck out the living meat. Just sort of hoover them up."

This piece of information was greeted by exclamations of disgust both genuine and feigned. Then one of the children called me and I was occupied for a minute or so. When I looked up Veronica had gone.

*

I did not see her again. I had planned another journey out to Karaki before we left, but somehow I never made it. I looked for her at the port, but she did not appear. The next summer several people told me she had gone to Paris to see Émile. I didn't know what to believe. It seemed impossible that she could have left the island. Again I was determined to visit her and again I failed. But the following year I made a point of doing it as soon as we arrived. I was resolved to skirt all distractions. Nothing would stand in my way. Filled with the old anticipation I boarded a caique, as though I were making a pilgrimage to a shrine.

The shrine was empty. It had not been whitewashed for months. The garden had returned almost to the wild, and the unpruned vines were creeping distractedly everywhere. I was horrified to find it so unkempt. But what surprised me most was that the doors were locked. I peered through the dusty windows. The bookcase was still there, and her bed and the candlesticks and all the kitchen utensils. Everything seemed just as she'd left it. I strained to see the octopus vase, but it did not appear to be in its usual place. Perhaps I was wrong, it was so dark in the kitchen. Perhaps she had moved it. Perhaps she had destroyed it. The thought that she might have filled me with panic. How ridiculous, I thought, running down the hill, climbing over the stone walls, grazing my knees and feet. With all that was left of my breath I shouted outside Alekos's door, but no one came. Suddenly Dmitri appeared. He was carrying a rifle, which startled me. He held it up, smiling, to show me it was empty, that he was only cleaning it.

"Veronica," I said, panting. "*Spiti*," and waved my hands in bewilderment. He signalled me to wait for a moment and fetched his aunt who seemed delighted I had come and embraced me and insisted I join her in her fly-blown kitchen for an ouzo. I had to give an account of all the children's progress before I could work the conversation round to Veronica.

"Back," she said.

"You mean she's coming back?"

"*Nai*," she nodded confidently.

"When?"

"Tomorrow. Next year."

"You don't really know."

"Next week." She smiled and nodded again and poured me another ouzo. I liked Irini, but she couldn't help me. It was evening when I left, and I was quite drunk. When I had stumbled as far as the broken gate (the same one) I turned to look at the house. I listened for the throbbing of the pump, but there was no sound other than the wind in the bamboo grove and the football game from Yorgos's television. He shortly emerged, stout as ever, and waved to me from his terrace. I knew in a flash that she had not sold the place, that she would never sell, and that she had left behind her small wilderness to be a token Arcadia amidst the encroaching commercialism.

I thought of her beauty, her isolation. Why had she chosen to live as she did? Was it egotism or contrition, some self-imposed punishment exacted by the puritan upon the hedonist? And in that case was her leaving as much a punishment as her staying? Or was she the idealist she claimed to be, a purist nonpareil?

People said various things: that she had returned to America, that she had died, that she had married a shipping magnate, that she had become a Buddhist nun in Nepal, that she had gone to live in an abandoned Byzantine village in the part of the island not accessible by car. None of these seemed to me to have any probability except perhaps the nun.

I sometimes visit the house. Every year it grows wilder and more haunted by her presence. I always arrive with the anticipation of seeing her there. Each time I am disappointed and go away saddened. But over the winter I gather hope and reassure myself that one day I will find her at home. Wherever she is, I know she is travelling light.

FLUFF

The children arrived unannounced, by air, in a pink plastic bag.

"Absolutely not, darling!" shrieked Angela. "No cats!"

"But, my dear," explained Kate who was experienced in these matters, "Greek cats don't make commitments." She pressed the tiny tabbies to her cheek. "A few din-dins, a little conversation, and they're on to the next sucker."

Angela scowled, not convinced. "I've never kept a pet in my life. Oh get that nasty thing away from me."

"But, sweetie, you won't keep them, I will." Kate nuzzled a bandit face, a raspberry-sorbet nose. "Besides, it's only for six weeks."

Angela lit a cigarette and smoked aggressively while reclining like an odalisque — a pose at odds with her greying crewcut.

"A lot can happen in six weeks," she muttered.

A lot can happen in an afternoon. Like a pink plastic bag slung over a garden wall and landing, as if it had fallen from the sky, in your simple, perfect lunch. Like the appalled unpacking of that bag's living contents.

"Whoever they are," fumed Angela, referring to the anonymous donor, "they have no respect for animals — or us — or themselves." She watched the wretched, half-blind creatures from a safe distance as Kate dribbled milk from an eyedropper into their toothless mouths.

"I mean we came here to get *away* from this sort of thing."

Angela had been divorced, burgled and made redundant — all in the space of five months. Kate, recently betrayed by a married lover, had been lucky to borrow this sweet Cycladic house for them. For six weeks they were escaping London, escaping husbands, escaping everything. They'd been reading, swimming, eating, communicating. They were each other's dearest friends, it was all so idyllic. Now this.

"You're right, petal," Kate answered kindly. She felt it her duty to keep Angela's mood up. Still, she was partial to fluff. How could you resist it when it was under your nose, in your lap, designed by sly Nature to appeal? Besides, she was an unemployed actress in need of an emotional outlet. She must, she would, save these orphaned babies.

Discreetly, of course. The nursing would work its miracles well away from her feisty friend. The kittens would grow and flourish and — in the customary way of Greek cats — promptly claim their independence, making confidently for the dry fields and cosy caves that rose up behind the town. She would think of them there during the drizzly London winter. Born free.

So Kate confined the orphans to her room, in a box lined with her Chinese dressing gown, an extravagance Angela would not admit to finding endearing.

"How are the *children*?" she would enquire scornfully as they breakfasted under the eucalyptus tree or shared the single mirror above the sink. Kate's taverna toilette always took longer than Angela's since she had hair, brown and shoulder-length, which she'd whisk inventively into tight sleek knots. Then off they would glide into the noisy island night, linen-trousered, silk-shirted, baubles in their neat ears. Confirmed fashion victims, they kept up appearances despite recent shortages of cash. Every day at four-thirty they went for a swim in their secret cove.

Kate was a selfless mother. The kittens grew and could not be contained. They escaped the nursery and ventured into the wide world — up three stairs to the kitchen, out on to the baking white terrace and finally up three more stairs to Angela's immaculate bedroom. They came by stealth in the night, demon twins, to take her by surprise in her vulnerable state.

"You sneaks!" she cried and pulled the sheet up to her chin. She was absolutely convinced they had done this on purpose. They boxed and tumbled and attacked her toes. The protective carapace in which she lived was shrivelling, withering. She was shedding it like a skin. She was defenceless. The kittens moved in on their weakened prey and she surrendered, without a struggle, to fluff.

They took time naming the children and kept ferocious watch over them, noting each nuance of character and behaviour. One sported a white triangle of fur, worn like a dinner napkin under his permanently expectant chin. Otherwise they were physically identical. In all respects. Naturally, Kate and Angela had been hoping for girls. They wanted daughters to identify with, project on to, shop for. So two sets of testicles came as a blow. However, their love was deep and unqualified, encompassing such deficiencies as only a mother's can.

The slight difference in the time it took for the twins to respond to stimuli, and the more pensive cast to he of the white bib gave Angela the idea at last. The boys were christened Adagio and Allegro, testifying to her devotion to music as well as her passion for symmetry. When a hard woman falls, thought Kate, she is always the soppiest.

The friends now lived as if under a spell, bewitched by the antics of the madcap orphans, cooing and fussing over them eighteen hours a day.

"It's a silly old fuzz-pants, it is."

"Who's my sweetest person? Who's my pussie-pie?"

"Look at the way he's cleaning his toes. Look at him spread them. It's too divine."

"Oh God, he's sneezed again. That's the second time in a week. Do cats get pneumonia? Are there vets in Greece?"

"You had them last night *and* the night before. I want them now. It's hell sleeping alone."

"Mother's perfect darling."

Six weeks pass quickly. Kittens turn to cats. Yet they showed no signs of wanting, as Kate had predicted, to head for the hills.

The women stopped going for swims in the secret cove. It was too far away, and they were reluctant to leave the boys alone. They glided less often into the night. The cats were therapy, love-objects, in-home entertainment. They made Kate and Angela forget the bitterness of life. There was absolutely no question of leaving them on the island.

But how to skirt the rabies restrictions? England was a fortress locked tight against foreign fluff.

"We need a bent doctor is what," was Angela's conclusion.

They located one in the person of Nikos Xenophantos who did not give a fig for finicky English rules and was pleased to dispense his pale-blue pills to pet-fixated middle-aged females, one of whom was not at all bad-looking.

"Half tablet one hour before board plane. No problem." He slid the prescription across his desk, and they practically kissed his hands before scurrying off to purchase a large straw carrier bag embroidered with a lime-green Parthenon surrounded by a border of prancing satyrs.

In the overcrowded Ladies at Athens Airport they administered the medicine.

"The poor darlings, they're hysterical." Angela wrung her hands.

"No time to cave in, precious, we've got to be tough." Kate was a pillar of strength.

But the docility with which the kittens swallowed their pills only increased the women's escalating guilt.

The stowaways were shortly quiet, if not unconscious, under Kate's shawl, and, blessing Dr X, they boarded the plane, the highly illegal hand baggage dangling from Angela's brown arm. They were desperadoes, flaunting international law, a gang of four.

Albania slid uneventfully beneath them. All was calm. Lunch arrived, and they managed to drag their attention from the basket nestled by Kate's feet to poke at pallid chicken limbs and over-salted vegetables, years dead. They exchanged glances that said so far so good. They dared to breathe normally.

It was after Belgrade that things began to go wrong. Small but unmistakable movements could be detected by eyes fastened anxiously on the lime-green Parthenon. From under the shawl came a disorientated mew definitely audible to pricked maternal ears. Angela's brown eyes were huge with fright. Instinctively the women grasped each other's hands.

"Darling," Angela hissed, "they're awake."

"Shhh."

"That bloody quack Xenophantos."

"To the toilet. Fast," Kate actually said.

The lavatory was a tight fit, and they had to dodge a disapproving hostess.

"My God, we still have two hours to London — plus customs." Kate clutched her hair which had fallen from its French twist.

It was Angela's turn to take control. "Open his mouth," she commanded and popped in a pale-blue pill, did likewise with Allegro, was bitten for her pains. They were now literally holding down their perversely adventurous pets. Kate returned to her seat so as not to provoke the air hostess's curiosity, leaving Angela to soothe the boys back into slumber. She sang them "I Got Rhythm", which usually worked. As they were crossing the Alps she slid into her seat with a newly immobile basket and an hour and a half to devote to dread and guilt. She vowed to report herself to the RSPCA.

Paris found the boys still unconscious, the South Downs comatose, Heathrow ditto. All might be well, provided the customs –

"They're not breathing." Angela froze, her hand in the basket as they waited in the passport queue. Tough as she was, she had been unable to meet the hostess's eye when they disembarked.

"What do you mean, of course they're breathing." Kate was now operating on sheer will. She snatched the basket from Angela who tried to snatch it back. Too late. It was their turn at the desk where Angela was nerve-wrackingly detained by a woman who checked her name against a book full of subversives. If only she knew. Finally she let Angela go. But the crunch was coming.

The man at the customs counter seemed to be expecting Kate. As hundreds of dodgy rucksacks and a parade of dubious hand luggage sailed past him, he beckoned her over and asked if she'd mind opening her bags — *all* her bags.

She gave him a smile of medium charm. (Mega-charm would have been thoroughly suspect. She was an actress, after all, and guessed she knew how to play this scene.) Amenably she unfastened her suitcases and displayed their contents as Angela waited, quaking, behind the barrier. Finally Kate opened the Parthenon basket.

The customs man, thirtyish with thinning hair and a rather striking aquiline nose, was looking at her hard and putting some pretty direct questions about agricultural samples, but Kate wasn't fooled. She glanced at his name tag. Clive Sheeky is on to me, she thought, but did not panic; and when he asked for her address and telephone number she gave him Angela's. She reassembled her muddled belongings with dignity, and no plain-clothes detectives stopped her at the exit and asked her to come along quietly.

Poor Angela was in a shattered state. She fell upon Kate whom she had expected to see next behind bars. "Darling," she gasped, where are the boys?"

Kate looked left and right before opening for her friend's inspection first one jacket pocket then the other. She'd made the switch amidst the chaos of the baggage claim. It was her greatest performance.

But freedom, it seemed, had been purchased at too high a price, for no amount of gentle prodding or whispered endearments could rouse the still-unconscious cats. Cursing Dr X and mother love and contemplating permanent brain damage, both women were in tears by the time they'd got a taxi. They spent their last money on it and wondered all the way down the Cromwell Road if they should go straight to the animal emergency hospital in Victoria and if they did whether it would mean immediate arrest.

"We've murdered them," Angela wailed, "the angels." No fate seemed harsh enough for her.

But cats are resilient. By seven o'clock there were signs of life from the basket. By eight reassuring, if not enthusiastic, response to coaxing with milk. By nine Allegro laid claim to his new territory by urinating on the Tibetan carpet.

Angela and Kate were ecstatic. They hugged and danced and opened a self-congratulatory bottle of wine.

"My dear, you were sublime."

"I'd have been nothing without you. Nothing."

"Nonsense. You're the bravest person I've ever known."

They felt redeemed. They drank to audacity, to risk and to that poor darling, whoever and wherever she was, the biological mother. They drank also to their new living arrangement, for Kate had decided to abandon her floating life and move into Angela's husband-free flat. They couldn't, they agreed, be so irresponsible as to separate now. What effect would it have on the boys? Children need a two-parent family.

At nine-thirty the telephone rang. Their nerves must still have been fraught because Kate gasped and Angela spilled her drink. Filled with foreboding she lifted the receiver.

"It's for you," she said, amazed, and passed the phone to Kate.

"Hello." Kate's voice was strained. Of course. This was the call that had to come.

"Miss Miller?" said a man. "It's Clive Sheeky. From the airport."

A cold hand closed on her heart. Had the hostess tipped him off after all? And did this mean six months of quarantine or worse for sensitive Adagio and high-spirited Allegro?

"I remember." She could barely speak since her stomach was where her larynx used to be. She could feel Angela breathing behind her.

"I was just wondering" — Clive Sheeky was polite, tentative — "if you were free next Saturday. You see, I've got these two tickets for *Cats*."

THE WHITE CLIFFS

(For Liz)

What are you gaping at?"

"It's a Valentine, isn't it?"

Auntie Lil squinted at the red paper heart I held up for her inspection.

"You been messing about on the sly?"

"No such luck. It's for Mr Papakiriacou. I found it just now in his trouser pocket."

"The Greek?" she sniffed. "Who'd send him a Valentine, I'd like to know."

I could have made an educated guess. I'm dead good at guessing. But I wasn't going to tell Auntie Lil. She thinks she's head of MI5 and it's her right to be kept informed.

"What's it say?" she suddenly called.

" 'Love from one who sees the beauty of your soul.' "

"Well," she huffed, "his soul had better be beautiful because his face is nothing to write home about."

"What would you know about souls?" I replaced the Valentine in Mr Papakiriacou's aquamarine trousers. He might not be Mel Gibson, but he'd got something. He was very defined, if you know what I mean, like someone had outlined him in biro. He had a big smile and soppy brown eyes and was sweet to the baby. And he'd always compliment me on my new perm or my leather skirt — things like that. His nose was — let's be polite — prominent. But I could understand what Mrs Tine might see in him.

'Course my aunt wouldn't. Not that she's stupid. She's made herself a nice little bundle out of the White Cliffs Launderette. (She named the place after a rude weekend she spent on the south coast in 1971.)

How did I know Mrs Tine was the love-sick admirer? I watch people instead of the game shows and cartoons my aunt gapes at all day on that old black-and-white telly in the office. It's a boring job, folding laundry, loading and unloading the machines. I need stimulation. So I get to know the customers. It's a real-life soap opera. Like I said, not much gets past me.

Except that Valentine. How had she slipped it into his pocket without my noticing? Mrs Tine's not exactly foxy, and her grasp on reality isn't what I'd call strong. She's a nervy type. I sized her up for a loony the first time she came into the White Cliffs dragging a wicker shopping trolley that was leaking water all over the pavement.

"The machine's broken," she gasped, nearly in tears. "It died right in the middle of the rinse cycle. All my bed linen." She stood in a puddle fumbling with her purse. Together we dragged out the dripping sheets and crammed them into the dryer. While they went round and round she straightened her hair, which didn't make that much difference, and tried to calm down. Well, we started nattering and she told me she lived around the corner on Uffing Road. Uffing Road is one of those pedestrian streets being all tarted up. I walked along it every day on my way from the estate to the White Cliffs. The address and her accent convinced me she was all right for dosh. Not that her clothes gave it away. She must have been forty-five but had a wardrobe my nan wouldn't have worn back in 1953.

So we're sitting chatting when in comes Papakiriacou, in a hurry for his laundry as usual. He drove a mini-cab and delivered and collected his clothes between fares. You always knew he was arriving because you'd hear one of those pirate Greek stations blasting away on his radio. I introduced him to Mrs Tine who was so polite it'd kill you.

"Where is your home, Mr Papakiriacou?" she asked.

"Cyprus," he answered proudly. "The birthday of Venus."

"A lovely place." She gave him a knock-out smile.

"You are been?"

"Oh yes. We enjoyed it so much." She actually blushed.

When he finally left, she stood at the window waving goodbye, and he waved back from the front seat of the car with its flashing red rose tied to the rear-view mirror.

Right away she starts pumping me for information, trying to be subtle and not succeeding. I told her he'd come to London last October to drive for his cousin who ran the mini-cab company. He'd spend the winter here then go back to Cyprus when the tourist season started and his brother's restaurant opened. He sent all the money back to his wife and four kids.

"The Greeks work terribly hard," she said.

I should have realized something was up when two days later she was back, this time with a couch cover and a counterpane. She claimed she was spring cleaning, but it seemed a bit early in the year for that kind of thing. The following Thursday she was in again with the sheets she'd only just washed and which didn't look that slept in. The Zanussi still hasn't been fixed, she tells me. Repair men are so unreliable. Next time she's buying a Bosch. Well she sat there for two hours, her nose in the *Home and Freezer Digest*. Turns out she's a freezer freak and keeps it stocked like she's expecting war or famine or the Russian winter. She never cooks to eat, only to freeze, so she has to thaw every meal. She said it made her feel secure to see a fridge full of all those future dinners. I call it bleedin' neurotic.

Still, Mrs Tine was a nice woman. She knitted my Cynthia a hat with a pom-pom and gave her a Peter Rabbit mug for her first birthday. And she was nice as could be when Cynthia threw it on the floor and broke it. I felt sorry for her too. I met her husband who was a narrow-shouldered geezer with a fat bum. He had a head of fuzzy red-blond hair that looked like a panto wig, though it was all his own, I'm afraid, and a complexion like tinned corned beef. And she'd had three kids by this prat.

The next week she comes on a Tuesday. Machine still kaput, so she says. Like clockwork Mr Papakiriacou drops off his wash between fares. They act like they're long-lost friends. He enquires about her Zanussi like it's dear relation. He kisses her hand and mine and drives off, illegal bouzouki music all over the street.

"Does Mr Papakiriacou live locally?" she asks.

Since I don't miss much, I did happen to know Mr P.'s address. It was one of the two unrenovated houses on Percola Road, the kind still occupied by three families, with a front garden full of weeds, crumbling Georgian masonry and a windowless Vauxhall that's been rusting in the drive since 1967. She knew that house, she said. Her husband was hoping the landlord would sell up and remove that eyesore of a car.

Well, no prizes for guessing that by the end of January Mrs T.'s turning up *only* on Tuesdays. Each time, she and Mr P. would have a fussy, affectionate little exchange. Then she'd sit and stare at the same page in her *Home and Freezer Digest* for over an hour.

She was running out of excuses. The Zanussi couldn't be on the blink for ever, and her husband could easily have afforded the Bosch. All her underwear — which I bet you she normally washed by hand — was being ruined by the dryer: elastic puckering, whites turning to dinge grey. She confessed she liked coming to the White Cliffs, me and my aunt were so friendly, she missed babies and adored Cynthia, she'd become a home-body since the children went away to school. For a while I believed her. OK, I thought, it's warm in here and she's lonely. Let her sit and dream about freezers. She's not doing any harm.

Then I found the Valentine and my lightning brain saw the plot. But what next? Would Mr P. follow up? And if he did, how could I make sure I knew about it? Like I said, the White Cliffs was a live soap opera, except I got to play around with the characters.

The Tuesday sessions got longer. All of a sudden they both had mountains of laundry to do. She must have stripped every room in the house, and he was doing his cousin's dirty socks as well as his own. They wouldn't let me touch it. Take a break, they'd say. You're on your feet all day. And they'd start slamming a small fortune in fifty ps into the machines. I realized I was playing Cupid. I'm not as cynical as I make out.

"What we've got here," said my Auntie Lil, "is a proper court-ship." Then she gave them her office.

As you've probably guessed, they were not averse to this, and by the end of March were trysting on Tuesdays *and* Thursdays between two and four. Once when I'd been to a hen party the night before and was feeling rough, they offered to look after Cynthia while I had a quick kip. This too became a habit. They brought Cyn sweets and cuddly toys and she got completely spoilt. Not only were they courting, they were babysitting. They'd coo over the pushchair while I filled and emptied the machines or scrubbed the floor in my stilettos and leather skirt. If there's one thing I hate it's looking a frump.

As far as I could tell the love birds never did much more than hold hands and moon over each other. He was too religious and she was too proper. She could only be daring to a point. I said I felt guily that so much of their precious time was spent preventing Cynthia from doing herself GBH, but they said they liked it. They were playing house.

219

Auntie Lil, who was that pleased with those fifty p pieces, took advantage of the situation to nip across the street to the betting shop or into Zia's Mini-Market for a packet of fags. She got her highlights done and made a couple of shopping trips to Brent Cross. It was all super-convenient.

In late April, Mr P. made his announcement.

"I have a community from my brother." He whipped out a letter which he translated from the Greek. Most of it was incomprehensible, and Mrs T. was catching every word like they were eggs that might fall on the floor and break. But the last line was all too clear.

"Restaurant open in two weeks. Return back fast, please. Vasilly."

Mrs T. went the colour of her underwear. I felt sorry for the poor cow. My aunt felt sorry for Mr Papakiriacou. We all spent a lot of time feeling sorry.

That Thursday Mr P. arrived with a purple-and-white rabbit for Cynthia. He gave Mrs T. one of those big cameo pins they sell at Brick Lane market and she acted like it was the Koh-i-noor. Lil and I got two boxes of chocolate Brazils. He kissed our hands, he kissed Cynthia's forehead. He kissed a tearful Mrs Tine on both cheeks. Then, weepy himself, he drove away, his red rose flashing, taking his beautiful soul with him.

No surprise, we didn't see much of Mrs Tine after that. The White Cliffs depressed her, she said. She was going back to her freezer.

I left the launderette in June. Cynthia was too hyper to take to work, so I was stopping at home until she was ready for playgroup. Colin said what a good mum I was, but I couldn't pretend I was happy. Pretend isn't one of my strong points. I was bored, if you want to know. I missed Mrs T. and Mr P. and the launderette soap operas. I even missed Auntie Lil. Thing I hate most in the world's the feeling of life going on without me. Maybe I'm not so different from Mrs T., except I'm smart enough to keep clear of the love department. I like to keep my mood up-ish.

So I strapped Cynthia in the pushchair and went to see my aunt. In the office I found Mr Zia from the mini-market reading the *Standard* while *The Young Doctors* ran without the sound.

"Mrs Lillian has gone to Brighton for the day," he beamed.

"And you're minding the shop?"

"No, no, no. I am visiting only."

"Visiting who?"

"Mrs Tine. Do you know Mrs Tine?"

I certainly did, and in she walked with a cake she'd frozen last year and thawed that morning.

"Hello, my dear. We've missed you." She kissed me. "Staying to tea, I hope?"

Next morning I rang Auntie Lil, who'd had a late night and was not best pleased.

"Why didn't you *tell* me about Mrs Tine?"

"Didn't know it was my job to keep you up to date. She comes once a week. I need a day off. The pace gets to me. I'm not what I was."

"Rubbish. Anyway I'm talking about Mrs Tine and Mr Zia."

"They're an item."

"Since when?"

"Since I found a Valentine in Zia's pyjamas."

"Not again!"

"Worked before, didn't it? But you got a lot of neck ringing at seven when you never come round any more. Now sod off and let me get my beauty sleep."

I don't know what Spam-face thought about his wife's working in a launderette. But they're still married, and she's at the White Cliffs three days a week now. I'm a regular visitor. We all drink tea and eat

Mrs Tine's cakes. Mr Zia doesn't join us now his wife's back from Kenya, but a nice man who works in a Turkish restaurant on the Essex Road kept us company today while his wash was drying. *Scooby Doo* flickered away in a haze of static. Auntie Lil still has that old black-and-white telly. She refuses to trade it in. My aunt's a bit mean. That's why she's rich, I guess.

THE BLUE WOMAN

Even when he was drunk, Malcolm's sense of direction was infallible. In fact drink seemed to enhance his gift for finding the right street in a sixteenth-century urban maze, the dirt track whose entrance lay shrouded in fog and brambles, the only tourist-free restaurant in the middle of July. Jane, who could not drive in London and frequently became disorientated in her own neighbourhood — never mind Xania — trusted absolutely in his instincts.

"I have no space perception," she would sigh.

"But you have other strengths," he'd console.

She did. Though Malcolm drove like a professional and excelled at water sports, his position on the magazine was less secure than Jane's who had been there four years and was in line for deputy editor. This state of affairs bred a resentment he worked hard to suppress but which surfaced occasionally when his competitive parts were pricked. Jane found these efforts admirable, endearing even.

They discussed professional matters over a dinner of soup with potatoes, onions and diverse marine life eaten at a table by the edge of the black satin sea. The restaurant was the last — and the best — on the port with its loops of lights strung along the curved Venetian harbour. Another of Malcolm's famous discoveries and the only place at which all the clientele were Greek.

She was reminding him that no one could afford to spend money on advertising now. Although readership was up, net income was down. It was the recession. If the magazine made cuts it wasn't personal.

"I don't think we should talk about work," said Malcolm.

"Neither do I. Oh this is so delicious." Jane ladled a second helping from the steaming soup pot. "You too?"

"Yes please. Another bottle of retsina?"

"Definitely. But let's get the one with the cap not the cork. I'm learning to love the taste of turpentine."

"You just like it rough," he teased.

"Sometimes." For a moment she relished an imaginary danger. They smiled and held each other's gaze.

They enjoyed looking at each other. Why shouldn't they? At thirty they could easily pass for twenty-five. They swam and went to the gym. They ate sensibly but well and, though they worked hard, had time to enjoy themselves. Their salaries were about the same, Jane having a slight edge. (Mal attributed the discrepancy to a tacit antagonism between the editor, Justin, and himself.) Both assumed they were *en route* to successful media careers. Occasionally each suspected that they might be more intelligent than the other, but these thoughts were never expressed and the general impression was that theirs was an entirely equal partnership.

Their affair was approaching that apogee that occurs at six months and is sustained for perhaps another two or three before reaching the straight gate at which it either terminates or attains a higher, if less intense, emotional plateau. Malcolm and Jane did not think about this sad but inevitable transition. Why should they? They hadn't even begun to exhaust their supply of jokes and endearments. Hundreds of biographical anecdotes waited in their mutual wings. They were still a mystery to each other. Small wonder

London-bred anxieties had made few raids on their exclusive holiday happiness.

When they had finished the soup they lingered a while, looking across the port to the causeway where pedestrians strolled. They fed the one-eyed cat, held hands across the table and took turns rubbing their toes against each other's ankles.

"You're so beautiful," said Mal. "You're all shining."

When they rose to leave Jane extended her hand, palm up.

"Take me somewhere," she said.

Inside the city, away from the water and the breeze, it was hot. Even at midnight the temperature hung in the high eighties.

The crowded arteries were busy and bright with the restaurants and shops where tourists idled. Human voices echoed off the cobble-stones of narrow passageways. Music from several opposing bouzoukis collided overhead where bright stars were visible even through the competition of so much electricity. The smells of cooking, the laughter of children, the octopuses drying on the backs of chairs: stereotypical Greece at the height of stereotypical summer . . . but no less lovely for that, agreed Malcolm and Jane. Simultaneously they stopped to admire a scarified pink-and-yellow wall that looked like an abstract painting.

"You give such wonderful hugs," murmured Jane as they held each other.

"I love hugging you," replied Mal gallantly.

"Why?" she laughed, but he was very serious.

"Because it makes me feel I really have you and that I can't lose you."

"You can't lose me." She liked his being strong enough to admit his insecurities.

They edged gradually towards the darker fringes of the city.

"Look at him!" Jane pointed at a gigantic cockroach making its insolent way along the pavement.

"In Mexico they're even bigger," Mal assured her.

As they spoke a lithe little cat sprang out of the night, snatched up the cockroach and trotted proudly off, the insect's feet waving between her jaws.

"Excellent," said Malcolm.

"Absolutely," said Jane. And for a while they discussed the agility and resourcefulness of cats. Both were confirmed ailurophiles. It was one of the many things they thought they had in common.

They walked on, hand in hand. They were in no particular hurry. Malcolm was taking them somewhere. Though he was not yet sure where that somewhere might be, he knew it was out there, waiting for him. He could smell it, and was following his brilliant nose.

"Mal's at his best when he's travelling," Jane would tell her friends. "Everything with Mal's a big adventure and he finds all the best places, secret places the tourists miss or are too lazy to look for. I suppose a lot of it is experience," she'd amend. "Mal's certainly been around." She was proud of Malcolm.

They had come to a very old part of town. Cooking aromas no longer hid the underlying smell of decay that seeped from ancient foundations and from the rows of long tubular boathouses where the Venetians had once dry-docked their beautiful ships and which were now warehouses or watermelon depots or else stood empty. Street lamps and pedestrians became infrequent. Rubbish lay in heaps beside the houses.

"Oh goodie," said Jane. "We're lost." And they stood for a moment relishing their directionlessness. Then from a distance came the sound of Cretan music — authentic Cretan music, not the Westernized sort that was pumped from loudspeakers at Zorba's taverna on the beach.

"This way," said Mal, taking Jane by the elbow. He had found what he'd known was out there.

Following the direction of the music they reached a small street which did not look in the least enticing. But experienced Mal knew that appearances in these cases were almost always deceptive. Unsavoury dives were his little speciality.

In contrast to the shadowy neighbourhood the café was blindingly bright. They stood in the doorway, over which there was no sign, adjusting their vision to the interior. A waiter beckoned energetically and pointed to a table at the rear. No sooner were they seated than another waiter rushed at them with two rakis which he placed on the paper tablecloth and made enthusiastic gestures so they might understand that the drinks were gratis. They understood.

Mal knocked back his raki and asked for a bottle of retsina. Jane nursed her fire water, more interested in drinking in her surroundings. In the glare of striplights and some bare electric bulbs which hung from the fly-speckled ceiling, the mustard-coloured walls looked slightly more yellow than brown. They were decorated only with a calendar advertising a restaurant in Suda and some aged posters of the Sumaria Gorge. The doors, she noticed, were a good green. All the chairs and tables had been pushed against the walls to leave a large open space in the centre of the oblong room above which volumes of cigarette smoke eddied, dispersed and regrouped.

The band, consisting of bouzoukis, a lyre, a clarino, a violin, a guitar and some bagpipes played loud and frantic music, the sinuous high spirits of which made Jane think alternately of snakes, goats and the stylized waves she'd seen on vases in the Heraklion museum. At the end of the room, not far from their table, was the busy bar from which waiters ran to and fro with rakis and beers. She could spot no wine drinkers among the almost exclusively male clientele. Only a woman, alone at a table halfway to the door, had finished a bottle of rosé and was in the process of ordering another. Her obvious familiarity with the waiter marked her as one of the café's regulars.

The woman was smiling—a dreamy indulgent smile that lingered at the corners of her mouth long after the waiter had made his way to the bar, skirting the customers with deft, practised movements. It was a smile so sweet as to be nearly plaintive, worn as it was with watery blue eyes ringed in royal blue with matching mascara, a thin face grown leathery from too many summers on the Mediterranean and hair that could no longer trust to holidays to maintain its original gold and so had been driven to desperate remedies. Her dress, made of that pleated cotton that Jane always regarded as the poor woman's Fortuny, was an aquamarine which clashed badly with the eye make-up. Plastic bangles of the same aquamarine decked toasted arms already braceleted by creased flesh. (Jane shuddered, resolved to switch her sun lotion from a twelve to a twenty.) She was long, dry and bony, as if the sun had sucked out all the moisture from the fruit of herself and left her a decorated hull.

"Look at that woman," whispered Jane, but Mal did not hear her.

Then she realized that it was not the waiter who had inspired that mesmerized smile but the dancers. The dancers. They had taken a break and were now back on the floor and forming a long line, their arms raised up to their shoulders, their hands joined, linked together like the strings of lights along the port. The music began and they set off in a row, turning and twisting and doubling back on themselves as they covered the entire empty space in the middle of the café, stomping, jumping, leaning towards then away from each other. There were twelve of them. They were all men.

"That's the snake dance," Mal informed her.

"The what?"

"Just watch."

The dancers laughed and cried out and bared their teeth, some of which were beautiful, some of which were gold and some of which were rotten. Ages ranged from twenty to fifty. They wore old black trousers and jeans, scruffy T-shirts and heavy shoes which they used to augment the thud of their stomping. A few of them had knives thrust into their belts. There were several excellent moustaches. ("It's a gun culture," Mal had explained as they'd passed another road sign that had been completely shot out. It was because of the War, of the Germans, he'd said with satisfaction. Cretans were fierce and brave.)

When they had executed a few turns the last dancer, the one at the end of the line, suddenly, as if at some secret signal, flipped his whole body over and kicked his heels in the air without letting go of the hand of his partner who looked as if, for a split second, he was supporting the other's entire weight. The audience clapped and cheered, the hero gave an exultant smile and the dancers continued on their endlessly weaving way.

Jane tried to imagine how she might describe their masculine hauteur in a travel piece: "Rough peacocks, unfettered male in all his archaic swagger, gender festivities in contemporary Crete, the Old Man is alive and well . . ."

"*Snake dance*," Mal repeated and took her hand. She nodded and smiled. There was an excited colour in her cheeks which shone through her freckles and her tan.

"It's very old. No one knows how old."

"Do you think it's related to the labyrinth and the Minotaur and all that?"

"Possibly."

"Look at that woman." Jane leaned close to him so as not to be overheard, though there was slight danger of it with the band at fever pitch. But Jane was always careful about other people's feelings. It was one of the things Mal loved her for, one he thought might eventually serve as an example to himself who judged more quickly and harshly and could find perverse pleasure in the leap to conclusions. They speculated in whispers about the woman's nationality. Malcolm thought German. Jane said Swedish then switched to American. They decided that the dewy smile was fixed especially on the tallest dancer, a swarthy, broad-shouldered man with a splendid moustache who, despite his size and his clumsy black boots, was surprisingly light on his feet. He was one of those with a knife in his belt. His hubris was impenetrable, and he betrayed no hint of any rapport with the besotted woman.

As was their habit, Malcolm and Jane quickly gave the pair nicknames. He was Boots and she was the Blue Woman.

Conversation was interrupted by a short fat man with a puffy face who tugged imploringly at Mal's sleeve. Mal flinched. He didn't like strangers touching him.

"Buy you drink," the man offered, his speech slurred but looking harmless enough.

"Thanks, but no thanks."

"C'mon, please, you Inglish, I think."

"No thank you, we're fine," Mal said firmly though with an afterthought smile.

"I been Ingland. Is good. You look friend called Mick. Nice man. Nice woman." He stared at Jane. "I buy you drink."

"Thank you," answered Jane and was about to add, "That would be lovely," when Mal interrupted.

"Sorry. We're having a private conversation."

"Why you not drink? Drink no good?"

"We like it very much," put in Jane. "And we like this place."

"You don't like." He leaned against Mal, his drink sloshing dangerously in his hand.

Their waiter appeared and escorted the man to his own table, smiling apologetically at his English customers.

"I come back, Mick," called the man, his boozy good-humour restored.

"Not too soon, baboon." Mal muttered then ordered another bottle of retsina and two rakis.

"I'm fine, Mal," said Jane gently.

"What's the matter?" He was suddenly petulant. "Don't you like going out? Don't you like having fun? You wanted me to bring you here."

"Of course. Of course I do."

"One retsina and two rakis," he ordered again. "And don't talk to me that way in front of the waiter."

"What way?" asked Jane, completely bewildered.

Mal didn't answer so she returned her attention to the woman. Again she traced the arc of her gaze to the tallest dancer. He wasn't handsome, having been cast in too coarse a mould, but his physique was impressive, and his magnetic field undeniably potent. Poor Blue Woman. Boots was indeed her *image de l'amour*.

"Am I boring you?" Mal suddenly asked.

Jane looked at him in amazement. The atmosphere between them had definitely soured. Of course drink did alter people's personalities, but was he becoming so regressive she'd better just say he never bored her? No, she quickly appraised. Still time to defuse him.

"Sorry," she smiled, determined to keep it light and save the evening. "Can't keep my eyes off the Blue Woman. She fascinates me."

"Is that why you wanted that little creep to join us?" he pressed, as if he hadn't heard her excuse.

The music stopped and the dancers dispersed to various tables where rounds of drinks awaited them. Jane and Mal watched to see

233

if the Blue Woman would be joined by Boots, but he had vanished.

"Probably doesn't want his mates to see him with her," said Mal, slurring his s's. "Probably picks her up later, screws her and goes home, wherever that is."

"How do you know he screws her?" Jane felt indignant for the Blue Woman and, in consequence, rashly returned the conversation to work.

"Helen told me Justin's having a prostate operation."

"I wouldn't believe anything Helen says — unless of course she has privileged information in this case. Anyway, why tell me now?"

"I've just remembered. I thought it would interest you."

"Well it doesn't." Mal maintained his sulk.

"There are worse people to work for, you know."

"He's a pillock."

"Just because he scrapped your article — "

"You always side with the landlord," he accused bitterly.

"That's unfair, Mal." Jane struggled to remain rational. "If it hadn't been for Justin, I wouldn't have got this freebie and we wouldn't be in Crete."

"Have you ever gone out with him?"

What she saw in his eyes shocked her: a wave of paranoia cohering, gathering force, cresting to break all over her. It was too late to advise him to stop drinking. Definitely too late.

"I know you, Mick. We meet London."

"Oh no," groaned Jane. The fat man was back.

Mal didn't answer. The fat man bent closer.

"Remember? Costa!" He smacked his chest. "Buy you drink."

"Go away," Mal enunciated and looked at Jane. "He thinks I'm *Irish*!"

"I been London. Is stupid place." The fat man was experiencing another mood swing.

"Sometimes, yes," Jane agreed as Mal kicked her under the table.

"Stupid people. Stupid place."

"Stop leaning on me!" Mal raised his voice. Customers at adjoining tables stared.

Again the waiter intervened, this time directing the man to the green door. "Mick," he cried, "Mick . . ."

"So long, Pork Chop," Mal smirked and ordered two more rakis.

"I don't want it," Jane insisted, but no one paid any attention.

More customers had come into the café, and the waiters flew about like the lizards Jane and Mal had seen running over the walls of their rented villa. The music grew wilder. The dancers were even more intoxicated. One of them slipped and fell to the floor, but his partners, without missing a beat, yanked him laughing to his feet. The audience cheered. Not one of them was a tourist. The Blue Woman sipped her rosé with the same entranced expression. She looked as though she were about to float up to the ceiling and hover there like a figure in a Chagall painting. No one joined her, and, aside from the waiters, no one spoke to her. Nor did anyone stare at her or accost her. Clearly they were used to her. She was a familiar fixture whose presence was taken for granted.

Mal signalled for more rakis, even though Jane's remained untouched. It was when she turned to say no thank you that she realized she and the Blue Woman were now the only females in the place. She also saw the stack of rifles behind the bar.

The waiter brought the rakis and this time Jane drank hers. As she did so Malcolm filled her glass with retsina. It was nearly toppled when someone stumbled against the table. Pork Chop again.

"Please leave him alone," pleaded Jane, but he took no notice. He seemed fixed on Mal the way the Blue Woman was fixed on Boots.

"Sorry, Mick."

"Piss off!" said Mal.

"I sorry. You sorry too, Mick?"

Mal turned his back. Pork Chop moved to the other side of the table in order to look in his eyes.

"I say sorry, man."

"Why don't you go boogie with the other yobs? Or won't they have you? Too fat and clumsy, huh? Too stunted."

"What mean stunted?"

"It means small but imperfectly formed."

"I no stunted, Mick, *you* stunted."

Mal rose to his full six feet. Pork Chop continued to glare at him.

"Don't like you. Stupid Inglish. Woman nice. You stupid."

Mal pushed him away hard, but he bounced back like a rubber beach toy. Everyone was watching. Mal seized his stained shirt front.

"Fuck off, you little Greek git, or I'll break your fucking jaw."

"Dazzle him with irony," drawled Jane.

For the third time the waiter attempted to rescue Mal and grabbed the fat man by the sleeve. But Mal maintained his grip on the shirt front. The waiter pulled. Mal hung on. Now Pork Chop looked worried. Jane was worried too.

Then the music stopped. At that exact moment he raised his voice and spewed a stream of Greek abuse at Mal. Apparently Pork Chop was a wit because everyone in the café screamed with laughter. Everyone except Mal and Jane and the Blue Woman who, also at that exact moment, tore her eyes from the dancers and looked at Malcolm and Jane. She looked at them as if she'd only just become aware of their presence, as if they came as a complete surprise to her, as if, for a split second, she really saw them.

Her mascara was melting in the heat, and her eyeliner and shadow had smeared calamitously, merging into two big circles so that she looked like a blue clown. Blue. The colour of the sea, the sea of love, of the Mediterranean that had seduced and desiccated her. What was her tragedy, Jane wondered in the midst of her own minor crisis. Where did she live and how? How did she get through the days waiting to be here — every night, here? Their eyes met. Then the woman assumed her smiling mask.

Jane blinked. That last raki was doing something strange to her vision. Loyally she placed her hand on Mal's arm, and the four of them stood like figures in a tableau vivant, two about to erupt, two attempting to prevent eruption, everyone else absorbed in the spectacle.

Once more Pork chop shouted in Greek. Once more they all laughed. Mal was sweating, red in his face and red in his brain. He felt rage, mortification. Most of all he felt his own physical strength. His blow would have landed squarely on Pork Chop's jaw if another waiter had not joined the first and extricated him from Mal's grip, tearing the fat pest's shirt in the process.

"Mick," he yelled as they dragged him away. "I love you. I give you shirt. Take shirt. Take everything. I love you, Mick." Then something more in Greek.

The customers were ecstatic.

Jane looked to see where they were taking Pork Chop, but the band started again and the dancers took to the floor, three more of them this time. She tried discreetly to make Mal sit down.

"It's all right now," she soothed.

Mal jerked his arm away. "You can stay if you want."

"Why would I want?" she began, astonished, but Mal was already moving to the door. His progress was halted by the dancers who were weaving their way towards his side of the room. Boots was now last in the line. As he passed Malcolm he executed the twist, the jump and the kick, leaping higher than any of the others had done. He glanced round in cool triumph, and it seemed to Jane that his eyes briefly caught those of the Blue Woman who looked as if she might swoon. Jane thought of the guns.

She pushed her way through the applauding clientele, more of whom were arriving by the minute. Mal was already in the street when she caught up with him.

"You don't have to leave, you know," he said, walking off.

"Of course I'm leaving. Why would I stay? How could I stay? I couldn't get home." It was the wrong thing to say.

"You wouldn't have to come home."

"Mal, that's crazy. I *want* to come home." Why did she feel like crying?

"Suit yourself." He was walking so fast now that she was half running to keep pace with him.

"Are you all right?" she asked.

"Look, if you want to go back, just say so."

He was impenetrable. She tried to take his hand, she tried to tell him how perverse he was being, she tried to keep pace with him. But he had finished speaking for the time being, so they went on in silence. The streets were empty except for the cats. They'd wandered very far from where they'd left the car and probably would have spent hours searching were it not for Mal's wonderful sense of direction. Even so, the shadows, the echoes, the real or imagined footsteps, the unfamiliar territory and the pursuing image of stacked rifles meant their Budget rent-a-car could not appear soon enough. It was only when they were at last unlocking its doors that Jane remembered Mal was too drunk to drive.

All the way to the villa she clung to the strap of her seat-belt, in spite of which she was hurled against the door whenever Mal took a corner at sixty. Glimpses of lovely familiar scenery flashed out of the night. She might never see it again, she thought. Yet she was unable to break Mal's implacable silence. For the sake of both their lives she decided to trust to his brilliant instincts and to the relative emptiness of the road. She stopped checking the speedometer. They approached the curve where the road swung sharply to the left and wound up a hill above a little bay. Lights in the taverna were still on. If only they could stop and sit somewhere quiet and safe. Just for a moment she thought of suggesting a drink, anything to make him stop driving, but already the taverna was out of sight. She must hang on to the end, her heart racing, her damp hands clenched. Barely slowing, Mal swerved into their dirt track, bumped violently towards the new white villas and pulled to a neat halt. He *was* a fantastic driver.

They sat in the dark, listening to their own breathing. Mal's came heavy and thick as it always did when he'd drunk too much. Jane's was quick and shallow. The lights in all but one of the apartments were out. It was their light. They'd forgotten as usual to turn it off. They felt trapped in the car, caught in the silence, each hoping and fearing that the other might speak. Jane knew for certain that Mal had not finished. He was letting the words rise slowly to the surface of his mind; they were gathering force, cresting to break all over her. Mal was picturing Jane's face in the café, happy and excited. She'd looked alive with curiosity and ready for anything.

"You'll end up just like her, you know."

"Like who?"

"The Blue Woman." He faced her. "You'll sit in cafés, wrinkled and ridiculous and menopausal. Watching dark men. Hoping to catch one with an empty slot."

"I don't find that a plausible scenario," she sniffed. But the thought frightened her. Once, she felt sure, the Blue Woman, too, had been "all shining".

"You'll sit there like her, imagining you're still beautiful. It'll take more and more retsinas to make you believe your own fantasy.

Especially when the time comes to go home alone. You'll be a sad case."

"Oh that's so corny." She was angry now. Then it struck her: they were having their first genuine row. And there was no stopping it. They had entered a war zone and must go on until one or the other surrendered.

"I know what you were doing back there." Mal abruptly switched gear, arguing like he drove.

"Really? Well, I certainly know what you're doing right here. You're trying to make me responsible for that farce in the café."

"What farce?"

"Your massive sense of humour failure. Your losing your rag at that pathetic little man. Your irresponsible driving."

"But I'm fine." He held up his hands, as if to indicate that he was unarmed. "Look at me. Do I look upset? It's you who's upset."

"Is that surprising when you've just behaved like a lunatic? Over nothing?"

"I thought I behaved quite well considering the way you tried to make a fool of me."

"Oh I see. I'm the Jezebel, I'm the traitor. I set it all up, laid a trap for you to fall into. I'm the villain and you're the victim."

"You're awfully young to be so bitter." Mal wore an expression of feigned concern. "It's a shame."

"Oh it's so cool now. If only it could have seen itself an hour ago . . ."

"Have you any idea how contorted your face is?"

". . . defending its threatened masculinity, its precious pride . . ."

"Will you please not shout. People are trying to sleep."

Mal had lured her into the argument then pretended to withdraw, leaving her alone with her conjured anger and nothing to confront. It was a sophisticated and original punishment for her equanimity.

But she had no intention of allowing him to abandon her this way. She would drag him back into the fray. It shouldn't be that hard now she'd got going.

She was right. In no time at all they'd returned to Boots and Pork Chop and the Blue Woman, using them like chess pieces to advance their attacks. People whose names they didn't even know. People who were only stereotypes.

"Why are we fighting over a few Greeks?" exclaimed Mal in desperation. She had him now.

"You're a proper English xenophobe, aren't you?"

They exchanged abuses until a light went on inside the villa and shone directly on to the bonnet of the car.

"One of those sleepers you're so concerned about."

"Now you've woken them. I hope you're satisfied."

"Deeply! Perfectly!"

The light had broken the malign spell that held them. They felt both observed and absurd. Escaping the car, they switched the scene of their drama to their apartment where they went on trying to shout in whispers until the tears ran over Mal's face and he collapsed and cried in earnest. Unwillingly at first, then with increasing tenderness, Jane held him. She was resentful of the Blue fate he had predicted for her, no doubt as an act of retribution for some pain centred in his own past; a revenge for accumulated, if unintentioned woundings. Blows not even delivered by herself but which he was returning by proxy. Yes, whatever has been suppressed must inevitably surface. And so she decided to believe this had all come about because he was unable to bear the thought of losing her, of their drifting apart, growing older. Hadn't he said as much many times? Wasn't that one of the reasons she liked him — his emotional vulnerability? Like everyone, he feared the future.

She failed to see how his tears came merely as the fitting climax to

241

an exhausting evening. In the end sleep, the great referee, called a ceasefire and they lay down on their hard, narrow, single tourist beds.

In the morning Mal had forgotten most of what had happened after they left Xania. He gave no thought to the events in the café. For him the characters in that play were already ceasing to exist. He woke like a child, primed for danger and discovery and fun. But first there was Jane. She would be reluctant, he knew, with the shreds of last night still clinging to her. Why did she tolerate such clinging when life was so patently short? Besides, she preferred sex at night. She would be tired still and damp with negative emotion. He would burn her awake.

He flung his whole weight down beside her and she groaned and pulled the sheet over her head. Nothing a little extra enthusiasm would not cure, though, so he bit her nipples and pried her legs apart and went at her for the next twenty minutes, during which time she felt sure the bed would split beneath them. Malcolm was not slight.

Now she was fully awake and wondering how soon she might safely shift him off her without denting his elation.

"That's the way Alexander the Great made love," he sighed, letting her breathe at last.

She hesitated before she spoke. Was he serious? "Raki and sex must have addled your brains," she started to say. Or perhaps "I thought you read history," might be more appropriate. Then he smiled at her. His curls were tight with sweat. His eyes were all attention, hers alone. She returned his smile. She'd wait until after lunch to remind him that Alexander the Great was gay.

THE SHOE GOD

I am not a violent woman," said Grace. "Oh, once when Anna was five I lost my temper and slapped her across the back of the leg, leaving a reddish-purple imprint of my hand. At the sight of it I burst into tears, and my daughter and I wept together in reconciliation. Apart from that regrettable incident I have harmed no one, man or beast. My voice has seldom been raised in anger. Yet here I sit, my victim helpless before me, poised to commit an act of surreal brutality."

Grace scanned her arsenal: hammer, handsaw, secateurs, electric drill, kitchen knife honed to a lethal brilliance. Where to start? She lifted the saw, but her hand shook so badly she dropped it and took a sip of the cold sherry she'd been drinking since the week her life had begun its downward spiral into chaos.

That week all she'd wanted was something a bit special to wear to Harold's Hallowe'en do. She and Gerald were seldom invited to parties, and she was looking forward to the occasion, though she knew her husband was not. She'd made a couple of preliminary forays along the High Street but had found nothing suitable for a woman of her age and Junoesque stature. It would have to be Long Tall Sally in Baker Street, she supposed. Then one lunchtime she passed Trotter's. As if guided by supernatural influences she entered, sank into a chair and removed her shoes with the customary relief.

"I've always had trouble with my feet," she informed the bored salesgirl.

With these words she had embarked upon the purchase of every pair of shoes in her life. She smiled hesitantly. "My feet are my Achilles' heel."

The salesgirl had no idea who Achilles might be, but she did betray a certain apprehension at the sight of what she was expected to fit. Grace's feet were a deathly white, nearly a handspan wide and a size eight. They looked like loaves of bread left too long to rise and bursting from the tops of their baking tins. Their corpulence should have provided cushioning akin to newly inflated car tyres, but for Grace a surfeit of flesh equalled a surfeit of sensitivity. She could not recall a day without discomfort save the few she'd spent in bed after the children were born. To walk was agony. She'd tried clogs, trainers, ballet slippers, plastic sandals, both Doctors — Marten and Scholl — wedgies, court shoes, plimsolls, flip-flops, Wellingtons and sheepskin moccasins. None of them eased her progress through a world in which other people went skimming past while she limped behind, able to concentrate on little besides placing one foot gingerly in front of the other. Podiatrists proved futile, and advancing middle age only refined the torture.

She was about to expand on her problem when she spied the monsters. There was no other word to describe their four-inch heels the thickness of broom handles, ankle straps like manacles and an aperture whose size and shape would mutilate the daintiest of big toes. She stared at their dubious charms. She could not look away. The monsters sang to her a siren song, scornful and flirtatious by turns. And the colour! Cerise, the girl called it, but it reminded Grace of the worst excesses of her mother's hybrid fuchsias. The shoes were impossible, outrageous.

"Let's try those," she said.

When they had fiddled and fumbled with the buckles, Grace rose tentively to her new height of six foot two inches and felt the easing of every metacarpal tension. Against all reason and experience the shoes were comfortable. She blurted her delight to the salesgirl.

"Suede gives," she answered cryptically.

Grace wore the monsters home, amazed at every step by the absence of pain. When she showed them to Gerald he did not comment on her extravagance but merely remarked that they were appropriate to the season. For the first time in years she did not have to soak her feet in Epsom salts.

She enjoyed the Hallowe'en party. Gerald did not. He was ill at ease with so much youth. (He'd been ill at ease with his own children.) And he mistrusted Harold. It was not only Harold's age that rankled but the fact that he and Grace were colleagues in an arcane world of computer terminals, tea-breaks and office gossip. Harold was twenty-six, a neat, slim redhead with a short beard carefully crafted to a point and a gold ring in his left ear. Harold was fond of Grace. She was a good sport with a sweet nature, eager for life but just a bit afraid of making a fool of herself.

"Actually, Hallowe'en is a survival of Samain, the beginning of the old Celtic winter," he informed Grace and Gerald who stood stiffly clutching his drink.

"*Really*?" Grace was charmed. Harold was always telling her such interesting things. He'd read widely, she was sure.

"What wonderful shoes!" he exclaimed. "Marvellously out of character."

Grace beamed. When she suggested to Gerald that they walk home, he looked at her as if she'd taken leave of her female senses.

She wore the shoes all weekend and to work on Monday. She hesitated at the door when Gerald glanced reprovingly over the top of the *Telegraph*.

"Comfort's more important than style," she said.

At work she seemed to sail in and out of Mr Berry's office, her characteristic (some said endearing) waddle replaced by smart clicks and hairpin turns. It was intoxicating simply to move from one point to another.

That afternoon she walked home via Shoreditch, as a result of which she and Gerald had supper rather later than their usual seven o'clock. He said nothing, though he checked his watch three times. She walked home the next day and the next. On Thursday she made a diversion through Victoria Park which she had not visited in a decade. This time Gerald complained.

"Right," she told herself, "no more diversions."

So on Friday she rose at six and walked *to* work not *from* it, reasoning that Mr Berry's displeasure would prove a more effective deterrent to wandering than Gerald's. For a few days the trick worked. But on the following Monday an urge she was reluctant to control sent her tangenting off Liverpool Street just within sight of the station. Nine-fifteen found her dawdling before the Roman walls. Grace had not been late for work for seven years. She was surprised at how unintimidated she was by Mr Berry's raised eyebrow. But for the next two days she kept her feet on a tight rein.

"Still, I am not made of stone," she sighed as at five-thirty in the morning she fastened the monsters' buckles, tiptoed down the stairs and set off for Leytonstone. The pleasure of the pavement beneath her confident soles made the dull light Atmospheric, the stale air City-Scented and the morning activities of drab Londoners Exotic. Her head reeled, her heart leapt. She was a great observing eye, seeing everything for the first time. Why was the city, for so long near-dead to her, suddenly resplendent?

She arrived only ten minutes late at the office, but that night Gerald went without supper.

"I was about to call the police," he said when she opened the door at ten-thirty.

"I went to Barnet," she confessed, then added, "to see Anna." It was the first time she had ever lied to Gerald.

She had a cold sherry and a bath but hardly slept, so eager was she to be up and walking at the crack of dawn.

"Today is my big day," she told herself as she reached Fleet Street. She was going to cross the river, and it would be an irrevocable step. Irrevocable — she said the word over and over again as she stared down into the grey water. It was moving so fast. She hadn't realized the tide came in that quickly. She understood its motiveless forward surge. She was at one with it. She saw how motion was the most divine of god-like attributes.

"God is a verb," she thought as she stood on Blackfriars Bridge and wept tears of joy.

Soon Grace was taking the Underground to the end of the line and walking from there: Theydon Bois, Elephant and Castle, Brixton, Morden, Edgware, West Ruislip. She missed three days of work and Gerald missed five consecutive suppers. And she knew now; she had to admit it: she was not in control. The wings on her feet were Another's. Something, some force, was using her to explore, driving her on like the tidal Thames, searching for an entrance or an exit, she didn't know which. And that power resided in the shoes. The monsters were haunted, she was forced to conclude.

Me, she thought, a rational person, not given to fantasies. This is the point I have come to. The point of no return.

She panicked. She would renounce the shoes, throw them away, limp through life as before. At least she would not be — she hesitated before the word — possessed. But one hour in trainers sent her back to the cupboard to which she had consigned the monsters. It was no good. They were just too comfortable.

The compulsion to walk, to travel the length and breadth of the city, was stronger than ever, and Grace surrendered to it without a blush. When, for four nights in a row, she arrived home after midnight, she found herself in an empty house.

"Have gone to Anna's," read Gerald's note. "If you're never here I don't see why I should be."

Grace shrugged, but when she removed the shoes she felt sad climbing into an empty bed.

The next morning Harold drew her aside and whispered that Mr Berry was dismayed at her chronic absenteeism. She'd used up all her holidays and her job was now in danger. He felt he must warn her. Grace smiled, thanked him politely and asked if he knew anything about ghosts.

Harold, who liked supplying information, explained that they weren't always spirits of the dead. Practitioners of Shinto, for instance (a most interesting Japanese religion; Grace had heard of it), believed that objects, animals or humans might become temporarily inhabited by a god, a sort of benign parasite who would eventually quit the premises to take up residence in another host. She resolved to bear this in mind.

She ate her meals "on the road" as she put it. That is, when she ate at all. As for sleep, she had little, for though she was exhausted, a pathological restlessness prevented her descent into the unconscious. Air was her element, air and light. Meanwhile her peripatetics became more ambitious. She even wandered to the fringes of Essex. And then one morning, hardly knowing how she'd got there, she stood before the ticket window at Euston Station, chequebook in hand.

"Single to Inverness." She smiled at the clerk and heard her own voice echo through a cavernous distance. She pictured herself in the cerise shoes, striding across the Highlands, the Orkneys, the Faeroes, the polar ice cap. Then she saw the ticket price flash red on the screen. She snatched back her Barclaycard just in time. It was then she knew that matters really had gone too far, and she thanked heaven she was not rich.

"Where to start?" she asked again, setting down her sherry and grasping the secateurs. Briskly she snipped off the buckles of the shoes which she had tied together in complicated knots in order to prevent or at least delay temptation. She hammered at the four-inch heels until they snapped lose and she tore them asunder. She inserted the kitchen knife beneath the sole and ripped it from the upper platform. Panting and sweating she set to work sawing each shoe in half. Finally she drove nails through the insteps where she guessed their hearts might be, like she'd seen in vampire movies.

The monsters lay in mangled segments before her, as ruined as her life. She finished the sherry, scooped up the carnage and deposited it in a plastic bag which she fastened with twine in the same elaborate knots. She took a taxi to Islington where she dropped the monsters' remains into the Grand Union Canal and watched them sink to a depth where they could do no more damage. She'd half expected to find a diabolical microchip in their innards, at least some tangible clue to the power they'd wielded over her for nearly a year. They might have gone up in a puff of smoke or expired with a mocking laugh. But there was nothing. Gods depart unseen. Like childhood, she thought, like love.

Gerald came home. At her request he telephoned Mr Berry and explained that his wife had suffered a minor nervous collapse. (Grace assumed he would interpret the euphemism as menopause.) She was now under a doctor's care and making an excellent recovery. Mr Berry expressed his relief.

"He says everyone misses you," Gerald reported as though he were telling her she'd got lipstick on her teeth.

Life resumed its tortoise pace. Grace stumbled to the bus stop and from the bus stop to the office and back again. Suppers were at seven. Anna and Gordon came for Sunday lunch. Every night she watched television with Gerald while she soaked her feet in Epsom salts. She'd had a narrow escape. Yet she missed her wanderings. She missed the morning light and sunsets on the river and anonymous suburban streets. She missed mobility. She regarded the cerise shoes and the spirit — whatever it was — that had so perversely animated them as dear departed friends and felt guilty at her role in their demise. She almost pined for the havoc they had raised and regretted her commitment to normalcy.

On Hallowe'en motion nostalgia overcame her and she paid a visit to Trotter's, just for old time's sake. The walk from the office was hell.

"Need any help?" chirped the new salesgirl.

Grace described the cerise shoes and asked if there were any in stock. Dangerous, but she must test herself. The girl remembered them but said they were part of last autumn's line. This year's styles were sleeker. Heels were low, straps were out, toes were square and the colour was paratroop green.

"You mean those shoes will never be made again?"

The salesgirl was frankly contemptuous of Grace's naivety.

"It's fashion, innit?" she snapped and turned to another customer.

Grace nodded, smiled and hobbled slowly off towards the handbag department.

BYE-BYE, BLACKBIRD

They'd come at last. She'd been waiting since noon, constantly pushing back the net curtains for a better view of the street. Now she laid aside her knitting with certainty. The rattle of Danny's motor was unmistakable. Once again Jennifer parted the curtains, watched the two of them separate with a kiss, lay their shoulders to the creaking doors and step out on to the pavement. Their vapour trails swirled and evaporated in the freezing air. It was three o'clock, and already the moon was rising.

She opened the front door, folding her arms to stop herself shivering. They were saying hello to Mr Flax, who was fussing as usual with his spare front garden. They were laughing. What could anyone find to laugh about with Mr Flax? But Megan and Danny laughed easily. They seemed to take pleasure in everything.

When Danny had first come, the neighbours stared. Jennifer had sensed that slight displacement of air that is the breath of hostility. Now they waved and helloed as if Danny had grown up in Dartwood, as if they'd known him all his life. He was such a charming young man; everyone was so fond of Megan. She strode up the path, holding his hand within her bright glove. She wore a black dress to her ankles, a vest sagging with pockets and what looked to Jennifer like a pair of old farmer's boots. Hatless, she pushed a long strand of golden hair back from her face. She was a beautiful mess and just too good to be true.

Once Jennifer had worried. Their relationship had seemed such a risk. But it wasn't a problem now. Most of the time she didn't think about the difference. She regarded them as very brave. Perhaps it was just as well, though, that Hugh wasn't alive.

"Hello, Mummy." Megan gave her a long hard hug. A proper hug. Her youngest was back in the house where she'd grown up, and everything that had seemed mean and shabby about it was suddenly fresh and alight, as if it held nothing but happy memories. Jennifer and Hugh had intended to sell it once all the children had left. They'd paid off their mortgage. They could move closer to the sea they both loved. Then the housing market had collapsed, and Hugh had quietly died, and Jennifer found herself alone at 26 Chester Terrace. Not what she'd wanted, and not what she'd planned. Still, she consoled herself with the thought of the children and of keeping a continuity for them; sustaining the familiar space, the place they could always come to. But the only one of the four to avail herself much was Megan.

She and Danny didn't seem to find it dreary. Quite the reverse. Jennifer had once visited the shambolic house in Finchley which they shared with four other people. No wonder Megan was glad to come home to a little order and cleanliness. That, or she simply loved her mother. Jennifer basked in the thought.

The tea table had been laid since twelve-thirty. She saw them smile at each other, amused by her old-fashioned fussiness, she supposed. But then she realized they were only anticipating the delights of sweet tea and cake. They were very simple, really.

When she entered with the Dundee cake (she had baked it the night before in case anything went wrong with the oven at the last minute) she found Danny inspecting one of her pictures. Jennifer "painted sometimes" and went to Mrs Dimsdale's weekly classes at the village hall.

"This isn't a new one, is it, Jenny?" He leaned forward to look, his hands on his hips.

"No, it's not. And you're very observant." She stood holding the cake. "I did it a couple of years ago. I don't really paint like that any more, but I wanted to see it again. I don't know why."

"Before my time," he smiled, as if, before him, there was no time. "It's good," he concluded. "I like it. It's a little like Lowry."

"All amateurs paint like Lowry," she laughed.

She studied him as he took his place beside Megan. His short dreadlocks were plump and shiny, expertly done. They looked to her like a nest of stylish tarantulas. She loved the smoothness of his skin and his sweet smile, which her conditioning could not help but interpret as exotic and Caribbean.

"Hurry up with the cake, Mum, we're ravenous."

They were beside each other on the couch. Jennifer sat opposite, the better to watch them. When should she tell Megan? Best wait for a quiet moment. She felt too shy to deliver her news in front of Danny.

"Delicious," he said.

"Delicious," echoed Megan, with her mouth full, spraying a storm of crumbs across the table, so that she laughed and sprayed more. Megan was the only one of Jennifer's children to eat Dundee cake now. The others were on diets or had given up white sugar and no longer wanted nursery treats. But Megan seemed to have no strictures. She forbade herself nothing. Jennifer noted the way she relished the cake. Suddenly she felt afraid for her daughter.

"Oh God!" Megan exclaimed, brushing crumbs from Danny's jeans all over the rug, "we forgot the present."

"Oh yeah!" He struck his forehead.

"Is it in the car, I hope?"

"Must be. I'll go."

Here was Jennifer's opportunity. A moment alone with her daughter.

"No, I'll come with you."

"What's going on?" Jennifer laughed.

"Never mind." Megan wagged her finger in mock reproof, and they went out. They could not be separated.

"There!" Megan triumphantly placed a crumpled paper bag on the table and gave her mother a loud kiss.

"What's this?" Jennifer peered inside and drew out something that looked like a bright orange tomato.

"They're persimmons. Aren't they gorgeous? Don't you love them?"

Jennifer removed three more. "I — I've never tasted a persimmon."

"Well, you'll taste one now." Megan produced a plate. "We eat them all the time." She looked at Danny as though this were a prize-winning achievement. Jennifer continued to stare at the persimmon. "Go *on*, Mum. It'll be a new sensation. You'll like it. You've got developed tastes."

"Have I?"

"Of *course* you have."

"But I'm not hungry, darling." It was true. "I'll try one later with my tea. Meanwhile I'll just enjoy looking at them. My goodness, they certainly are exotic. I don't think I've ever seen such a colour."

"We knew you'd appreciate it."

"They leave a funny taste in your mouth," Danny informed her, "but you get used to it."

"I'm sure I will. Thank you both so much for thinking of me." She was touched but deeply wary of the persimmons and their funny aftertaste.

"Don't you like them?" Megan pouted. "You're not going to be a fusty old Brit, are you, Mum?"

"Don't put pressure, girl." Danny gently shook her shoulder. "People do things when they're ready."

"Thank you, dear." How kind he was, thought Jennifer.

Should I tell them both, she wondered. Tell them now? Make a little joke of it: your mother's human after all, that sort of thing.

"So what's the news, Mum?" As if her daughter had read her thoughts. Was her state that obvious? Megan bounced herself into a more comfortable position. They'd called her Tigger when she was a child.

"Oh," Jennifer touched her greying curls, "a bit of painting. My little job at Tesco's. Everyone squabbling about Sunday trading. And the birds come. My special friends, you know," she confided to Danny who nodded sympathetically. "I feed them and in return they keep me entertained. It's a good arrangement."

The cat entered, opening the door with a practised paw.

"And of course there's Mimi to keep me on my toes." Mimi jumped into her lap and purred noisily.

"No conflict of interest there?" Danny grinned.

"You always say the same things, Mum," Megan chided.

"That's because nothing changes." (Except for one thing. The most important thing. Why not tell them? But, as always, their news seemed so much more exciting and interesting. She was thrilled when they shared their information and their trials and their gossip with her.) "I don't lead a hectic London life like you two. The pace, as you know, is slow in Hampshire."

Everyone, they told her, was outraged about the cuts in student grants. There had been protests and demos all over the country. They were fed up with their Student Union and were agitating for direct action. Their newly formed group was planning to occupy the library. They complained of the general apathy, amazed that people could just submit while the government attacked their lives. And all the while his brown hand fondled her ear, and she drew patterns with her fingernail on his knee.

Jennifer agreed, yet she felt worried for them, frightened of the punishments inevitably administered for rebellion and bravery. Hugh would not have approved. Neither, probably, would Bill.

Yet she wanted him to meet them. Silly, she knew, a delusion. Yet she couldn't help it. She wanted to show him her treasure, her shining, best girl and her lovely young man. And what would he think when he saw them? Would it make any difference? The question bothered her.

Megan and Danny had moved on to the subject of a dream machine by which they were very intrigued.

"A guy in Hull's done years of research on it," Danny enthused. "The machine registers your REMs and gives you a tiny shock to remind you you're dreaming. So you're awake and asleep at the same time."

"Really?" What were REMs?

"When you're in this lucid state you can start to control your dreams. It can stop recurring nightmares, let you dream whatever you want."

"Perfect dreams."

"Yeah."

They fantasized about getting involved in the programme. They wanted to register for the experiments and develop the capacity to direct the workings of their unconscious. Why, Jennifer wanted to ask, when all they'd choose to dream about was each other.

"But perhaps it's better just to let dreams happen," she suggested. "How else will you know what's really going on inside yourself?"

They found it difficult to understand such passivity.

Mimi flirted and whined and clawed the couch. She wanted her tea, and soon.

"Mimi doesn't understand passivity either." Danny grinned.

She followed Jennifer to the kitchen, flicking her great grey tail.

Standing by the worktop, cranking the old wall-attached tin opener that made a grinding sound, Jennifer could see into the sitting room through the partially opened door. Megan and Danny were kissing. His hand was inside her black dress. Jennifer stopped turning.

She waited for what seemed an appropriate length of time before walking in on them. They separated without embarrassment and smiled at her. Megan, who was holding Danny's hand, suddenly held his palm upwards and thrust it towards Jennifer.

"Look," she commanded sweetly, "isn't it amazing? Look at the contrast." She flipped the hand over then back again. "The pink inside and the brown outside. It's so lovely. And the lines" — she traced them — "so dark, you can see every little crease. Aren't they wonderful, Mum?"

Danny laughed.

"And his nose," she went on, stroking it with the tip of her finger. "Look. It's just the right combination of elements: hooked like Indian, splayed like black, thin like white. It's just so perfect. All of him is just perfect. Don't you think he's beautiful, Mum?"

Jennifer hesitated. Her daughter's candour could be so unnerving. How had she managed to produce such a child?

"Yes, I do," she answered softly.

After they had departed with numerous hugs and endearments, Jennifer stood by the dining-room window watching the starlings and blackbirds and pigeons and sparrows finishing up the bread she'd scattered for them the day before. She liked to see them bicker and prance about on the grass, lifting off simultaneously at the first hint of danger. She was especially fond of the blackbirds — so common and so uncommonly gifted. The way each one practised its little aria enchanted her, choosing its own special spot at the end of the day, working out variations on its particular theme from television aerials and garden sheds and the top branches of the apple trees. It wasn't yet time for them to sing, but, come April, Jennifer would stand in her small garden and whistle back to them their unique melodies and they would answer her with the same musical phrases. It seemed such a privilege, this allowed participation in their mysteries. She smiled at how little it took to please her. If she let herself, she could stand for hours like this, just looking. (She wondered what the neighbours made of such idleness. Did they see her alone in semi-darkness and think poor thing, she has nothing to do, no one to care for, all fledglings flown the nest. She is only waiting for teatime when she will turn on the news and open herself a tin of Scotch broth.) The starlings, as usual, were making off with the best bits. Sometimes — a great occasion — a pair of jays visited. It had been a week since Bill had phoned her.

She thought of Megan and Danny, clattering happily along in that antiquated car whose heater sometimes worked and sometimes didn't. What would have been the point of telling them? What would she have said, after all: "I have a man who isn't beautiful and never touches me and yet I want him"? She'd been haunted lately by something one of the children's friends had said long ago. It must have been during Charles's A levels, but even then the remark had struck her. He'd brought a boy home to do some revising, and she'd overheard a snatch of their conversation:

"My Mum's fifty years old, and she thinks she's in love!" The contempt with which that child had spoken. And she, at fifty-six, was nurturing a stupid dream of middle-aged passion with an unsuitable man, a man many would call unworthy of her. Thank heavens she hadn't told the children. It would have been utterly premature. She'd been mad, carried away by their sexiness and their goodness.

The phone rang and she went to answer, much faster than she had intended, but it was only a woman selling double glazing. No, said Jennifer. She was sorry. She couldn't afford it just now. Thank you for calling. She began to do the washing up. (Danny had offered, but she'd forbidden him.)

Bill had joined the painting class six months ago. After a few weeks Jennifer found that he always sat next to her. They had similar problems with perspective and laughed over their mutual disability. One night Jennifer boldly confessed that she often did paintings with no perspective at all. Like in the Middle Ages. Flat as a pancake. "But don't tell Mrs Dimsdale," she cautioned. He said he'd suspected her all along of secret vices, and they'd giggled and gone for a coffee.

He was married but separated, he told her forthrightly. He had three children. Attachments remained strong. Being independent was hard but good. Did she find that too? No, she said, she didn't. Hugh was gone. Except for Megan, she hardly saw her children. What was good about that?

Coffee led to suppers, but not, as yet, to sex. He'd kissed her a few times. She'd seen her reflection in his glasses, smelled his acidic aftershave and whatever it was he used to flatten his straight grey hair. His kiss was hard and not at all sensual, administered with lips that neither yielded nor explored. Not a kiss to warm her to life. Still, she wanted more. Just stubbornly wanted more. It had been so long since a man had held and kissed her. Somehow his kisses affirmed her.

They talked of going on holiday together. She was blindly,

263

stupidly excited. But he began to have bad moods. She caught the scent of alcohol on him, and he grew unattractive, his face blotchy and his skin pale. He didn't kiss her when he was like that. His thoughts were elsewhere. There was something wrong with Bill. And still she wanted him.

Last week he had not turned up at the painting class. Of course he might be down with flu, or his children might be ill. Or even his wife. Jennifer tried never to think of Bill's wife. Maybe he'd gone back to her. She told herself she didn't mind so long as he phoned. They could work out an arrangement, even if it involved a few lies. That was the way her mind had started working. And there were still the painting classes. But he might have dropped them altogether. Her heart missed a beat at the possibility.

The afternoon was nearly over. She'd forgotten to turn on the lights, and the house was filling with darkness like water rising in a tank. How long had she been standing here at the sink, washing the persimmons? She placed them in a dark-green bowl, intending them for décor rather than consumption. Perhaps in a day or two she might take a small exploratory bite. Meanwhile they would grace the coffee table with their malevolent glow. She saw that the last of the day would be beautiful, with a delicate mist settling over the houses and the sky turning to pink. The white moon looked down, watching the world as she watched the garden.

Mimi was sitting on the brick wall. She sat absolutely still, her ears pricked, all quaint attention like a cat in a Chinese scroll painting. Mimi was lovely, grey and fat. Jennifer thought she might try to draw her in that very pose. What, she wondered, could be the object of such innocent but fixed enquiry. Then, quicker than a breath, Mimi disappeared over the wall, only to reappear with a male blackbird between her teeth.

"Mimi, Mimi," Jennifer cried, and raced for the back door. As she ran into the garden, Mimi shot past her and through the open door into the house, her jaws clamped on the vainly struggling bird. She was determined to enjoy its torture and slow death in comfortable surroundings. Jennifer followed her. How could such an overweight cat be so nimble? Indoors she was just in time to see Mimi reach the top of the stairs and make a sharp right into her bedroom, her preferred spot for leaving tokens of esteem, the majority of them still twitching.

"No," shrieked Jennifer, "no!" Somehow she must save the blackbird, save her friend. She went down on her hands and knees to reach Mimi who sat under the bed, bunched over her prey. Just as Jennifer was about to grab her velvet collar, she sped out the door and back down the stairs. Again Jennifer ran after her, the blood pounding in her temples. My God, I shall have a stroke, she thought. The house was so dark now that it was difficult to follow the cat's wicked progress. Jennifer switched on the hall light.

She realized she'd better change her tack. She must get Mimi into a room, lock the door and corner her, whatever the consequences for her hands and arms. Oh why had the perverse beast waited until Megan and Danny had gone? She needed help, another person to head the cat off and herd her into a small room where she could find no hiding place. Mimi turned and bolted again for the stairs and Jennifer's bedroom. Hot and panting, Jennifer followed her, resolved this time that she would not escape. In her haste she banged against the coffee table, hurting her thigh. She thought she heard the persimmons tumble to the floor, but she did not stop to investigate.

She slammed the bedroom door and switched on the light. She stalked Mimi to the right and to the left, reading in her eyes defiance mixed with incomprehension. Finally she managed to grab her, quite brutally, but it could not be helped, tried to extricate the bird from her pet's grasp, but ended, in desperation, by wrenching it free in a manner which, she realized with horror, had probably compounded its injuries.

On the landing, Jennifer held the trembling creature in her hands.

"Oh you," she whispered, "poor you. I'm so sorry, I'm so sorry. What should I do?" Trembling herself, she assessed the damage. Perhaps it was only stunned. Meanwhile Mimi whined in desolation and scratched at the bedroom door. I must get him out of here, Jennifer thought. Outside where he can hide and recover. I must return him to nature.

She carried him to the back garden. Thin clouds covered the moon, but there was still enough light to see. "Life," she prayed, "don't leave him." She intended to release the blackbird between the viburnum and the cotoneaster whose branches stretched low over the grass. There it could find immediate shelter. She kissed the tiny head. Between her fingers the bird's heart still beat.

"Goodbye," she murmured, feeling not at all ridiculous. "Good luck. God bless you."

She set down the blackbird. It hesitated then hopped with difficulty towards the cotoneaster. Jennifer thought of Megan and Danny and the long drive still before them. She thought of narrow slippery Cornwall lanes with their high hedges and poor visibility.

Suddenly, as if by teleportation, a ginger tom appeared on the top of the fence, his eyes bright with malice. How could he know that so vulnerable a creature had just been turned loose as if for his personal gourmandizing?

"Get out!" she shouted, and he fled. But she knew that some-where near by he'd be waiting. And she realized that, in her panic, she had done everything wrong.

She knew what to do, she *knew*. She should have wrapped the bird in a towel and put it in the airing cupboard, bathed its beak in sugar water — what had she been thinking of? She subscribed to Bird Aid. She'd rung them before in similar emergencies. Usually they referred her to that nice man Barry at the garage who'd been so helpful. She'd never actually met Barry, only spoken to him on the telephone, but his voice was so — but what had she been *thinking*? Her head had been all muddled with Bill and Danny and persimmons . . . This was entirely her fault. She must retrieve the bird and follow the correct procedures this time. She might still save him, but she'd have to act fast, and it was nearly dark.

Ignoring her tights and skirt, Jennifer dropped to her hands and knees and crawled through the cave-like opening between the viburnum and the cotoneaster. Its shape and the blackness behind made it seem like an entrance to the underworld. She could hear the bird fluttering miserably and imagined cruel eyes that could penetrate the night, huge paws pouncing with ease upon the stricken victim. She inched forward, her hands and knees covered with mud, her tights torn, shivering in her thin cardigan. From the corner of her eye she could just see him, his wing hanging limp. Unless she could reach him quickly he stood no chance of survival. It might be too late anyway. Why interfere? Why not let him die in nature? But no, not yet. She grabbed for him and he hopped away, but not far. He was weakening. As she tried again she stretched, lost her balance and fell.

Beneath her the ground was cold and wet, strewn with small stones and twigs that dug into her breasts and stomach. Alone, shivering in the dark with a dying animal, she could feel the indiscriminate force of gravity. It pulled on her prostrate body, as though wanting to drag them both down into the tomb of the earth, the tomb over which she walked, unthinking, each day of her life. She was afraid. Why had Megan and Danny gone and left her like this?

Somewhere a telephone rang, its sound trajectory cutting the air like a bullet. Jennifer could not tell if it was her phone or Mr Flax's. It rang and rang. Perhaps it was her phone, but she knew it would not be the call she waited for because that call would never come.

Away from home, in maximum danger in the darkness of night, the bird waited for death. Jennifer, flat on her stomach, stretched to her full length, groping one way then another, determined to snatch him back. "Fuck," she whispered. "Fuck it." She nearly had him, but he moved an inch or two beyond her grasp and out of sight completely. The phone stopped ringing. She squirmed forward, feeling her way, straining through blackness to reach the black bird.

BEYOND BARKING

Does that gate fasten securely?"

"It does, my dear."

"Double lock on the door?"

"Check."

"How about the restrainer?"

"Here we are." Nurse McHarg patted the garment that lay neatly folded and out of sight in the drawer.

"Pine's obviously expecting a spot of bother." Something in Nurse Tupper's voice told Nurse McHarg that she rather looked forward to the bother. Tupper was easily bored.

"This is his last chance, poor old thing. Of course no one's saying that, but any more nonsense and it's the hospice and the nuns for Mr Wilberforce."

"Or else those daughters."

"They look a vicious lot."

"Termagants. Anyway," snapped Nurse Tupper, "we'd better get on. Commode tidy?"

"It is."

"Drugs in the fridge?"

"Yup."

"OK, Margaret, we're ready to rock."

Tina Tupper and Margaret McHarg were ready. They'd had a briefing that morning from Dr Pine. There was nothing for them to worry about since, as Pine never tired of repeating, Shady Meadows was better equipped, better staffed, better trained, better funded, and better natured than any of the competition. When it came to intractable patient care, it was state-of-the-art and handled crackpots that other retirement homes wouldn't touch. The words "hopeless case" were never uttered within its walls. He'd had them banned, and stiff fines were imposed on any member of staff who slipped up and spoke them within his hearing or that of his spies.

Dr Pine felt confident when assuring anxious and exhausted relatives that, yes, Shady Meadows could guarantee them the peace and freedom they craved and that they richly deserved. Their relief, gratitude and forthcoming cheques were very gratifying to Dr Pine. He had no doubts about his establishment's ability to deal with the most hardened offenders.

Mr Wilberforce's three daughters had wept and wrung their hands and cleaned their spectacles and dabbed with lacy handkerchiefs at their silk blouses. They'd begged him not to refuse.

"Daddy's a sweet man, really. He has his little ways, but he's never harmed a soul. You should have known him as he used to be. Such charm, such — "

"We know he upset a few people at those other places, but it wasn't his fault," pleaded Mrs Partridge. "We hope you won't hold a few misdemeanours against him. I'm sure if they'd been keeping a proper eye on him — "

"Besides," Mrs Delisle stabbed out her cigarette, "you couldn't call those women exactly blameless. It takes two, you know."

"Not to urinate on a clivia, Mrs Delisle." Pine frowned at Henry Wilberforce's copious notes. He was keeping the women in suspense, exercising his power a little.

"Oh well, a *clivia* . . ." Mrs Delisle waved a new cigarette dismissively. She was not as easily intimidated as her sisters.

He cleared his throat. "The clivia happened to be a patient's ninetieth birthday present. Mrs Goswell was having a party, and it seems your father's behaviour rather spoilt things."

That shut her up.

Mrs Pridell then caved in completely. "We know he's been bad," she sobbed. She had the right attitude.

"Now, now," soothed the good doctor, "at Shady Meadows, there is no such thing as a hopeless case. Here we have tamed the wildest. With gentleness, patience." (And a lot of money.) Dr Pine smiled benevolently. "We've developed unique methods of caring for the high-spirited elderly."

Their faces lit up. They were worn out, exhausted, on the brink of despair, ready to pay or promise anything.

"And that is because" — he folded his hands carefully and rested them on the desk, the women leaned towards him — "Shady Meadows is better equipped, better staffed, better trained . . ."

As always, Dr Pine was correct. Shady Meadows was ready. Shady Meadows was prepared. Even for Henry Wilberforce and his little ways.

The Duchess was in a snit. For the second time Mustafa had failed to bring her the new issue of *Cosmopolitan*. She'd particularly wanted to read the article on fellatio and was so frustrated she'd nearly snapped at him. Thank God she'd caught herself in time. But what a miserable excuse to say they were sold out. *Sold out*? When the boy knew quite well no one else in Potty Park ever read *Cosmopolitan*. The Wingeing Winnies went for *Woman's Own* and the Prancing Percies took the *Telegraph*. She'd had to settle for *Hello* but ended by hurling it across the room. Got a lecture from McHarg for that little display.

Anyway, screw the collaborationists, the important thing was not to have offended Mustafa; not when he kept her supplied with something far more vital than a magazine. She felt under the mattress. It was there. She already knew it was there. She just enjoyed the sense of physical verification. It was about as physical as one ever got here in Crappy Corner. She looked at her twisted hand then stuck it under the blanket, out of sight. With the other hand she fondled her nipple. Not a lot of response. But she had to admit, though she'd never tell anyone except maybe Ada, that it felt damned and surprisingly good to have surrendered the bra at last. The tears began. She wished they wouldn't, but she could not control them. What if McHarg saw? She knew what the result would be. And here she lay helpless, prey to unsolicited visits from The Creature. Please God, keep that damned animal away from me. Bring another Tinky into my life. I'm just a poor old woman who wants to make love one more time and can't even get hold of a dirty magazine any other female in the country can lay her hands on as easily as a box of Tampax or a dozen eggs.

She stopped crying. Why did they think she was depressed? She wasn't depressed, she was furious.

She hated Shady Meadows. She hated being trapped in this room with its Laura Ashley-type wallpaper, bed-bound by arthritis, surrounded by a bunch of decaying monetarists and Home County toadies. She feared she was fading into the pastel environment. She longed for some fuchsia, a little gamboge. Those touches of bad taste that make a house a home. She wasn't paying for pastels.

The Duchess cursed the night she'd let May Mahoney drag her off to the Mecca Bingo. Who could have predicted they'd win on that full house? They'd split the take — £18,000 each. Fuck money. Without money she'd now be tucked up in a nice crumbling NHS establishment. Of course the place would be a wreck. But who'd care if it hadn't been decorated since 1963? At least she'd be with real people (by whom she meant Londoners), people with a sense of humour who'd worked and got by on their wits like she had. There'd be someone to talk to, crack a few naughty jokes with. But here, locked up in Potty Park with the W.W.s and the P.P.s? Dream on, Florence. Mustafa, who could barely speak English, was better company than they were. At least he didn't have one of those poncey accents. Of course neither did Tupper nor Rawlings nor McHarg, but they were collaborationists. Hang on, wasn't the word collaborator? She couldn't recall. Her memory was unravelling, it was frightening. She confused her suffixes all the time. Suffixes, that's what they were called. Suf-fix. She clung to the word like a liferaft. These days no one knew what a suffix was. Bet McHarg didn't know. Or Ada or Mustafa or the Home Bodies. Her education, what she'd had of it, must have been OK after all.

Why, why had she ever let May talk her into that private patients' plan? She could have spent the money on make-up and shoes and trips to Mexico. Even a toy boy if the price was right. Why not? She'd at least have something to remember as she sat in her rusting bed in her curtained cubicle in a draughty ward with people who might be rotting but with whom you could carry on a decent conversation and sneak off for a fag.

"You'll have a nice place," May had argued. "Good care with a room to yourself and all your nice things — the photos of you and Max and Tinky and the group, your old costumes, the stuffed flamingo. Be lovely."

The Duchess looked around at the room she now had to herself. To herself alone. Why had she committed the one "sensible" act of her life? And May, where was May? In a canister in Braintree. Fat lot of good the £18,000 was doing her there. Her son-in-law had spent it on putting in a pool. Tore up an entire garden for a bloody swimming pool you can't use but three days a year in this dumpsville of a country. Christ, the pretension of it all. She reached under the mattress and removed the bottle. Oh it was Upminster. Totally and completely Upminster.

Deirdre's toenails clicked on the gleaming linoleum. She ambled placidly along the corridor, checking for dust. Everything seemed shipshape. Mr Bigsby struggled past on his walking frame and stopped to stroke her head. She gave him a look that mixed affection, understanding, encouragement and humility, an all-purpose look that she'd entirely perfected. In a way it came naturally because of her breeding. But you had to work at these things too. Deirdre had a repertoire of expressions and bestowed each one according to what she deduced to be the requirements of the sufferer. Instincts did make life a good deal easier, she reflected. But not her next assignment. Florence Fox was a real challenge, even for a person who'd come tops at the training centre. She hadn't yet discovered that magic look, the one that would at last elicit a positive response. Perhaps if she paraded around with her blanket between her teeth. That never failed to raise a laugh, even among the Terminals. It was worth a try. She congratulated herself on possessing infinite patience and, despite her exquisite sensibilities, a thick skin. One day the Duchess would succumb. For the moment, however . . .

Deirdre pushed open the door of Room 25 and got the reception she had anticipated.

"Get out!" shrieked the Duchess and hurled half a bread roll. "Keep your distance, you flea-bitten cur!" The bread roll missed and bounced off the television. Deirdre knew it would. The old girl's eyesight had deteriorated over the past few months. And her reactions were slowing down. Normally she'd have whipped that bottle out of sight so quickly that only the sharpest eye could detect it. Only Deirdre's eye, large and golden brown.

She turned those eyes on the fearsome Mrs Fox. She was trying out a new tactic. She waddled to the bed, placed her chin on the counterpane and gazed at the Duchess with a look of supplication to which she added half a gram — no more, no less — of pity. She was still trying for the right combination.

"Come to gloat, have we?" snarled the Duchess. Deirdre sighed.

"Getting off on other people's misery is sick. Anyway, I'm Lab-proof."

No one, thought Deirdre, is Lab-proof.

"I know you're supposed to be therapy. Potty Park's Secret Weapon. Well, what bloody good are you if you can't crank my bed up or get me some ice? You swan around here getting fatter and fatter. Look at your stomach, it's practically dragging on the floor."

She was a fine one to talk.

"I'd be ashamed of a gut like that. Why don't they put you on diet dog food? Or let Pine pay for a tummy tuck. He's rich enough."

Deirdre continued to gaze at her.

"You think you're clever just because you had twelve children. Well, let me tell you, anyone can breed. And I hear you can't even do that any more." She was losing her train of thought. Just a couple of sips was enough to do it these days. She groped for the accusation she wanted. Deirdre tried a bit of tail wagging. Sometimes the old tricks were the best.

"Stop that damned carpet-beating. It gives me a headache. She was silent for a minute. "What makes you or them think you're qualified to understand an artist? That wally Dr Pine has this idea that you can be a substitute for an interest in life. Well, my only interest in life is under the mattress. So piss off, you parasite!"

Deirdre sat and wagged.

The Duchess hauled herself to the side of the bed and with great effort brought her face close to the dog's. She reached down and lifted the black velvet flap.

"I'm serious!" she shouted into the sensitive ear.

She was very trying, that Mrs Fox. Still, if she derived satisfaction from abusing her, that was all right too. It was a kind of response. But the remarks about her figure were uncalled for. She didn't realize — most humans didn't — that it was precisely her figure, especially her waddling bottom, that was the source of a Labrador's universal appeal. They were the most desirable mates, the sex-objects of the canine world. Even at her age, visits to the park could still produce the odd annoyance: Jack Russells, Yorkies, setters. Size didn't seem to matter. It was very stressful, even for someone as well balanced and beautifully brought up as herself.

With a pang of pride, she thought of her children, equally top-drawer. Yes, she was fulfilled. With one glaring exception, her patients adored her. She'd risen to the top of a very demanding profession. Yes, women were the great communicators. If only her mother were alive to share in her success.

Deirdre made her way to Room 30. Next assignment: Miss Parish.

They got him in fast. Rawlings was an expert in quick manoeuvres that skirted goodbyes. Saved everyone a lot of heartache. After all, most relations couldn't wait to get home and celebrate their liberation from geriatric hell. Especially those three daughters who'd probably inherit a fortune when the old boy snuffed it. They wanted to be good to him, just in case, but they wanted him out of their hair. Best put Deirdre in with him straight away. Settle him down. (The theory was that the Secret Weapon not only saved the nurses' energies but cut down on medical expenses. It had worked pretty well so far. Pine was pleased.)

Henny sat on the bed in his new eau-de-Nil room. He wore a tweed suit that had grown too big for him, a green waistcoat, a mustard-coloured shirt and a Paisley tie. His collar sat loose around a neck like a withered cabbage stalk. He'd once been a well-dressed man, and his youngest daughter struggled to maintain the illusion.

He placed his spotted hands on his narrow thighs. He was thinking — he did not know why; it was unusual — of his wife. He saw the two of them, whiskies in hand, standing in the long front window, gazing at the lawn that sloped down to a lazy stream. It was summer, and the light was tender and rosy.

"Wonderful," he heard himself say, "how these summer evenings seem to go on and on for ever."

Edwina looked at him hard. "That's the *dawn*, Henny," she said, disgusted.

The news had rather startled him, but he soon recovered himself. "Oh well," he'd said, "not to worry."

"Not to worry," he said aloud. "not . . . to . . . worry . . ."

"That's the spirit," chirped Rawlings. This was encouraging. Henny hardly ever spoke.

It occurred to him that his wife might be dead. Was she? He couldn't remember. Who could tell him? He watched the strange woman who was opening suitcases and putting underwear and pyjamas into drawers. He looked around for his wife but could not see her. She'd disappeared among the plants, fed up with him. Who wouldn't be? Oh well. He reached for the whisky he'd put down by the oleander twenty years ago. His hand closed on nothing. He looked on the floor. An image crossed his retinas; an impulse propelled his arm. His hand closed on Nurse Rawlings's ankle.

"Uh-uh-*uh*!" she scolded. "That sort of behaviour is not encouraged here, Mr Wilberforce."

Henny blinked at her, switched his gaze to the wall, smiled

sweetly at a print of the Severn Bridge. "No nonsense, or it's the Romper Room for you, my lad. But we'll forget it for now, shall we?" She held out her hand which he did not take. "Come along, Mr Wilberforce." He showed no inclination to join her, so she grabbed his wrist and pulled him to his feet. He backed away, attempting to extricate his hand.

"We're only making a little trip to the loo. It's what's known as a pre-emptive strike."

Whisky, he was thinking as she led him to the bathroom, petrol, Bath Oliver, Polyfilla, five foot two, eyes of blue, has anybody seen my — whisky . . . and the dawn comes up like thunder out of Moscow . . . Dar es Salaam . . . Huddersfield? He wondered who was the woman holding his hand. Expertly he stole glances at her figure. She had a fine large bosom, but also a determined look in her eye that alarmed him. Perhaps she could tell him if his wife was dead. He wouldn't feel so anxious if he could be certain there was no danger of Edwina turning up. But what came out was not the question he was trying to frame.

"Bath Oliver."

"Baths at nine," snapped Nurse Rawlings.

"So what do I owe you, lovey?"

"It makes £18.36, Duchess." His smile shone radiant out of his dark face. She liked the little cap he always wore. Mustafa passed her the bag, and she slipped it under the mattress.

Her mood had improved this morning. She'd put on mascara and some lipstick and a clean dressing gown. She usually did this for Mustafa's visits. Not to impress him — he'd seen her at her worst — but to reignite her waning sense of occasion.

Mustafa had arrived not only with the gin but the *Cosmopolitan*. It promised to be a diverting afternoon, provided there were no doggy visits or nurses forcing her to listen to Mozart. "Eine Kleine Nachtmusik" was all very well, but not when her whole being craved Ethel Merman. Just one act of *Gypsy* or *Annie Get Your Gun*. But would Pine let her play her precious 78s? Would he hell. That horse-faced bitch next door complained of the noise.

She asked about Mustafa's sister's betrothal. She was rebelling, poor girl, and wouldn't have the git. Family were raising hell. She was in love with the plumber, but they didn't know. Mustafa knew.

"All right," said the Duchess, looking at her watch, "we'd better get on with it. It's now or never." Emptying the old bottle, she poured a large glass of gin and settled herself. "Well," she encouraged him, "don't just sit there. You know what to do."

They hadn't "done" it for two weeks. Florence took a long sip, closed her eyes and leaned back into the pillows, savouring the pleasure to come. She heard him take the key from the drawer, go to to the cupboard and open it. There were some fumbling noises, followed by the squeak of wheels. A few inches from the bed they stopped.

"Duchess," whispered Mustapha, "it is here."

She opened her eyes. There he stood, beautiful as ever, the glistening pinks of his plumage undimmed by the years. Walter had gone a bit mangy, so Max had had him restuffed back in 1978, just before he died. At great expense. Only the best for Max. She'd loved that about him. He knew what was really important. (Sadly, Louise could not be saved.) She could not look at the flamingo without thinking of Max and the tears rose in her blue eyes, rose and fell. Mustafa hastened to bring her the box of tissues and she yanked several out and applied them to her nose.

"Thank you, my dear," she sniffed.

"Is very pretty bird, Duchess," said Mustafa, who was sixteen and stood only three inches higher than Walter himself.

"Artists need to contemplate beauty, Mustafa." Her chin trembled and she turned away.

"Then why you don't keep bird always in bedroom?"

She stopped crying and looked at him, aghast. "And be mocked by those monetarists? Not on your Nellie. Bad enough they found out about my career. They're always creeping around asking questions. But I tell them nothing." She leaned towards Mustafa. "We used Walter in the act, you see. And for one or two other things."

He nodded, mystified. For a while they contemplated the flamingo in silence.

"Duchess," whispered Mustafa, "I must leave."

She shook herself. "Of course you must. Put Walter away, there's a good boy, and off you go."

She waved a damp tissue at him as he left, taking the empty gin bottle which he would smuggle off the premises.

She was sorry to have to confine Walter to the cupboard. But his presence there sustained her, an old and true friend. Ten minutes after Mustafa had gone, she was woken from her nap by the ear-splitting sound of Rawlings's voice.

"Mr Wilberforce, when are we going to learn to be a tidy person? This is uncivilized behaviour, Mr Wilberforce. Margaret, fetch the mop! No one will invite us to their birthday parties, Mr Wilberforce, if we carry on this way."

The Duchess smiled with satisfaction. Pine had forbidden the nurses and staff to lose their tempers. Another of his stiff fines was imposed if they yielded. She enjoyed watching Potty Park test their patience to the limit. She closed her eyes. She'd been dreaming of the Lilac Room in Bournemouth. Of Teddy and Eddy and Chico and Walter and Max. Especially Max.

*

282

Nurse McHarg was trying to change the subject. How many times could she be expected to enthuse over Nurse Tupper's grand-daughter winning the Bonniest Baby Contest at Clacton-on-Sea? Tupper had trapped her in the supply room for fifteen minutes now and she was beginning to panic.

"Duty calls, Tina. Must get on," she sighed, as if reluctant to terminate their mesmerizing exchange.

"I suppose so."

"What news of our Henny?" Margaret, who had been on holiday for a week, had a soft spot for Mr Wilberforce, despite the extra work he made for her. There was something in his vague blue eyes she found endearing. Even Mrs Rufus had asked who that attractive new man might be.

"One step forward, two steps back."

"No luck with the Secret Weapon?"

"He likes her and all, but — "

"Give her time." Margaret had faith in Deirdre's charms.

"He did make an attempt to clean up after himself once or twice."

"This is progress."

"And on Friday he was actually moving in the direction of the toilet, but something seemed to distract him at the last minute."

"Dreaming of Bath Olivers."

"Or Gatling Guns."

"What about the — um — Other Problem?"

"So far, so good." Tupper looked disappointed. With the exception of her granddaughter, she was easily bored.

On the Road to Mandalay, where the flying, flying . . . at the dawning of the day, and the sun comes up like H-bombs out of sticky buns, Martinis, Gatling Guns, ICBM, B 42s, Harriers . . . Give me some men who are stout-hearted men who will fight for —

There was a sound outside the door. Henny laid aside his *Guinness Book of Naval Blunders*. The door opened. It was that black person again. She came to him, glossy and fat. She sat beside him. He watched her movements, stared into her moist and glowing eyes. There was something . . .

"Anthea," he said.

The Duchess looked out of the window. God, the country was boring. So depressing. Nothing going on. She'd have given anything for a stroll down the Kingsland Road with her shopping trolley and a look-in at the Dog and Dumplings. What was she doing here, practically in Essex? Jugged-up in foliage, choking on the stench of chlorophyll. She supposed she was a malcontent, but this was even beyond Upminster.

There were cries of consternation in the corridor.

"Dirty! Dirty, Mr Wilberforce. This time it really is the Romper Room."

She was tempted to open the door. No, Florence, don't do it. Restrain yourself. Never let them catch you taking an interest. They'll assume that beast is "restoring you to wholeness" and she'll be all over you. Nevertheless, she tiptoed to the door, turned the knob carefully and opened it a quarter of an inch. The hall was deserted. Just as well. But who was this Wilberforce geezer who was always getting nicked and what kind of poncey name was that anyway? Still, if he was giving them aggro, good on him, whoever he was. She checked her watch. Time for Ada. She never left the room except for Ada.

She adjusted her pink leggings and pulled on her extra-large T-shirt with the gold sunglasses printed across the front. She'd had to wear a bra, otherwise the joke didn't exactly make sense. The bra wasn't comfortable. She tugged at the strap. Which shoes should she wear? She narrowed the choice to the patent-leather stilettos with the *diamanté* heels and the polka-dot wedgies and settled for the former. She knew that others might not find a visit to the hairdresser a state occasion, but for her it was — well, something from the past. She'd spent many a happy hour under the hairdryer and got a lot of good advice from manicurists. She hoped she wouldn't cry.

The article on fellatio had been a disappointment. They never did go the whole hog with these things, but went all coy at the critical moment. What a swizz. And the stilettos were murder. But what could she do? If you go about in four-inch heels for fifty years, something funny happens to your calf muscles and you are no longer able to put your heels on the floor. Even in bare feet, you still have to walk tippy-toe. Try that with rheumatoid arthritis. She'd started wearing the heels at sixteen, as soon as she ran away from home. (Personal adornment was the first step on the road to damnation, according to her mother.) Five foot one and a half inches just wasn't *enough* of Florence Fox. She wanted more of her, the way you would a strawberry ice-cream cone. Everyone wanted more of her. Then.

She checked her lipstick in the mirror and gazed for thirty seconds — as long as she could bear — at what had been the exquisite tiny body which she had draped in clouds of organza and pink and purple feathers and sequined gowns that stuck like Clingfilm; at the ears from which she had dangled gold and coral and silver and jet, and at the arms over which she'd drawn black satin gloves that buttoned above the elbow. She'd made a kind of signature of their slow and ostentatious removal prior to laying her ringed white hands on the keyboard. Now she looked like a barrel with limbs. Only her arms and calves were still shapely, but the skin on her arms was so wrinkled that she kept them permanently covered, and did the same to her neck with a leopard-print scarf. Her legs were, well, more like Walter's.

But somewhere beneath the puffiness and the wrinkles and the foundation with which she masked it all were vestiges, hints, and tributes to what had been her flirtatious little face. And the adorable nose was still intact, not yet metamorphosed into a prickly pear. She intended to persist with the leggings and the lipstick, the *diamanté* and the nail varnish to what would certainly be the very bitter end. No surrender. Not an inch. *La luta continua*. Why, she wasn't sure. Except that *la luta* was life and all else the grey corridors of Shady Meadows that led inexorably to the grave.

The nurses arrived. As always she was ready for them, standing as upright as her condition would allow, pretending she could still balance successfully on the stilettos.

"Now, Mrs Fox, we'd like you to use your walking frame and no nonsense, please."

"Over my dead body."

"Then we'll have to hold your arms."

"Absolutely not."

"You need support, Duchess."

"I need a cigarette."

They arrived at the usual compromise: Tupper and McHarg on either side, and the Duchess between them, walking in agony but unaided. On the way to the salon they passed the community room. This was the stretch that worried her; this was where no stumbles or wobbles must be made. A lively group was assembled in front of the television watching *Blue Peter*. Would the adjective were true, the Duchess reflected, her back straight, her head high, her gaze unwavering. No way would she give those W.W.s and P.P.s the slightest cause for gossip or comment, especially with The Secret Weapon snoring content and adored in their midst. She maintained a stature regal as her nickname until she was well past them when she collapsed and clung, humiliated but grateful, to the walking frame. Just at that moment Henry Wilberforce shuffled along. So that was him. Furtively she looked him over, reluctant, as always, to show an interest in anyone or anything at Shady Meadows.

Ada was her usual permed and perfumed self. Ada was the only person at Potty Park with whom the Duchess enjoyed a decent conversation. Perhaps because they shared similar backgrounds. Ada was a young woman, of course, but she was always so cheerful, always ready for a laugh. She did the pink rinse beautifully. Above all she was a good listener.

For the twentieth time the Duchess recounted her memories of the Lilac Room and Pete's Palace and the Liverpool Garden Hotel and cruises on the *Canberra* and Teddy and Eddy and Chico and Max. (She did not mention Walter. Walter was her's alone. She shared him with Mustafa because she had to and because he was discreet. And in a funny way, he understood.) Ada didn't mind the chatter. She liked elderly people and thought the Duchess was a lovely old thing.

"Now the Lilac Room, that was the best. It's in Bournemouth. Do you know it?"

"No, Mrs Fox."

"Well, I expect it's gone now. That was when Teddy and Eddy had just joined the group. We were called the Constellations — did I tell you? Teddy was West Indian, a beautiful trombonist, and Eddy, he was from Newcastle, the best sax player I ever worked with. Then there was darling Max on base, Chico on drums and yours truly tickling the ivories."

"*And* you were the vocalist, Mrs Fox." Ada was proud of her favourite client.

"Oh you bet, and I was pretty good, though I was much better at the piano. I was a natural, you see. No training to speak of." She held up her hands. "Well, no more tickling for poor old Flossie. That's what Max used to call me when he was feeling playful. It was Teddy who called me the Duchess and that was the one that stuck." She dropped her hands in her lap.

Ada's reflection gave her a wistful smile and patted her shoulder. "Never mind, love."

"I don't mind. It was great while it lasted. I had my applause and my fun and my share of rumpy-pumpy. I do regret not going that little bit further, though. I did all right for a gal from the gutter. I had ambition, but not the real stuff. Not the sort that — inflames you."

"Like Ethel, you mean."

"Oh Ethel! What a voice, what a personality. That go-ahead style. Never saw anything like her in *Call Me Madam*. Incandescent, she was. Always my heroine. She was titchy too, you know. But that didn't stop Ethel. I heard once that she voted Republican, but I'm still not sure I believe it. People are mean, you know, they talk rubbish out of spite. And of course it was a major boo-boo to marry that Ernest Borgnine. He was never for her. I could tell by his eyebrows. Marriage lasted five days."

Ada shrugged. "We all make mistakes."

The Duchess was close to tears. Ada really understood. In a way, that made her even sadder. "I regret no children, I must say. Didn't want 'em then couldn't have 'em. It hurts me. Then when Max went — "

"You poor thing. Shall we try a bit more red in the rinse this time?"

"Whatever you think, darling. I leave it to you." She looked at her ruined hands. "Be nice to play again." She sighed then smiled. "And a bit of the other wouldn't go amiss either. Ach! It's all so Upminster. What's in the new *Marie Claire*?"

*

Lay da *dee* da da. Lai lai lai lai. None but the lonely hearts get apple pie ... Tchaikovsky, Catherine the Great, Ivan the Terrible, Gorbachev, Yeltsin, cabbage soup ... soup ... liquid.

Henny stood and pondered. There was an urge he knew he must control. Why? He could not remember the reason for the Must, only that this Must must be obeyed and that it had become a new and unpleasant factor in his life. He turned towards the bathroom. As he did so, Mrs Rufus emerged from the door opposite. Mrs Rufus was a large splendid woman, soft as a duvet with huge brown eyes and yellow-grey hair and a luxuriant moustache. She smiled at Henny.

He watched her waddle slowly away.

The Duchess was planning her suicide. It was a regular pastime and got her through many a bad night. But the last one had been a real stinker. She'd had to have a gin at six and listen to *Farming Today* which she found mysteriously calming. Thank God she'd cleaned her teeth and sluiced her mouth with Listerine because Tupper and McHarg arrived twenty minutes early to change the bed linen. She sat sullen as they worked. Her nose was in the *Mirror*, but her ears were tuned VHF to their gossip.

"No doubt about it, Henny's improved."

The Duchess was sorry to hear this.

"Wonderful how a couple of nights in the Romper Room focuses their minds."

"I hesitate to say we've got a cure here, but it's looking hopeful."

Worse and worse. *En route* to Upminster.

Tupper savagely plumped the pillows. Once in place, they were still not to her satisfaction so she plumped them again, harder.

"You keep beating it like that and it'll come," said the sprightly Mrs Fox and was ignored.

"Shame about the other little incident."

McHarg sighed. "Mrs Rufus was that upset. Had to be sedated."

"I heard."

The Duchess perked up. What was this?

"She overreacted is my opinion."

"Let's hope it was a one-off regression on his part."

"Can't believe he'll start all that again when he's been such an angel lately."

"I think it's Deirdre, you know. She's had a miraculous effect on him."

"Dotes on that animal, he does."

Tupper gave her a saccharine smile. "Well, don't we all."

The Duchess simulated a choking fit which was also ignored. In walked the canine in question.

"Hello, my old darling. Come to say good morning to Auntie Margaret, have we?"

"Get that fat slag out of my room!"

"She'll be leaving in a minute, Mrs Fox. She's coming with us." It was time for Deirdre's daily round of love-ins.

The Duchess rattled the paper at Deirdre. "It says here that cats are about to replace dogs as number one British pet. A quarter of all households have 'em. Twenty thousand families have *more than six*. The streets might be safe again without all that filth and aggro from you lot." Deirdre's tail continued to beat the carpet, which further enraged Mrs Fox. A headache was coming on. "Just remember your days are numbered. Prepare for extinction, bitch. You're history!"

"That's enough, Mrs Fox. There's no need to abuse the poor animal."

The Duchess raised her newspaper and waved it menacingly at the nurse. Enough, eh? She'd hardly begun and intended to rouse herself to a proper frenzy.

"Poor animal? What about these poor girls on the street in front of the Royal Hospital in the freezing cold? Why aren't you two out there supporting them?"

"Some of us have work to do," sniffed McHarg.

"It's a disgrace. Don't you have any sense of solidarity with your sister nurses? Doesn't it bother you how scandalously little they're paid? No, it does not. All you care about is the tidy packet you pocket each week for coddling rich wrecks."

"We have patients to look after," Tupper airily informed her. "We don't have time to be batting our eyelashes for the telly cameras."

That did it.

"Fascists!" screamed the Duchess. "Collaborationists!" as she pelted them with the contents of the bedside table.

Deirdre whimpered but held her ground. The nurses approached with caution, dodging Sprite tins and plastic hair rollers and packets of All-Sorts. They grabbed her arms and pinned them to the chair.

"Now see here, Duchess. This is as far as it goes. These tantrums must and shall end. Do you want to go back on to that other medication? The one you didn't like?"

"No."

"Do you want to spend twenty-four hours in the Romper Room?"

"No." She was crying, damn it.

McHarg sighed and released her arms. "Then what *do* you want, Mrs Fox?"

"Sex! Sex! Sex!"

Phew, that was harrowing. Lucky Labs have stable personalities. There are times, though, and that was one of them, when even we feel taken advantage of. Doesn't it ever occur to anyone that I might suffer from compassion fatigue?

But Deirdre did not hold the thought. She was incapable of sustained resentment. She was only sorry she hadn't had the opportunity to try out her new expression on the Duchess. It was custom made, and she had been working hard on it. She called it simply Adoration and felt certain it would be a breakthrough.

Oh do you know the Gattling Gun, the Gattling Gun, the Gattling Gun. Oh do you know the Gattling Gun that lives in Drury Lane. Henny stopped singing in his head. He was suddenly terrified. He was sure he heard Edwina's footsteps in the hall. He scrambled under the bed, his heart pounding. And just when he'd been convinced she was really dead. There was a light knock. Someone entered. Why hadn't he locked the door?

"Mr Wilberforce." The voice was gentle, hesitant. Couldn't be Edwina. Whoever it was crossed the room and stood by the bed.

"We wondered if you'd care to join us in the giant jigsaw," said the voice to the furniture and the empty air.

Henny saw a pair of fluffy blue slippers. Ankles and slender calves encased in support hose and an elastic bandage. His hand seemed to have a mind of its own. It reached out and groped its way up Miss Parish's leg.

The Duchess was dreaming. She was Flossie Fox the Five Foot Duchess, the Dishy Duchess from Dagenham. She and Max were performing in the Strangeways Hotel in Eastbourne. Teddy and Eddy had gone on to greater things in Doncaster, but Chico was still pounding the drums. Walter and Louise had been added to the act. They and some potted palms among which the Duchess was belting out, "Bongo bongo bongo, I don't want to leave the Congo, oh no no no no no," to an audience of grimacing, delighted geriatrics. She did not think then, in her leopard-print sateen trouser suit and multi-layered bone necklace that one day she would join their company. The scene changed, and she was fondling her adored cat Tinkerbell, who then weighed a mere stone.

She groaned, rolled over with difficulty. The image went fuzzy like a telly screen in a thunderstorm. She was awake. A major disturbance was taking place in the corridor. Shouts and screams, the sounds of a scuffle, running feet and Nurse Tupper's voice yelling, "Chill *out*, Henny!"

The Duchess could not restrain herself. Fuck dignity, fuck pride, something jolly interesting was going on. Her hair was in a frightful state, she wore no make-up and her torn draylon nightie was slipping from her blubbery shoulders. Getting out of bed unaided was excruciating. But she gave no thought to her appearance and reached the door with teenaged alacrity. When she opened it, she found Tupper and the new night nurse attempting to subdue a confused and naked Mr Wilberforce. Another nurse arrived with a blanket in which they quickly wrapped him, though not before the Duchess had had a good look.

Near by, Nurse Soames comforted an hysterical Mrs Langston. Henny, now being hurried off to the Romper Room, seemed completely mystified by their behaviour. Someone arrived with a syringe and a stretcher, Mrs Langston was removed and that was that. The Duchess closed the door.

Well! So there was life in some of these cadavers. And, surprise, surprise, Wilberforce was no Prancing Percy. She felt suddenly but not unpleasantly faint. Her fingers and toes were tingling. Blood pressure. Back to bed, Flos. She groped her way there and poured herself a large gin. She sat on the edge of the bed, slowly sipping. She needed to think. She'd known Henny was a live wire, but Tupper and McHarg always talked in such euphemisms, it was difficult to tell what he was really up to. She took a long swallow and with an effort crossed her legs. Her ankles were still beautiful and her arches dizzyingly high. You could see what they had once been despite their webbing of blue veins. Keeping time with her dangling foot she began to sing an old Nat King Cole song. "Straighten up and fly right. Cool down, poppa, don't you blow your top."

The Duchess was getting the picture.

It was a freezing February day, and Dr Pine had told Mustafa to make a fire in the office. The comfort and elegance of a real fire always impressed the relatives. It seemed to diminish their sense of guilt, and the three women before him had plenty to diminish. They were nervous. Their eyes alternated fear and supplication and every so often a hint of penitence.

Pine assumed a stern demeanour. He was going to enjoy this. He would play them like he played the salmon in the Tay. Then he would let them off the hook — if the price was right.

"We don't know what to say, Doctor," Mrs Partridge opened. "Naturally we were horrified."

"Mrs Partridge, it wasn't you who assaulted Miss Parish and trapped Mrs Langston in the loo." He was the soul of fair play.

"Oh honestly." Mrs Delisle shifted irritably on her chair. "One would have thought by his age — can't you *give* him something?"

"That is one of the things we're here to discuss."

Mrs Pridell was crying. "Poor Daddy. He'll be a vegetable. He'll have no soul. There must be an alternative — "

"Oh stress less, Camilla." Sandra Delisle lit another cigarette. Her baby sister had always been a pain in the arse. She'd never see her at all if it weren't for this bloody inconvenience with their randy father. Why she was suddenly feigning such concern she couldn't make out. Really the woman was a complete nincompoop.

"Please explain to us what's involved," pleaded the rational Mrs Partridge. "The effects of the treatment."

"The fact is, Mrs Partridge, we've already increased your father's dosage." He pretended to consult Henny's notes. "He is now on Trianolymanoscaline, a new drug and very expensive. But so far we haven't seen much improvement. Frankly, ladies" — he closed the book with a snap of worrying finality — "I'm not encouraged."

"But he's *better*," Camilla shrieked. "You said he was."

"In certain respects." Dr Pine paced in dignified style before the fire, his noble brow furrowed, turning over the case of Henry Wilberforce in his great brain. He could feel their six eyes upon him. "About which you know. However, in another respect there has been a deterioration of behaviour. To be blunt" — he faced them — "he's a very upsetting influence on the other patients. And this we cannot allow. Moreover, he requires extra care. I have administrative costs to consider, increased drug prices, overtime, overheads, taxes . . ."

"Oh if it's only a question of *money*." Mrs Partridge and Mrs Pridell gushed in unison, their eyes alight with hope. They'd had visions of keeping their father locked in the cellar, hearing his screams during dinner parties, having to lie to the guests, or, worse still, having to tell the truth. Then there was the astronomical expense of a round-the-clock nurse. Moreover he was healthy and might live indefinitely.

Dr Pine did not alter his expression. He waited. He let the implications sink in.

"J-Just how much money would be involved, Doctor?"

Still he did not answer. He was pretending to consider.

"I mean we'd be happy to make a, well, contribution."

"Aren't there nurses' pension schemes or something?" Sandra was still reluctant.

"Daddy's so happy here." Camilla wiped her eyes. "And we feel so relieved that he's well looked after. I mean it's really wonderful . . ." Her voice trailed off.

Pine waited exactly thirty seconds. Then he smiled.

One more night and Henny was free. He was serving his term in the Romper Room, and the Duchess felt like a moll waiting for her mobster to break out of jail. She was in hiding from the police, planning their getaway. It was delicious.

What a fool she'd been, locking her door every night. Why hadn't she twigged? No regrets, Florence. Just concentrate on making up for lost time.

She prepared carefully. She realized it might not happen the first night or the second or even the third, but sooner or later he would be unable to resist the sight of her open door.

She sat propped against a mountain of pillows, the bedside lamp glowing through the scarf she'd draped over it. She was wearing her best dressing gown of chartreuse satin, which had not been removed from its box since 1985, gold (why not?) eye shadow and a lot of, though not the maximum, jewellery. No rings, though, too grotesque on her ruined hands. She didn't want to look like some corrupt and decaying Manchu empress in a pink wig. Speaking of pink, she'd wheeled Walter out just to keep her spirits up. For she was nervous.

A terrible thought occurred to her. What if Tupper and McHarg had decided to lock Henny in his room? Never mind. He would escape them somehow, she felt sure. The mad are fiendishly clever, and Henny was a five-star loony with bath. Clearly when his gonads were teeming nothing could restrain him. She'd hold the thought.

Was he really any good in the sack, she wondered, or was it all PR? Oh well, what did it matter when both of them were only invoking a vanished past, play-acting to conjure up lost fun? She'd been on the pull for so long, and this might be her last chance, the one she'd dreamed of. Somehow she knew that life at Shady Meadows was unlikely to present such a golden opportunity twice.

It took a while. Friday and Saturday were quiet, so they must have had him under lock and key. But the Duchess knew he'd appear. She just knew. So each night she sat and waited in full kit; and each night ended with a thin dawn which found her nodding and dishevelled, with an empty glass in her hand and the telly flickering in anticipation of *The Big Breakfast*. But she was not discouraged. She had an interest in life.

On the Monday, *en route* to Ada, she saw him in the corridor, hurrying along in his green-felt slippers as if he actually had somewhere to go, singing a tuneless and meandering song whose meaning was comprehensible to him alone. She willed him to look at her. He did. Remember me? said her answering glance. I certainly got a good look at you, and what I saw was not without interest, an interest in life. He stopped to watch her continue on her haughty painful way.

Then it happened. Quite early, thank God, before her slap went caky or her hair turned matted and sticky with dozing. She was drunk, but not too. (She'd filled a tumbler with the last of the gin, enough to get her through to the next evening provided she was careful. Mustafa would come on Wednesday. It would be dodgy until then, but she wasn't thinking of that now.) Henny peeped round the door. She wasn't sure whether or not he recognized her, but what did it matter? She wasn't in this for her ego. She smiled and beckoned to him. He smiled back, then hesitated. He could not believe such a bird of paradise was inviting him into her nest. What should he do? He was used to shrieks and flight and punishment, and clearly she was not about to flee. Was it a trick? A trap? A test? Recent experiences had confused and frightened him. She smiled again and threw back the counterpane to reveal her ankles and her tiny painted toes. Henny gaped. Then just what she'd hoped would happen did happen. She'd kick-started 3,000,000 years of biological determinism. Henny became an organism in pursuit of its atavistic goal.

He walked to the bed, a bit unsteady. He touched each of the Duchess's toes, turning them gently between his fingers as if they were pearls.

"This little piggy," she quipped and took a sip of her gin. It seemed unwise to offer him any just now, but he didn't notice she was drinking, so engrossed was he with her feet, which he caressed with an astonished expression, and with her blue-and-white legs which he began to kiss, working his way along to her knee and thigh. She was ashamed of her thighs, but there was no way of avoiding them, since they were the pillared entrance to the atavistic goal.

"Here, darling," she said and put his hands on the straps of her nightdress. He was well-versed in this manoeuvre and had them down in a flash. Then he dived for her breasts. The force knocked her sideways, and his face vanished into her bulging tummy. My, this was fun. And she hadn't forgotten a thing. Libido still lived in the deep-freeze of herself. She had only to take it out and pop it in the microwave.

All the while he was muttering and singing to himself. She made out a word here and there: Gattling Gun, sticky bun. Five-star loony with bath. Who cared?

He was a bit too absorbed in her navel, probably because it was so deep and dark. She hoped he wasn't confusing one hole with another.

"I'd skip the foreplay, sweetie," she advised. "Too risky at our age. We could both be dead before we get to the interesting bit."

Henny drew back and fumbled with his trousers. He kept singing something about Peter Rabbit and awful habit. Then suddenly it was out. It was up, sort of up, and he had her dressing gown and nightie off and really he was quite deft, the Duchess was amazed. Then he actually attempted to roll her on to her stomach.

"Um, this might be difficult, old thing. Not sure I can manage it." But she could, she could, and he was nipping at her large white bottom and then she was on her back again, breathless and laughing. Laughing! He opened her legs. They would not go very far, but she assumed they would loosen up. Everything else had.

Henny stopped singing. Something was pressing on his excitement and his happiness. Two things, in fact. One came from the recesses of his own body and was intimately connected with his lower regions and his current activities. The other was a voice, a terrible voice at which he trembled.

Mr Wilberforce, thundered the voice, *when are we going to learn to be a tidy person*? The awful Must that must be obeyed.

"What's wrong, darling?" asked the Duchess. "Look at the bird if you're having trouble. Look at Walter. Max always did towards the end and it worked wonders." Then she laughed, realizing his problem. Sometimes it happened even at the critical moment. There were a couple of incidents with Chico and even Max — should she think of Max? Use this poor old ram to imagine him back into her bed? With a twinge of guilt she turned out the light. She assumed, in the darkness, that Henny was headed for the loo.

It was too urgent. It could not be controlled. Henny thought again of the voice and panicked. In the shadows he could make out the lunar glow of the sink. He went to it and relieved himself into the pristine basin.

Now what had he been doing? Then he saw that the thing in his hand was swollen in the most interesting way. He remembered the Duchess. He heard her call to him. "Max . . . Max . . ."

The voice reminded him that what he had just done was most unsanitary. The voice was right. He wanted to be good; he wanted to be tidy. Especially for Anthea. Gently, inaudibly, he removed the large glass of water from the bedside table and dutifully rinsed out the sink with its contents. Now he could proceed with a clear conscience.

Mr Wilberforce fell upon the Duchess who gasped with surprise and pleasure. It was all going swimmingly. But she was having trouble conjuring Max. Perhaps a little drinkie would help. She reached for her glass. Her wrecked hand closed on air. She groped the top of the table, panic rising.

"Henny?"

"Anthea?"

"Who the hell is Anthea and where's my gin?"

He was doing his best to persuade her to resume their previous activity.

"No bonking until we find my gin!" She heaved him off and switched on the light. She opened the drawer, took out her spectacles and glared at him. Their lenses magnified the smudged gold eye shadow and black mascara. She looked as if someone had hit her. Who could have been such a brute? He explored her cheekbones with quizzical tender fingers. She pushed his hand away.

"Don't try to distract me. What have you done with my gin?" This must be sorted out. Now. "Did you drink it, you batty old — "

Henny shook his head. He felt incapable of achieving goodness. He despaired of being invited to any more birthday parties.

"You did," shouted the Duchess. "Don't lie to me. That was the last of my gin, all I had, and you took it, you greedy, guzzling, mean-minded sneak. You seduced me for my booze!"

Henny was alarmed. The bird of paradise had turned suddenly dangerous, all beak and talons and burning black eyes. Her pink hair stood up in tufts like the young people's he'd seen on telly. Was she what was called a punk? Or was it Pinko? He was very confused.

With surprising strength she shoved him off the bed.

"You're a low type, Wilberforce," she snarled. "The lowest. You pretend to be mad so you can steal the only thing that gives meaning to life. You're worse than that bloody dog."

She began to cry. Really this was most distressing. Even more than Miss Parish. He tried to speak.

"I'm . . . I'm . . . s-s-s-s —"

"Out!" she cried imperiously, indicating the door.

As he moved away in fear he bumped into Walter who tottered then fell with a crash and a flurry of pink feathers on to the floor.

The Duchess was enraged. She dragged Henny towards the door, tears streaming down her face. Then she remembered the others. On no account must they know. Somehow this must be kept quiet. Wilberforce would probably have forgotten by tomorrow if not before. But there must be no more shouting. Carefully she opened the door and thrust Henny into the hall. Never in her life had anything been so Upminster.

"Go to your room," she hissed. "Stay there. Never come here again."

She closed the door and locked it. This time it would stay locked.

Of course everyone knew. Impossible to keep secrets in a place full of insomniacs. Rufus next door had heard it all. The Duchess was mortified and would speak to no one. Deirdre was given a particularly difficult time until Mustafa paid his next visit. After a few days the Duchess calmed down and agreed to receive a delegation made up of the Wilberforce girls and a deeply concerned Dr Pine. They'd come to consult and console her about her "dreadful ordeal".

"Nothing wrong with me," she insisted, observing each of the daughters and beginning to pity Henny.

"We feel awful about it," cooed Camilla.

"Don't."

"You won't be — pressing charges, will you?"

"Why would I do that?"

"Well, that's most handsome of you, Mrs Fox, but we feel we must make it up to you somehow. Offer some kind of, well, compensation."

The Duchess looked up. Pine was smiling his starchy smile. Had she ever in her life met such a tosser? She looked at each of their phoney faces. Was she mistaken, or did she detect an interesting offer squatting behind them? She waited.

"We heard he attacked your flamingo."

"Walter's seen worse."

"Was there any damage?"

Florence Fox said nothing. She concentrated on looking very sad. Partridge made a definite movement towards her handbag.

"Of course, money can't make up for — "

"No, it can't." The Duchess looked at them hard. She saw right through these Wilberforce bitches. They wanted Dad incarcerated at just about any price. And they did not want aged pink-haired floozies complaining to this or any other establishment.

"In other words, Mrs Fox," said the doctor gently, "is there anything we can do to make your life at Shady Meadows more comfortable?"

Mrs Fox replied that she would consider the matter.

The Duchess adjusted her headphones. She hadn't quite got the hang of them yet, nor of the chic and very expensive black gadget to which they were attached. She fiddled with some dials. There. Now

Ethel came through, as always, loud and clear: "The hostess with the mostest on the ball." The Duchess stroked the machine, awed by its mystery and power. The Japs must have a hotline to some source of divine inspiration. She contemplated her stack of CDs. All those gorgeous digital reissues — a lifetime of listening pleasure.

The walls of her room had been redecorated in "Samoa", a rich peach which was, however, barely visible behind the scores of photographs. Max, Tinky, Teddy and Eddy, Chico, May, friends and admirers from over fifty years, and many of the Duchess herself, covered in feathers and fake pearls, seated at a grand piano or standing with a microphone between Walter and Louise against a backdrop of plastic ferns. It was lovely.

Next to her bed stood Walter, resplendent in his restitched feathers. She was wearing Mustafa's cap on her pink-rinsed head. It had been a parting gift when he'd left to work in his uncle's restaurant in Walthamstow. She missed him badly and had cried when he left, but she was glad he was escaping Pine's servitude. He'd promised to visit, then just as he was leaving, he returned to her bedside.

"Duchess," he said, very earnest, "do me a favour before I go?"

"Anything, my dear."

"Tell me, please, what means Upminster?"

"It's the last stop on the District Line, isn't it?"

"But why do you always say it like you're upset?"

"It's just an old joke of mine and Max's. Whenever anything was completely crackers, barking mad, proper Wonderland, we'd say it was Upminster."

"But why Upminster?"

"Because it's *beyond Barking*. Even further east. You see?"

He considered it. Then he laughed. Indian men, she thought as he went out the door, have really got something.

Yes, life at Potty Park had greatly improved. She was no longer hiding her past. It was her life, herself, with all its plumed and sequined contradictions, and anyone who wanted to look at it was welcome, whether they understood or not, and if they didn't want to look they could stick it. She was proud of her life. What the hell. Of course Shady Meadows was still a den of corruption, packed with fascists and collaborationists. But she had her sanctuary, her shrine, her inviolable fortress from which to thumb her nose at them with impunity. And it helped to have a regular, and legal, supply of drink. And listening to Ethel day and night was sublime, with no complaints from Rufus, now that she had the magic headphones. The music centre had been a grand gesture, despite the Wilberforce girls' motives. In a way she had a lot to thank old Henny for. "Have a kumquat, Mr Goldstone," the Duchess sang along, adding the appropriate hand gestures.

Anyway, whatever other bribes they'd offered hadn't worked because Henny had gone. As of five days ago. There had been no screams, no fainting, no alarms at night. She was burning to know what crime had been so heinous as to have him banned for ever from this haven of hopeless cases. She liked the thought of him raising hell in some other defenceless institution, still up to his old dirty tricks, taking the rest out of rest home. But what had he done? She must know. She'd drag it somehow from Tupper and McHarg. They'd had instructions to treat her with kid gloves and cater to all her little whims, one of which involved the eighty-sixing from her sanctuary of a certain dog.

That alone was enough to brighten her days. And who knew? Someone might get her out of here. Didn't she have a sister in Mitcham? Or Teddy and Eddy would swoop down and rescue her. They'd been playing on a world cruise and only just returned to London. Horrified, they'd discovered her absence. It had taken them months to find her, but at last . . .

The fantasy was shattered by the arrival of McHarg and Tupper, followed by Deirdre who waited, a model of obedience, outside the door to Room 25.

"Cross that threshold and you're dead meat," called the Duchess. Victory was sweet.

Deirdre tried the Adoration look. Labs live in hope.

"So where's he gone?" asked the Duchess.

At first they just clucked and muttered and wouldn't spill. It must have been pretty bad. The Duchess persisted. She reminded them of the new consideration she was to be shown. Anyway, they were longing to tell. She could see. Especially that Tupper. McHarg seemed positively gutted. She'd been fond of the old boy. The Duchess was too, in a funny way.

Tupper leaned close and whispered in the Duchess's ear. "It was that poor dog."

"You mean her?" The Duchess pointed, amazed. She couldn't imagine Wilberforce actually hurting anything. "But he was soppy as the rest of you lot. He liked her."

"Well . . ." Tupper looked embarrassed. "That was part of the problem." Then, still unable to meet the Duchess's eye, she gave an account in more explicit terms. Apparently Rawlings had caught Henny in flagrante delicto, frankly admiring Deirdre's posterior. And they were alone together. In his *room*. Naturally she was horrified. It was, as she put it, beyond the pale. How long had this been going on? All of Shady Meadows was in an uproar. Everyone adored Deirdre, including Pine. The stench of perversion was not to be tolerated. Never had this sort of scandal been associated with the good name of Shady Meadows. The Wilberforce daughters had protested at the lack of hard evidence, but Pine would countenance nothing short of complete removal from the premises. So Henny had left, as hastily, as well dressed and in as baffled a state as he had arrived.

Nurse McHarg patted the dog's head. "Imagine," she said, her voice breaking, "an innocent animal."

The Duchess raised an eyebrow and gave Deirdre a sceptical look. She sipped a gin in full view of McHarg and Tupper.

"I'm not so sure. Takes two, you know," said the Duchess.

NOT QUITE ARCADIA

In the dark she hardly recognized him. He spoke to her and passed before she realized he was Stevie, the butcher's assistant. He had made her a cup of tea last week in Mr Agrippa's shop and brought her a stool to sit on until she stopped sweating and the room had ceased to rotate. He was a kind man, Mr Agrippa. He kept Stevie on and didn't mind that he was damaged. A birth defect? Myra didn't know. She had problems of her own and never thought much about Stevie.

She could not remember what he had said. His voice was thick, like a patient under morphine. It was difficult to understand Stevie. It was difficult to look at him — small and thin, his face too long and his eyes too large, favouring his left leg and speaking in a mumble. Myra descended the steps to the door of her basement flat and turned the key. The cat came to greet her, wanting Whiskas. The envelope on the mat contained an entry form for a £135,000 prize draw, the third such letter this week. She would enter, as she had the others, and with the money she would get a face-lift at one of those clinics that advertised in the back pages of *Vogue*. Clearly, the Very Emollient Nourishing Night Cream With Placenta wasn't working.

Myra changed into a dressing gown; resolved not to glance in the bathroom mirror. But she couldn't help it, she turned and ended as she always did, searching in vain for her lost looks. What she found were puffy eyes, a crumpled mouth, and gaping pores surrounding her roseate nose with its smatter of remaining freckles. She switched off the overhead light and stood in the dark, panic rising. The cure was to lie down, play "Casta Diva" and breathe deeply. This she did, assailed by the scent of hyacinths dying on the table.

"Happens to all women," her GP had said. "Not as if it was fatal, is it? You're not the only one."

"Yes, I am. To myself I am," she whispered to Lily who sat purring and grooming on her tense abdomen. Oh, to be as beautiful as her broad-faced cat whose green eyes looked only outward. What *had* Stevie said?

Returning from the library with her Friday stack of soiled novels, she again failed to see him approach. He was suddenly beside her, speaking in his damaged voice.

"Come in, Stevie," she said.

He followed her down the stairs. Lily fled, the cat door going flap flap behind her.

"It's dark."

Myra could understand him now. "I don't like bright lights," she answered as he handed her a white packet stained red and tied with butcher's twine.

"What's this, soup bones?" How could she be speaking to him this way, familiarly, without preliminaries?

"For you." The sight of his teeth repelled her. "For your problem."

"Really?" She opened it. "Ah. Organs."

He nodded.

"Are they fish, fowl or mammal?" It was hard to tell.

"Mammal."

"I love mammals." She now returned his smile. "They're all that interest me."

For three days after cooking and eating the organs she aired the flat but could not get rid of the awful smell. The saucepan was put out with the rubbish.

She felt very well until the following Friday when she came home with her stack of new novels, changed into her dressing gown and bravely faced the mirror. She saw with alarm that her face had begun to pucker and bubble like the white of an egg when it was fried too quickly. On Monday she called the office and feigned illness.

When she awoke at 4 a.m. her face was itching, not unpleasantly. She stumbled to the bathroom and watched her reflection scratching at the base of its neck. She pushed with her fingertips, carefully inserting them under the loose skin. Gently she pulled and lifted. The dead face peeled off in its entirety like a layer of warm wax. She dropped it into the toilet where it floated, a bloodless afterbirth. She pulled the chain and flushed away her face.

Myra gazed at herself with satisfaction. Her pores had tightened and the circles had gone from beneath her eyes. In eight weeks the marbled tracks of cellulite on her thighs and bottom had vanished and the flab on her upper arms had firmed. Within a year she acquired a waist and ankles.

Myra's boss, Mr MacKenzie, asked her out. Her GP asked her out. She dined with them, slept with them, did the same with a bricklayer she met in a pub. She began affairs with a handsome married man on the second floor and with her bank manager, also married. She left them all. They were too old for her.

She went to a gym. She swam. She needed release for the energy coursing through her nice new endocrine system. She wore dresses that exposed her apricot skin. Every few years she peeled off her old face and threw it away. She disappeared into London, changing her name and acquiring a new set of friends and lovers. She married a lawyer, divorced him, and bought a flat in South Kensington. She moved on before anyone noticed the change in her appearance.

THE BLUE WOMAN

Her memory began to fail. It was as if she had never known what Celsius was, or a 747, or a duvet. Everything was unfamiliar and fresh. (It was just as well she had money because she could not have held down a job.) She felt a compulsion to learn all the things she had forgotten and decided to begin at a butcher's shop in E8.

Mr Agrippa scratched his head and laughed. "You do *look* familiar." She wanted to ask which animal's death had been the price of her youthing. Instead she asked if he remembered a customer named Myra Dent.

He snapped his fingers. "The daughter!" And Stevie? Stevie was gone.

She enrolled in an A-level college, but didn't like studying and failed her exams. She preferred to go skating, listen to the Everly Brothers or paint by numbers. Her periods stopped. She was hungry all the time and wanted to see her mother. Furtively she bought a doll. When one day she discovered she had been wearing her shoes on the wrong feet, she knew she could no longer look after herself.

A suitable woman was engaged, but Myra escaped her. She unlocked the gate to the communal gardens and squatted in the dawn light, watching the worms at work. She rejoiced in the taste of dirt she consumed by the fistful. The police found her wandering down the Fulham Road. She could not answer any of their questions, and they had no choice but to have her taken into care.

She was now a toddler, spilling her orange juice and building yellow and red cities out of plastic bricks. She was an infant, a small helpless mammal who screamed to no avail, suffocating in the heavy air that pressed her to her cot, panting for a liquid world.

An ambulance brought her to St Bartholomew's, the ancient hospital that stands opposite Smithfield Meat Market where men in stained white coats and huge rubber boots wheel beef carcasses to and fro like frocks on a rack. Myra was not aware of her surroundings. Her tiny fists seemed to the observing nurses to beat at nothing. In fact she was knocking, pounding, at wet red gates. She pounded soundlessly until they opened and swallowed her whole into the inner darkness.

A NOTE ON THE AUTHOR

Mary Flanagan is also the author of two acclaimed novels *Trust* and *Rose Reason*. Her work is translated into many languages and she lives in London.